No Man Required

CJ MORROW

Tamarillas Press

This book is written in British English.

Cover image: **istock.com/pixabay.com**
Cover design: ©CJ Morrow 2023

ISBN: 978 1-913807-36-8

For my family – strong, independent
women and men.

Other books by CJ MORROW

Women's Fiction/Romantic Comedy:
No Man Required
Save the Date
Escape to Christmas Cottage
It's Pamela Rigby Actually
Sooo Not Looking for a Man
We can Work it Out
Little Mishaps and Big Surprises
Mermaid Hair and I Don't Care
Blame it on the Onesie
A Onesie is not just for Christmas

Psychological Thriller:
Never Leaves Me
Kill For You
The Builder

Fantasy:
The Finder
The Illusionist
The Sister
The Family

One

'I'm home,' I shout, dropping my work bag on the hall table and sniffing the air for the aroma of something tasty.

Nothing. No response, no smell of cooking, just silence.

I kick off my shoes in the hallway and stomp through to the kitchen enjoying the coolness of the tiles on the burning soles of my feet. Maybe he's left me something I can microwave. I hope so.

But no, there's nothing. No sign of Gary, my fiancé of just over a year. He's not been at work today and said he'd cook me something lovely when I came home because he knew I had a hell of a day lined up at work.

'Anyway,' he'd said as he lay in bed this morning watching me wriggle myself into my business suit – yes it was going to one of those days. 'It's almost our engagement anniversary so we should celebrate that too.'

It's not actually. Our engagement anniversary, if such a thing exists, was two weeks ago, well no, seventeen days to be precise. It passed unnoticed by either of us, which says a lot for our relationship.

I glance around the kitchen looking for a note from him, sometimes he leaves a sticky note on the fridge or microwave. There's nothing. I stomp back to the hall balancing on my heels – the fire in the balls of my feet after wearing heels all day is excruciating – to retrieve my phone from my bag. Apart from a text from my dentist reminding me it's time to book a hygiene appointment, there's nothing. Not one little courtesy message from Gary.

Still standing in the hall, my stomach rumbling and my feet throbbing along with my temple, I fire off a message to him.

'Hey, where are you?'

He doesn't reply although I can see that he's read my message. So I ring him. It goes straight to voicemail but I end the call without speaking.

I'm really pissed off with him.

In the kitchen I revert to my default meal when there's nothing else, cereal. Sultana bran to be precise because after a day of sitting in a permanently clenched pose and eating only biscuits, and a dryish roll for lunch all washed down with far too many coffees, I think I need something healthy. And clearing, if you know what I mean.

After the cereal and a large glass of orange juice, I wince my way upstairs to have a shower. I really need to wash the grime and bad taste of today away.

I'm never going to get used to shafting people, even though sometimes it's my job to do so.

I've been at an industrial tribunal all day, hence

the outfit and the crippling shoes. My job as Head of Human Resources is to represent the company and make sure we win such cases although fortunately we also haul our lawyer in. Often, and today was definitely one of those, I don't agree with the company stance. I felt so sorry for the woman who lost her case today, she was in the right, we were in the wrong, but we had better legal representation and she left with nothing. The bitter taste it leaves is horrible. But what choice do I have? If I don't do my job properly I'll be the one without a job, without a salary. It's a hard world out there.

My phone pings as I walk from the shower into our bedroom towelling my hair dry. It's Gary.

Hey, how was work?

Just as good as expected, I ping back.

Oh shit. Shall I pick up Chinese or Indian on the way home?

I thought you were going to cook. Where are you?

Hey, did intend to but Nige called. Wanted a golf partner. We're just finishing up on the last hole.

Nineteenth, more like. It's getting dark out there; how would they even see the balls? He must think I'm stupid.

Chinese or Indian, he asks again because I haven't answered.

Neither for me, I've eaten. Get what you want. Then I drop my phone onto the badly made bed and hunt around for my hairdryer. It's not where it should be and it bloody infuriates me. Gary's had it, drying his luscious locks before he went golfing no doubt. He does have thick hair and he is very vain about it; he spends more on styling products and haircuts than I do. I've asked him not to use my dryer, told him to buy his own and even offered to buy him one for Christmas which he adamantly refused saying he didn't need one. Which was obviously a lie because he keeps using mine. I shouldn't have taken any notice of him and just bought one.

After a hunt I finally find it on the floor on his side of the bed, plugged in and the cable kinked where he's rested the still hot dryer on it.

Maybe I'll buy myself a new dryer and let him have this one, although it riles me because this one cost me a fortune, it's ionic and other fancy things that make my frizz-prone hair smoother. I only use it when I wash my hair every three or four days, he's at it every damn day, sometimes twice if he's going out, and he's wearing it out. He laughed when I said this to him, said I was being a drama-llama. That annoyed me even more.

By the time I've finished blasting my hair and get around to checking my phone I see that he has messaged me three more times. All the same question; why did I eat without him? He's got to be joking.

I'll tell him in person when he gets home.

An hour later, and two chocolate mousses and an old KitKat that I found in the bottom of the treats tin – his idea, no wonder I've put weight on since he moved in – and he comes bowling through the door.

'I got you Chinese,' he says, sticking his head round the living room door on his way to the kitchen. 'Thought you'd probably be hungry by now.' He grins before disappearing.

I jump up and follow him to the kitchen before he gets a chance to dish me up a giant portion and then pull sad faces when I don't eat it.

'Don't do any for me,' I say, sounding even grumpier than I feel. 'Like I said, I've eaten.'

He frowns as he runs two clean plates under the hot tap to warm them up. I wince at the waste of water and the extra pennies on the water bill. 'What did you have?' he asks.

'Cereal.'

'That's not dinner, that's breakfast. Have some of this.'

'No, I really don't want any. I'm full up.' I'm not admitting to the mousses and KitKat. 'Put it in the fridge for another day.' I don't even like Chinese that much, it's his favourite not mine. I'm not that keen on Indian either, I'd much prefer a pizza, but he doesn't. But what I really would have liked would have been the salmon and new potatoes that he promised me this morning. I suppose I'll have to cook that myself tomorrow evening.

'God, you look tired,' he says, putting the plates down and coming towards me. 'Come here.' He pulls me to him and hugs me tight. 'Hair smells nice,' he says.

'Yeah, just washed it. And dried it once I'd found my dryer.'

'Oops,' he says, laughing. 'Sorry, I was in a rush.'

I shrug him off, step back and force a smile before wandering back into the living room and flopping down on the sofa from where I can hear him clattering around in the kitchen.

Sometimes I wonder what we're doing together. No, I wonder this more than sometimes. A lot lately, if I'm honest with myself.

We met three years ago and ours was an on-off, well, more off than on, relationship. It was casual and that suited us both. I was – as he jokingly called me – a strong, independent woman. He then jokingly described himself as a man about town, whatever the hell that was supposed to mean. I was thirty-six when we met and definitely not looking for a long-time partner. Hooking up occasionally suited me just fine. Then, he invited me on a weekend away, a lovely country hotel where we went on walks and talked too much about our jobs. On the last evening he went down on bended knee in the restaurant and asked me to marry him. I could hardly say no in front of a dining room full of people, could I? Anyway, even though I'd never even imagined it before, I rather liked the idea. The whole weekend away, the meal, the proposal, it was romantic. I was swept away with the romance.

So here we are, a year later.

He saunters into the living room carrying a plate of steaming Chinese food and a can of lager.

He sees me glance at the plate. 'Had to nuke it in the end,' he says. 'Not too late to nuke yours?' He raises his eyebrows in question.

I shake my head in response and watch him stuff a forkful into his mouth before spitting it back out onto the plate. 'Fucking nuclear,' he says.

'Well, yes, it would be.'

He glances at me before taking a swig from his lager can, irritation evident on his face, but he doesn't say anything.

He's younger than me. When we first hooked up he said he was three years younger but the gap between us is six years which means he was still in his twenties when we met. He doesn't look younger than me, he says that's because I look so young, so hot. Well, that's what he said at the beginning, he doesn't say it now.

I've had my thirty-nineth birthday and he'll be thirty-three soon.

'I've been thinking about the wedding,' I say, just as he stuffs another steaming mouthful in. I haven't. And that's when I realise I never think about our wedding anymore.

But then, I don't think Gary does either. When we first got engaged we used to talk about it endlessly, what we wanted, who we would invite, where we'd go for our honeymoon, but now we never do.

'Esme,' he says, after he's swallowed down his noodle something or other. 'Is this really the time to be discussing this, when we're both knackered?'

'Nah,' I say. 'Suppose not.' I let him off. And myself. There's never going to be a wedding. I'm certain of that now.

'Hey, did I tell you, got a message today, my tenant's moving out.'

'No, you didn't.' I wonder when he thinks he told me that?

'Yeah, served a month's notice but actually moving out before that. Bloody nuisance. Means I might be a bit short this month. I might have to dip into the savings, see how it goes. I told the agent to get on and find another tenant pronto but with all the checks and shit they have to do I bet the flat sits empty for weeks.'

I laugh. The savings that he so glibly refers to are actually our wedding fund. After he moved in, having rented his flat out, I opened a joint savings account which he said he would put the money he received from the rent in every month and I would match it. He managed it for three months, me four, because I didn't realise he had stopped. We, or rather he, has dipped into it a few times. There is exactly eleven-hundred-and-twenty-three pounds in there now. I don't know what he spends his money on, he has a good job, well paid and with bonuses. Too much golf and the nineteenth hole I suspect.

'There's not much in the savings,' I say.

'Yeah, I suppose we have had a few pounds out of it.'

'You have,' I snap.

'Last time was for that nice little spa weekend and I didn't see you complaining then,' he snaps back, before shoving another forkful of food into his mouth. Grease slides down his chin.

'Yeah,' I say, defeated and far too tired to have an argument about it.

'Anyway,' he says. 'We've got plenty of time for that, not like we're in a rush, is it?'

Evidently not.

He's gone to work early today and I'm going in a bit later because of yesterday. At least I can make the bed properly instead of standing on the other side of the room and hurling the duvet at it and hope that it actually lands on the bed like he does. He's used my hairdryer again too; I heard it whirring away while I pulled the duvet further over my head and tried to get back to sleep. And he's left it on the floor again. He really needs to get a hairdryer of his own. But I won't be buying it.

After my shower I can't find my dry hairbrush – yes I have a special hairbrush I only use when my hair is dry, it's supposed to prevent breakage and calm frizz. I bet Gary's had it. I hunt around in the bathroom getting increasingly annoyed when I don't find it.

Is it my imagination or is Gary doing more things to irritate me than he ever has? Is he doing it on purpose?

Or is it me? Am I just a grumpy cow? I'm not premenstrual; Gary says he can always tell when I'm premenstrual because I snap at him. The last time he accused me of this I most definitely was not premenstrual. So he trotted out the drama-llama epithet again. I don't call him names, not even behind his back.

Oh my God, a horrible thought strikes me. Can I be perimenopausal? I'm nearly thirty-nine. Could it be that? I slump down on Gary's side of the bed and sigh. I hope it's not that. I want a family. I want to have babies before it's too late. Maybe my jibing

Gary last night about the wedding was a deep-seated cry for help. How do I find out if I'm perimenopausal? Does that mean I don't have any more eggs? I don't know much about fertility or menopause or anything like that really; I've spent all my assumed fertile years trying to avoid getting pregnant. But now, sitting here wallowing, I'm beginning to wonder. Maybe I've never been fertile. Maybe all those years on the pill, with a coil, insisting on condoms, maybe all that was futile.

How do I find out how much time I've got left to have a baby?

Ovulation tests. The answer pops into my head almost unbidden. I've seen them on the supermarket shelf in the medicine aisle. I'll get one next time I'm in there. If I'm still ovulating I can't be perimenopausal, right? I don't know.

I lean over to close Gary's bedside drawer which he's left slightly open; I'm sure he does it to annoy me. Just as my hand reaches the drawer, I see something, I yank it open. My brush. What the hell? It's got hair in it too. I hate that and it's not my hair. Gary has fair hair, not exactly blond but much lighter than my own. I start to pull out the fair hairs while heading for the bathroom bin. As I walk I pull out a very long blonde hair. I stop. Very long. My hair is not very long, I have a sleek, very dark, chin length bob. I pull out another strand and examine it. What the hell? I throw the brush in the bin, then fish it out and lay it on a piece of loo roll. Evidence.

I wash my hands and use my 'wet' hairbrush.

Maybe I don't need to bother getting that

ovulation test.

I'm home before him so I start dinner. The salmon and new potatoes he said he would cook for me last night.

I've just finished eating mine when he finally bursts through the door.

'You're late,' I say, keeping my voice light.

'Yeah, sorry.' He kisses me on the cheek as he passes. 'Mine in the oven?' he asks.

'Yes. I didn't realise you were working late or I would have waited.'

He turns and looks at me, silent for a moment too long. 'Yeah, no, had a quick catch up with Nige. Just a quick, cheeky pint.' He grabs the oven gloves, pulls out his plate. I covered it with tin foil so it didn't dry out, very generous of me really.

'But you spent all day with Nige yesterday, didn't you? Golfing.'

He swallows and his Adam's apple bounces. 'Yeah, well, a lot can happen overnight, he's having a few problems. Lady problems.' He grins, he thinks it's funny that Nige has no luck in relationships.

I wonder if he'll think it funny when he realises he doesn't either.

Two

I saw Gary this morning.

I was driving to work and at a standstill in traffic; he was standing in the queue outside Costa waiting to get his customary latte with an extra shot. God knows how much that costs and he has at least one every day, he knows how to waste money.

He was chatting to a girl in the queue, an animated chat that involved a lot of smiling and laughing. I can't remember the last time he laughed like that with me. Then just as I pulled away, he wrapped his arms around the girl and kissed her, proper kissing, an embarrassing public display of affection that he always claimed to hate. When he was with me. The girl was blonde, and she was a girl, much younger than Gary and very much younger than me.

I suppose that's her.

His new fiancée. Yes, that's right, the new future Mrs Prendergast. When *we* were first engaged I used to practice writing my married name, Mrs Esme Prendergast instead of Ms Esme Haste. I was quite sure I was going to change my name. I know it's sad, juvenile, the sort of thing a teenager does, but I liked it. I used to draw a heart and put our initials inside. God, I was pathetic. Whatever happened to the strong independent woman that was supposed to be me?

Well, she's back now.

The evening of the day I found the evidential hairbrush was shocking in its brevity. I accused Gary of having an affair with a blonde woman who had also, and this enraged me far more than the affair, been in my house and used my hairbrush, and now I come to think of it, probably my hairdryer too. What woman in her right mind uses another woman's hairbrush? I mean, urgh. But she wasn't a woman, not a grown-up one. He didn't even deny it. Didn't make any excuses, didn't try to justify it, just nodded silently.

Then he asked if he could stay until the tenant moved out of his flat.

That was it.

I wanted a big row, I wanted tears – from him – contrition, begging for forgiveness, not that I was ever going to forgive him, but nothing. He just accepted his fate, resigned to it, seemingly not bothered at all. I don't understand infidelity. I mean, I really don't. If you want to be with someone else then be with someone else. Everyone changes their mind. It's the same as buying a house or a car, a big purchase, sometimes a lifelong commitment, especially a house, but you're allowed to change your mind. You can decide you don't like the area, or the street or even the kitchen. It's acceptable to decide you want something different and move on. Nothing is for ever. It's not a great thing but it's okay to change your mind in a relationship. But at least have the decency to move on properly, to finish with one person before you start with another. At least be honest and decent about it. This is why hook ups are so much better; there's no pretence at fidelity, everyone knows the rules.

'You can go and stay with your new girlfriend,' I spat.

'Can't at the mo,' he said. 'She still lives with her parents.'

I felt sick. 'What is she? A child?'

He shrugged in that way that had always irritated me; like hey, nothing matters much, nothing to see here.

'So can I?' he ventured again. 'I can sleep in the spare room.'

'No. You can't. You're out tonight. I told you right from the start that to me commitment and fidelity mean everything. It's why I never got myself tied down before you. And, and, may I remind you, *you* asked me to marry you.'

He didn't answer, just stood there looking stupid. I mean genuinely stupid as though he didn't know what to do. So I dragged out one of his sports bags, flung it at him and told him to pack what he needed for a few days and I'd sort out the rest of his shit in due course.

'Sling yer hook,' I'd screeched. God knows where that came from; I'd never used that phrase before, not in my entire life. He didn't call me a drama-llama then I noticed.

He left without much fuss after that. Apparently turned up on Nige's doorstep unbidden. I heard on the grapevine that Nige wasn't best pleased to see him having not had any contact with him for months before that night – so much for the golfing days. And Nige's girlfriend – yes, he had one after all – was even less pleased. He outstayed his welcome there for almost two weeks before he finally got his flat back and moved back in. In the meantime, he'd been round for a few more clothes and I'd been ready for him, waiting on the doorstep with another one of his sports bags full of his clothes, clean and not so clean; well I wasn't doing his washing ever again. I'd changed the locks too so he couldn't get in.

'You've no right to do that,' he said through gritted teeth. 'All my stuff's here. No right at all.'

'Every right actually. I've taken legal advice.' I had too, unofficial but he wasn't to know that; I'd spoken to our legal boff at work.

He didn't comment on that, didn't dare. 'I'll be round for all my stuff when I move back into my flat.' He gave me the date and I nodded my agreement before slamming the door in his face.

I pre-empted his next visit by sending all his stuff round to his flat via courier. It cost a fortune because there was a lot of it and it included his golf clubs – not used in a long time. Unfortunately – for him – he wasn't in when the courier called so they took his stuff away and didn't deliver it for a few more days.

Apparently he had a couple of days without clean underwear because the washing machine at his place was broken. Oh dear, so sad. Perhaps his little girlfriend should have rubbed through a few pairs of his baggy boxers for him, or better still, lent him some of her own. He sent me a message calling me a bitch, I countered with arsehole. We were as immature as his little friend.

I deducted the cost of the courier bill from his half of the eleven-hundred-and-twenty-three-pounds and sent it to his bank account. On the bank reference I wrote Cheating Bastard. I wanted to write a lot more but there wasn't enough room in the online box, which is just as well really because it wouldn't have been as polite as cheating bastard.

And this must be her. I wonder if she's moved in with him yet? Maybe her mum and dad won't let her.

Bitch. Me or her.

Bastard. Definitely him.

But that was months ago and I've moved on.

I have a clinic appointment immediately after work. A fertility clinic. I'm both petrified and excited. It appears that I'm not perimenopausal at all. I have eggs. Many eggs and they've been harvested. They managed to extract twenty. Who knew that little old thirty-nine-year-old me could make so many. I'm so grateful, so relieved. They've also been fertilised. And two have been implanted. Yes, I started investigating IVF the day after Gary left. Call me hasty, Haste is my name after all.

I might be pregnant. Driving on my way to work

and I might be eighteen days pregnant with twins because it's eighteen days since implantation. I've not taken a pregnancy test. I've been tempted but the clinic told me not to. Wait until you come back here, they said. I've taken their advice because if I'd got a negative test I would have been taking another and another until who knows when. This way I'll get a definitive result.

I don't feel any different. Would I feel different? I don't know. The clinic suggested chatting to other prospective mothers, getting into a nice support network. I haven't. And I haven't shared this with anyone yet, not even my mum. I'll tell people once it's confirmed I'm pregnant. Will I tell them how I've achieved it? No, well, maybe my mum.

We've always been honest with each other. She's on my side, my true confidant. She'll understand; she won't judge. She brought me up single-handed after my dad did a runner when I was two months old. She tried to contact him, wanted him to be involved but he vanished into thin air. Until I was seventeen. Then he tracked her down and declared he wanted to be part of our lives. Mum wasn't interested. She'd moved on by then, ironically she'd just married Tim, though they'd been together for a few years by then. He's lovely, my stepdad. But she encouraged me to meet with him, my real dad, my biological dad. Tim even drove me to the pub to meet him; Dan, his name is. Dan my dad.

I get my looks from Mum, we have the same snub noses, the same blue eyes, even the same slightly wonky teeth – although Mum insisted on braces for me, which I thank her for now though not at the time. But I get my colouring from Dad Dan. Dark hair and a soft, olive tone to our skins.

'Hello, darling,' he said, standing up to greet me; we exchanged an awkward and swift hug. It felt uncomfortable and I was sad because I'd expected something else, maybe fireworks and instant love like it is on TV when they match up long lost families. I don't know how long he'd been there but he had a pint in front of him and an empty whisky glass. Mum had said to cut him some slack because he'd be as nervous as I was. Maybe this is what nerves looked like on him. With me it just meant I kept going to the loo and talking too much.

'Glass of wine?' he asked.

I glared at him. 'Coke,' I said. 'I'm not old enough.'

'Just this once. Won't hurt you. No one will know. You don't need to tell your mum.'

I shook my head because Mum never encouraged me to drink. She didn't like it at all. She knew I drank with my mates, of course I did, I was seventeen, but she never bought me a drink or openly approved of my having alcohol.

'No thanks.' I shook my head. I was disappointed in him; Dad Dan. Parents aren't supposed to cajole their kids into underage drinking, are they?

He shrugged. 'If you're sure,' he said, eyeing me suspiciously. 'You must be nearly old enough anyway.'

He got me a Coke and I sniffed it before I sipped it, not quite trusting that he hadn't slipped a vodka in it. I remember thinking what a good-looking man he was. I felt a little buzz of pride – look at my handsome dad. He looked older than Mum although I knew they were the same age because they'd been at college together. He'd carried on and finished his course but Mum had had to abandon hers to have me. Then he ran away.

He started talking, wittering on about his life, where he'd been – Thailand seemed to feature a lot – what he did for a living then, scaffolding. He had never married or had children, so there weren't any siblings for me to get to know, well, none that he knew about anyway – he actually made that joke. He didn't ask about me so I never bothered telling him. I thought he was odd. Sad. At seventeen I didn't have that much life experience but even then to me he seemed like a lost person, no, a loser.

I'd asked Tim to pick me up after two hours and those two hours seemed to drag on for a long time. Conversation did not flow. Dad Dan had another three pints during that time, and I had another Coke which made me burpy. I was glad when Tim waved from the pub door and I was able to escape, letting out a loud burp as I scurried away.

We had a few stilted phone conversations after that and then he came, at Mum's invitation, to my eighteenth birthday bash. I tried my best to make him welcome but honestly, I didn't want to sit holding my stranger-dad's hand all through my birthday party. Tim and Mum were great hosts with him, chatting and behaving as though he hadn't abandoned me and Mum all those years ago.

Then he disappeared again. I've heard from him maybe ten times in the last twenty years and seen him twice.

And that's enough of Dad Dan, biological or not. I much prefer Tim, who treats me like a proper daughter. It's a shame I won't be getting married because Tim would have walked me up the aisle. He'd have been proud of me and I would have been proud to be on his arm.

But there you go. Maybe I'll be making him a granddad soon. He'll love that. Don't know what Dad Dan will think; his track record with babies isn't exactly good. Baby will probably be five before he even finds out it exists.

'Esme Haste.' My name echoes around the waiting room. There's only me in it so there was no need for shouting. 'You just need to do a urine sample before you go in.' She smiles and thrusts a tiny tube at me, it is already labelled with my details.

Inwardly I wince. When I've done samples at home I do them in a jug then pour some into the tube. I wished they'd let me do this at home but apparently they wanted a *fresh* one. Outwardly I smile and trot off to the toilet she's indicating.

At first I can't go – well I went before I left work, like I always do. Then I have to tell myself to get a grip and just wee in the tube. I'm just about managing it when there's a knock on the door and I jerk.

'Everything okay?'

'Yes thanks,' I squeak back.

I've filled the tube, and some. The label on the outside is wet. I spend the next five minutes dabbing it with toilet paper and holding it under the hand dryer. I hope the heat doesn't affect the sample.

She's hovering outside the door when I open it, blue-gloved hand held out waiting for the tube. 'Oh, it's still warm,' she says, then giggles because that really wasn't very professional. 'Take a seat and we'll call you soon.'

Ten minutes later I'm sitting in the doctor's room and she's smiling at me. It must be good news, it must be; she's smiling.

'I'm really sorry,' she says. 'No luck yet.'

I feel myself physically deflate on the chair; it's as though someone has let the stopper out of me.

'It would have been exceptionally lucky on a first go.' She pushes a box of tissues at me and asks if I'd like a drink.

'Are you sure? I mean…' Do I really want to tell her that I had to hand dry the tube? 'Really sure?'

'We can do a blood test to make absolutely sure.' She drops a soft, sympathetic, humouring smile at me.

I wonder how many times she's delivered this shit news in this shit office with its shitty plastic chairs and dusty, lopsided venetian blind? You'd think, with all the money they charge, that they could afford decent décor and furniture. I've gone private because I don't qualify for NHS treatment and I wanted to speed up the process. I hate this room.

'What now?' I ask.

'We start again. I suggest you have a little break

first.'

'So I stop taking the drug?' I've been taking drugs daily since implantation to give the pregnancy a chance. Fat chance.

She nods.

'So when can I book my next implantation?'

She frowns, doesn't answer but flicks back the notes in front of her, then spins round to her computer.

'After we extract some more eggs.'

'But you got twenty.'

'And only two were viable after fertilisation which, at your insistence, we implanted.'

'Oh, I hadn't realised.' I thought I had the possibility of another eighteen goes. I sink lower in the chair, though I don't know how that's even possible.

'So give it a month,' she says. 'Then come back and see me and we'll start again.'

I think of all those drugs, the mood swings, the two days I had to have off sick because of feeling so bad. And I wouldn't tell anyone so I had to lie and say I had a sick bug. All for nothing. And I have to do it again.

She stands up. 'You stay, I'll get someone in to do your blood test.'

'Is there any point?'

She gives me a benign smile and leaves, letting the door close behind her.

I go home and drown my sorrows because that's what strong, independent women do, isn't it? I feel wretched. Then I feel guilty. What if I *am* pregnant, what if the wee test result was wrong and the blood test says differently?

I spend the next two days feeling evil and consumed with guilt until the clinic ring and confirm that my blood test was also negative.

I get a WhatsApp message from Carol-Anne reminding me that the final payment for Kerri's hen do is due this week. Great! Not. I had hoped I could cry off that due to being pregnant. It's in six weeks' time, a very long weekend in Cardiff.

Kerri is twenty-eight and constantly bleating on about being an old bride. One of the drawbacks of being single at my age is that once your peers move off and settle down you end up with friends who are younger than you, well, going out friends anyway. When I first started hanging around with Carol-Anne and Kerri, who I met through work, although she no longer works where I do, we had a lot in common. All out on the pull, or not depending on our moods, and no commitments. Now Kerri is the last one standing. Except for me. I only told them about Gary's departure a month ago, which was two months after I told him to 'sling yer hook.'

I dutifully pay the money into Carol-Anne's account and reply to let her know I've done it. She immediately messages me back and invites me out with her and Kerri later in the week for a quick catchup. I'm almost tempted to refuse when I realise that I haven't got anything else to do, have I? Other than sitting at home and moping on my own. The fertility doctor said take a break, so why not? Though I won't drink alcohol when I'm out with them.

'Hey.' Kerri jumps up and air kisses me when I arrive in the wine bar they have chosen. They already have a bottle on the go and three glasses. Carol-Anne waves the bottle at me.

'No, I won't. Still recovering from a hangover,' I say with a grin and a wince. It may be a few days since my pity party for one drinking binge but it's affects are still lingering. The fur coating on my tongue is only just starting to go.

'Urgh, know what you mean. I find the older I get the harsher the hangovers are,' Kerri says with a laugh before realising what she's just said. She looks embarrassed but decides, wisely, not to pursue it. You can, after all, only backpaddle so far.

I get myself a lime and soda water and make it last far longer than the wine bottle does.

'So what have you been up to?' Kerri asks, putting her arm around my shoulder and pulling me in tight. Has she really only had half a bottle of wine?

'Not a lot,' I say.

'Is it still off between you and Gary?'

'Very much so.'

'Good,' Carol-Anne says. 'Because I bumped into him in Waitrose the other day and he had that girl-child dangling off his arm. She clings to him like a limpet.'

'Probably afraid of getting lost in the shop,' I quip, and we all giggle.

'Yes, she looks a bit lost,' Carol-Anne says. 'No disrespect, but what does she see in him? He's almost old enough to be her dad.'

'He's not that old.' I don't know why I'm defending him.

'No, sorry, of course not.' Now Carol-Anne is embarrassed.

'He's younger than me.'

'Nooo,' they chorus. 'Nooo.'

'Six years.' When we first got together and I found out about our age gap I made a conscious decision not to tell my friends how much younger he was.

'Are you sure about that? He doesn't look younger than you.' Kerri stops then looks at me. 'Or maybe it's just that you look so young.'

'That's it,' I say, trying to make light of it. I don't know why we're all focussing on my age this evening. Maybe we're not and I'm just hypersensitive.

'We'll have to find you someone worthy of you,' Kerri says.' I'll talk to Garth.' Garth is her fiancé, soon to be husband.

'No, don't. I'm really not interested. I've decided that I prefer life without men. I really don't need one.'

'But I thought you wanted a family and all that, you were all talk about getting married last year. We were all expecting our invites, we'd even started thinking about your hen party.' They both giggle.

I shudder to think what they had in mind; I'm sure I've had a lucky escape there. 'Nah,' I say.

'Shall I get another?' Kerri waves the empty wine bottle around, before trotting off to the bar. When she comes back she has a barman in tow carrying a tray with the new wine and three new glasses.

'Got you a glass just in case,' she says, grinning at me.

'Oh, go on then.' What the hell? Why not? It's not work tomorrow. I might as well. I am going to limit myself though, I can't bear another hangover like the last one.

Several glasses and another bottle, or possibly two, later and I'm spilling my guts and telling them all about the fertility clinic. They listen wide-eyed and speechless. The alcohol has loosened my tongue and it's running away with itself. I'm blabbing all my secrets.

'You can try again, darling,' Kerri says, hugging me again. 'My cousin's best friend did it and she had twins just like that. Course they were prem and had to stay in hospital for months.' She sees my face drop. 'But they're absolutely fine now. Great in fact.' She smiles a bit too broadly.

'Yeah, I know I can go again.' I can afford to financially because the clinic persuaded me to buy a package. They said if I got lucky the first time I would get a partial refund. The offer was too good to refuse. 'I just can't bear the thought of it at the moment,' I say. 'All those drugs, injecting myself every day to stimulate my ovaries, plays havoc with your emotions.' I take another swig of wine. 'Then the extraction, the fertilisation, the implantation…' I shudder. Maybe I need to take a longer break than a month. But age is against me, I'll be forty before I have a baby even if I get lucky immediately.

'Who's the father?' Carol-Anne says, her normally smooth brow furrowing in puzzlement.

'Oh, I chose a donor.'

'How?' She's crinkled up her nose now.

'Like from a brochure?' Kerri asks.

'A bit. A database. You tell them what you want, they find some suitable choices, you pick from them.'

'Really? Wow. What did you ask for? Tall, dark and handsome?' She giggles.

'Yes, that's almost exactly what I asked for.' I giggle now. It does sound faintly ridiculous now I say it out loud. 'That's the easy bit, for them too, just knock one out over a porny mag.' We all start screech-laughing now, and someone on the other side of the wine bar shushes us.

'Bog off,' Kerri whispers, and we giggle some more.

'As usual it's the woman who has to suffer,' Carol-Anne says. 'I think you're very brave, Esme. I really do. Like you say, all those drugs and procedures and stuff.'

I smile. I don't honestly know if I can go through it again, or face the possibility of failure again. That's the hard bit. Maybe when it's successful it's all worth it. If it had been successful this time I certainly wouldn't be focusing on that now. Where's my inner strong independent woman when I need her?

As if reading my mind Kerri says, 'I read about a woman who got lucky on her sixteenth attempt, and she was older than you.'

'Kerri!' Carol-Anne snaps.

'Sorry. Shut up my big mouth.' She grabs her wine glass and takes another glug. So do I. 'Couldn't you, you know, just, well, you know…'

Carol-Anne and I stare at her. 'What?'

'Meet someone and just do it, you know, a one-night stand. Make sure you're ovulating first, get one of those kits. Keep doing that until you strike lucky.'

'Urgh no, Kerri,' Carol-Anne says. 'You don't know where they've been. At least a clinic tests the stuff, doesn't it? For germs and STIs and things, I mean.' She turns to look at me.

'Yes, they do.'

'You should check out one of those Facebook groups.' Kerri looks between me and Carol-Anne.

'What Facebook groups?' I ask.

'You know where there are donors, men obviously, who are willing to… donate.'

'Oh yeah, I've heard of them,' Carol-Anne agrees. 'Some of the men are proven to be very fertile, got like five kids themselves and don't want any more but are happy to spread the l-u-r-v-e.'

We all giggle when she says that.

'Sounds sordid,' I say.

'No, I don't think it is. Well, not completely anyway.' Kerri picks up her phone and starts flicking through it. 'Here,' she says. 'Here's one.' She thrusts the phone at me and sure enough there's a Facebook group called Sperm Donors and Receivers. It gives a brief intro but to find out more you have to join.

'I don't think so,' I say, handing her phone back.

'It all sounds a bit dodgy.'

'Yeah, better to st..stick with the ch..chemicals,' Carol-Anne says, slurring her words slightly. 'You know where you are with medical procedures.'

'Yes, keep it clean and neat and tidy. Clinical,' Kerri adds.

'Quite,' I say, helping myself to another glass of wine.

Three

I've joined the Facebook group. Well, two to be exact; two groups.

I know what you're thinking. I know what I said. I know all this. But I was only investigating, like you do. I joined one of the groups the day after our catch-up and Kerri's words were still spinning in my head. And my hangover wasn't as bad as the last time, so at least I could focus on what I was reading.

I was just curious. Where was the harm?

So I've postponed my next appointment at the fertility clinic. Put it off for another month. I'm questioning the wisdom of this but I need a break from the drugs, the moods, the stress. I'm being pathetic, I know, because if I really wanted a baby I'd just suffer it, wouldn't I?

And I do want a baby. I just wanted one in better circumstances.

Anyway, I've been communicating with Roger. He's fifty-two, has four children of his own, two very young grandchildren and he's fathered six babies via donation and says his maximum will be ten. After that he will stop. We've been chatting via

WhatsApp and yesterday we did a video call. Roger and his wife Sue, who was also there. They showed me pictures of their children and grandchildren. It all sounded very genuine, I mean *very* genuine, but how can you tell? Judging by the photos, their kids and grandkids are beautiful. I asked what's in it for them and they both laughed. Roger said he just wanted to spread joy and Sue agreed with him. And Roger is tall, dark and blue-eyed, so fits my criteria.

So, we're giving it a go. I made this decision after I'd spoken to two of the women who'd already had successful pregnancies via Roger's donation. Of course they could have been fake. But they both had children with them. One a little boy of about three months and the other a little girl aged four, that mother was also pregnant again via Roger. Both these women have infertile partners and couldn't afford private IVF as neither fitted the NHS criteria.

Roger and Sue live over a hundred miles away from me which is good because I'm not likely to bump into them in Sainsbury's or Asda one Saturday morning, am I? Also, if I do have success the distance reduces the chances of my child meeting a half-sibling sometime in the future. Although in this global world you cannot ever be sure of anything. I've put that thought out of my mind, it's the only way I can cope.

Roger has sent me a contract which basically says he won't charge me for his donation and I won't ever ask him for money for child maintenance and he won't be named on the birth certificate or have any legal rights at all. Which all sounds good to me.

I have to bring it with me when we meet in person.

I've been plotting my cycle and I've got one of those kits to check my ovulation and well, we're having a go this week. The kit has more in it than just an ovulation test. Sue had sent me the Amazon link and told me to buy it, it cost just over thirty pounds. We're meeting on Thursday. I'm taking the day off work and the Friday, too. I should be fertile then and well… I'm scared.

We're meeting half-way. No money has been asked for, not one penny, but I have had to book and pay for two rooms at a hotel they've chosen. I've done it. I'm only staying one night, they say they might stay longer but I'm only to pay for the one night, they'll pay extra if they decide to stay on. It depends on the hotel and the area, they said.

So we're doing it.

I just hope it doesn't turn into the same fiasco as the last time.

Yes, that's how desperate I am. Roger is not as they say, going to be my first rodeo.

My first contact was with Jeremy. I thought he sounded cultured, or at least his name did anyway. Although to be fair my judgement was severely clouded by alcohol. I blame Kerri for what happened.

No, I take full responsibility myself. I am a grown up, a strong independent woman. Ha ha.

Kerri grabbed my phone when I went to the toilet and joined me to one of the Facebook groups. Within half an hour I was getting messages and I was so intoxicated with both the idea and alcohol that I allowed myself to be hooked up with Jeremy.

Giggling and stupid we hurriedly worked out when I would most likely be fertile – given how many drugs I'd been on for the IVF I really don't know how we'd worked it out. Before I knew what was happening a date was arranged, my address given and Jeremy was booked.

'But how does it work?' I asked the girls who both roared with laughter. 'No, I mean how do I, you know, get it up… in the right place?'

'Good point,' Kerri said, grabbing my phone again and tapping away furiously.

Ten minutes later Jeremy replied to say not to worry he would bring the requisite – he used that word, which I rather liked – kit.

The date agreed was the following Saturday and more than once in the week preceding, I considered cancelling. I messaged Kerri and Carol-Anne and told them I was going to pull out, they dared me not to. Many messages flew between us before I agreed to go ahead. As Kerri pointed out, it wasn't costing me anything, other than my time.

The appointed time arrived and there was no sign of Jeremy. Once sober I hadn't been very happy about Kerri giving him my address anyway; what if he was an axe killer? An hour passed and there was still no sign of him; I felt so relieved. I felt light, as though a weight had quite literally been lifted off my shoulders.

I checked my phone in case he'd messaged, but he hadn't. He was a scammer, or at least a bullshitter.

I was sitting with my feet up, flicking through a

glossy magazine, half-watching a cheesewhiff film on TV and enjoying a cup of strong, black coffee when I heard a roar outside. I leapt up to see what was going on. A beaten-up car had pulled onto my drive. Oh God was this him? Should I just hide and pretend I wasn't in?

My phone beeped and a message came through on Facebook.

Hi Ellie – great start, he couldn't even get my name right. *Jeremy here, sorry I'm a bit late, bit of a trek from my hometown. Anyway, ready to do the deed now.*

I didn't reply. He wasn't deterred.

Success rate is higher if done the natural way. I knew he was dodgy. I turned the TV off and dashed to my front door to put the chain on. And I didn't reply.

Or I can just drop you off a fresh deposit, no contact required.

I thought for a moment. If I did that he could just leave his deposit and go. The sooner the better.

Yes please, I messaged back, expecting a swift knock on the door.

Cool. Won't be long.

I stood to the side of the front window and watched his car. In my naivety I expected him to climb out of the car immediately. When he didn't I wondered if he wanted me to go and collect it.

Then I realised what he meant by fresh.

It wasn't long before his car was rocking to and fro, gently at first and then the momentum got up. His head was rolling back and forth, I could see his shoulder jerking. Jerking. Yes, definitely jerking. It was so obvious what he was doing. On my drive.

What was he thinking? It was broad daylight, the middle of the afternoon, a Saturday when there were people about everywhere. What if one of my neighbours saw him? What if one of their children did? My drive isn't exactly hidden. It, like everyone else's in the street, is very open.

I slumped down on the floor and wanted to die. And I couldn't bear to look out of the window again.

'Hurry up, hurry up and go,' I muttered to myself, saying it several times like a mantra.

But when I heard nothing, no knock on the door, I assumed he wanted me to go and collect it. I stood up, looked outside and saw that the car was still rocking. Oh my God, how long was this going to take? He was obviously having a few problems knocking one out. On my drive. Yuk.

Then the car stopped moving and no more than thirty seconds later the door was flung open. Out climbed a man in his forties, I think, it was hard to tell. He looked scruffy, baggy jogging bottoms hung loose around his skinny arse. He sauntered over to my front door carrying a supermarket plastic bag. Then he rapped hard on the door.

I steeled myself to face him, scuttled along the hallway and opened the door. I kept the chain on.

'Hello Ellie,' he said, grinning at me. I was fixated by his teeth, he only had a few on the top row. He thrust the carrier bag at me. 'There you go, two lots in there to give you a better chance.'

I didn't want to take it; I didn't want it at all. But if I took it he would go, wouldn't he? I snaked my hand out through the gap between door and frame.

He pushed the carrier bag into my hand. It was sticky and inwardly I recoiled. I swallowed to control my gag reflex.

'Okay then.' He turned to walk away. 'Use it while it's still warm, more effective that way.'

'Thank you,' I called, suppressing the urgh to gag again. 'Thank you very much.' I felt disgusted with myself for taking the deposit but also for being so ungracious, for being so disdainful. He was doing me a huge favour. He wasn't charging me. No money had been asked for or given. Yes, he'd suggested sex but he hadn't demanded it. 'Thank you,' I called again as he reached his car.

'No problem. I'll be back in an hour for me equipment back.' With that he climbed into his car, started the engine and backed off the drive while I stood with the sticky supermarket plastic bag still in my hand and dangling out of the door, my mouth hanging open. As he drove off he tooted his horn several times and waved.

I had to take the chain off to bring the *deposit* inside. My heart was beating fast and I felt sick. Yet I couldn't prevent myself from looking inside the bag. Nestling in the bottom was a turkey baster – the last time I'd seen one of those was at Mum's house when she was basting the Christmas turkey. I'll never be able to look at that again without gagging.

What had he said about coming back in an hour for his equipment? He meant this. Oh my God, it had been used before.

I hunted around under the sink until I found a pair of seldom used rubber gloves. Once I had pulled them on I retrieved the turkey baster from the bag; the bulb was still warm. I gagged. I ran with the baster to the toilet, yanked off the bulb and tipped the contents away, then I filled it with hot water and tipped it in the toilet again. I could smell the warm, salty tang of semen. I filled the sink with hot, soapy water and washed the turkey baster out. Then I used toilet paper to dry it as best I could. I took it back to the kitchen, put it back in the bag then ran back to the toilet and scrubbed the pan and basin.

Afterwards I threw the rubber gloves in the bin.

I considered putting the bag outside the front door in the hope that he would just take it, but what if someone came along, a child, or a dog, and took it? No, I'd have to wait.

Exactly an hour later he was back. He stood grinning on the doorstep at me.

'Okay love?' he said.

'Yes, thank you. And thank you so much.' Now it was my turn to thrust the bag at him. 'I've washed it out,' I said, as he looked inside.

'Cool. Let me know if it's successful. I like to keep a tally. So far we're fifty-fifty on the success chart.'

'Okay. Will do.' Please go away now, please.

He smiled and turned away.

'Did you come far?' I asked, mad politeness kicking in.

'Only twenty minutes,' he said.

'Can I give you some money for your petrol?'

'Oh no, Ellie. I do this for love, not profit. I'm an altruist. A philanthropist. Like Bill Gates and them.' He gave me his toothless grin and jogged the few metres to his car. He beeped his horn this time before backing off the drive.

I don't think Bill Gates would count that in his philanthropy.

I told Kerri and Carol-Anne that it was an unmitigated disaster. I didn't give them all the details, but they do know I didn't go through with it. And that's all they know, because I haven't said a word to anyone about Roger.

The drive to meet Roger and Sue is a pleasant one. Where we're meeting is also very convenient for me because it's on the way to Cardiff and it's Kerri's hen weekend. When I've done the business with Roger and Sue – I do feel as though they are both involved which makes it slightly less tacky than with Jeremy – I'll carry on down to Cardiff. I'm booked onto the train with the others. When I told Carol-Anne that I wouldn't be getting the train she said she'd try to sell my ticket – I think she means get a refund but it's probably too late for that. Actually driving is better because it means I won't have to get involved in the boozy party that will start as soon as the train journey does. Obviously, as it will increase my chances of getting pregnant, I'll be watching my alcohol intake carefully over this weekend.

The hotel is lovelier than it looked online. It's small, boutique, in a large leafy garden that leads onto a larger leafy area and overlooking water at the back. A public lake, apparently.

I'm sitting in the bar at a table in the corner as prearranged when Roger and Sue come in. I know them immediately from our video call but they're both taller and slimmer than I expected.

Sue spots me first, coming over and hugging me like an old friend. Then Roger, less ebullient, does the same. He goes off to the bar and orders drinks, coming back with a white wine spritzer each for Sue and me as well as what looks like orange juice for himself.

'I hope you don't mind, I took the liberty,' he says, putting the drink in front of me.

'No, absolutely. Thank you.'

I ask about the contract and then we all sign it, Sue acting as the witness. I don't know if this would stand up in a court of law and I haven't taken any legal advice, official or otherwise. I'm trusting them, they're trusting me.

We've booked a table for dinner. The plan is we'll eat and chat, do the deed, sleep well and go our separate ways. We're soon told our dinner table is ready and as we sit down to eat I've already decided that this is not going to be a repeat of the Jeremy incident.

We chat about ourselves, our lives. It's easier than I expected. Roger is a telecoms engineer and Sue is a nurse. I bore them a little with my job then we chat about holidays, family, more about work and finally, why I want to do this.

'Before it's too late,' I hear myself say. 'I'm not getting any younger.'

'You don't look old,' Sue says.

'If this is successful I'll be forty by the time the baby is born.'

Sue and Roger exchange looks. 'You definitely don't look forty,' Roger says, while Sue frowns at him. 'I'm surprised there's no nice man for you.'

'Roger,' Sue says, but she smiles.

'There was. That was the plan, but then he turned out not to be so nice.'

'I see. So you're going it alone. I admire you for that. It won't be easy.'

'I know. I really do. But I was brought up by a single mum so… And I have a good job with good maternity leave and pay.' I feel a little guilty now because I still haven't told Mum what I'm up to. No point worrying her and Tim with this.

'Very important that.' Roger tucks into his steak.

We don't talk about the actual deed as I've come to think of it. Only checking that our rooms are adjacent so that the transfer will be speedy. This is their talk, transfer, speed.

It's as we're tucking into our dessert that I ask Roger and Sue why they do this? I asked on our video call and they just said it felt right.

Sue glances at Roger who nods.

'Well,' she begins, 'Our sister-in-law couldn't get pregnant. She's Roger's twin brother's wife. They'd been together far longer than us and we had two children by then.'

'It was my brother who wasn't fertile. Turns out I got his.' Roger half chuckles to himself.

'Men,' Sue says, shaking her head. 'They went down the IVF route. No luck. They were despondent. So that's when it started.' Sue finishes her Eton Mess and dabs her mouth with her napkin.

'And they're identical twins so…'

I imagine Roger sneaking into his sister-in-law's bed and impersonating his brother.

'Took several transfers,' Sue says. 'But it worked in the end. I did the inseminations myself.'

'Twice,' Roger adds, waving the waiter over to order coffee. 'They have two children now.'

'Wow. Are they included in the six?'

'Oh yes. But please keep it to yourself. We don't usually tell people.'

'Oh absolutely.' Because I won't be telling anyone anything.

Eventually it's time, we're leaving the table. We've paid the bill – split a third and two thirds at Sue and Roger's insistence – and we're heading up to our rooms.

'I'll come and collect the kit now,' Sue says. 'Did you get the exact one I suggested?'

'Yes, yes I did.'

'Excellent.'

I'm ready for bed and waiting in my room when half an hour later Sue knocks on the door. She's grinning. She comes in and shuts the door behind her.

'Would you like me to put it in the syringe for you?' She holds up a little half full pot.

I nod. This is definitely what I want; the less I can do the better. She goes into the bathroom and comes back minutes later with the syringe on a towel.

'All yours,' she says. 'Good luck, and don't forget it increases the chances if you can have an orgasm afterwards.'

'Thanks,' I say, not able to even look Sue in the eye.

'Give me a call if you have any problems.'

'Thank you,' I mutter.

After she's gone I do the deed, well the two deeds and, trying not to think about Roger and Sue in the next room, I tell myself it will all be worth it in the end.

The next morning we have a leisurely breakfast together. No one mentions what's gone on and Sue says they've decided to stay another two nights as there is a lot to see in the local area and the weather is supposed to be good.

I hope I'm able to contact them soon with good news; they're good people.

Another good thing about driving to Cardiff is that I can go shopping and not have to worry about getting my purchases back on the train. I have a lovely time on my own. I feel really happy. I could be pregnant. Already. If Roger's a twin does that mean I could have twins?

Stop. Don't get carried away. One healthy baby will be sufficient.

I'm sitting in the hotel reception area – it's a nice enough hotel – but seems very plain after the boutique one I was in last night – when they all fall through the door. Kerri is wearing a white tutu and is red in the face, the rest, about twenty of them, are giggling away. They obviously had a good time on the train, not sorry I missed that.

'Esme, hey,' Carol-Anne shouts. 'We missed you.

Need to tell you something.'

Oh dear, not sure I like the sound of that. She goes to the desk and checks us all in, a process which seems to take ages with her calling people over to take their key cards and giving instructions about dinner and what we're doing later. I'm tired just watching them. Finally, there's just me and her left.

'Come on,' she says, waiting for me to drag my wheely case along.

In the lift I notice she only has one key card in her hand. I suddenly have an ominous feeling but I say nothing, letting politeness and patience get the better of me. I have decided that being zen is the way to go if I want this pregnancy thing to work.

She leads the way to a room, opens the door and waves me in. It's a pleasant enough room, very corporate and chain hotel looking, but clean and tidy. I expect her to give me the key then trundle off to find her own room but instead she comes in and shuts the door.

I frown at her.

'Right,' she says. 'We're sharing.'

'No. I paid extra to have my own room.' I sorted this out months ago. Everyone was sharing, some were bunking up three in a room, but not me. I'm too old for that shit. 'There's only one bed.'

'Yeah, but it's enormous.'

'It's a standard king size.'

'Yes, and we're both slim, so it's okay. I promise I won't attack you.' She cackles, and it's more than obvious that she's had a lot to drink, also her eyes are slightly glazed. I hope it's just alcohol but nothing would surprise me.

'I can't share a room, not even with you, much as I like you.' I'm trying to placate her. 'Can't we just book another room?'

'Well, here's the thing. I sold your train ticket at the last minute to Kerri's cousin, who couldn't come originally but then could, anyway, so I got you your money back. I'll give you the fifteen-pounds-ninety in a mo.' She starts glancing around the room for her handbag seemingly unaware that it's slung across her body. 'Anyway, I know you don't know Kerri's cousin so def wouldn't want to share with her so I said I would, cos we're mates, aren't we?' She pulls her lips together in something that's a cross between a pout and a pucker.

And this is exactly why I didn't want to share a room. With anyone. At all. I'm a good ten years older than most of them and even though when this was all booked I wasn't on the having a baby journey, I knew that after a while I'd tire of them all and would want to escape and have some privacy.

'It'll be great,' Carol-Anne says, launching herself across the bed and making a starfish shape. I bet she sleeps like that too. Or worse still, urgh, she'll mistake me for her husband and start cuddling up to me.

'I'll go down to reception and get another room.' I don't even mind paying for it, even though I've already paid extra.

'None left,' Carol-Anne says. 'I already asked. They're fully booked.'

Oh God.

She turns on her side, tucks up her knees, closes her eyes and falls asleep. I look at her, glance around the room, imagine what it will be like later when everyone troops in here for pre-dinner drinks because I know they all have bottles and glasses in their cases. I feel as though I'm going to cry. Why is this bothering me so much? Could it be pregnancy hormones already? Pull yourself together.

I pick up the phone and ring Reception, but Carol-Anne's right, they are fully booked. I stare out of the window, notice a hotel across the road, get out my mobile, find their number and ring them.

Success, they have a room. It's pricey but it's going to be worth every penny.

I shake Carol-Anne awake and tell her I'm moving to another hotel.

'Sure, shee you lates,' she says. 'Check your itineraryrsh, it's on the WhatshApp group.'

I'm almost tempted to just get in my car and drive home. But not tempted enough, it seems.

Once checked in across the road, this hotel is a class above the other one, I check the itinerary and see I have plenty of time to run myself a nice scented bath. This hotel provides some very nice toiletries.

I turn up deliberately late just as the predinner drinks, or more likely the preloading drinks, are finishing. Carol-Anne hosted the event in her/my room, as I suspected she would as she's the organiser. I'm so relieved I decided to move hotel. I refuse a drink and wait while they collect themselves up to go for dinner.

Everyone is wearing a pink t-shirt with Kerri's name stretched across their breasts, everyone except me. Kerri looks me up and down then yells to Carol-Anne who comes over to explain that Kerri's cousin has my t-shirt and do I mind? I assure her I don't. However, there are plenty of sashes to go round and I end up wearing two, criss-crossed and dissecting my breasts perfectly. It makes them very much a focal point.

Five taxis have been booked and we stand on the street in a great, except me, drunken gaggle shouting and laughing. I feel sorry for anyone who has to pass us, but when a stag party stumbles along and a lot of raucous screeching takes place I know what sort of evening I'm in for. But really, what did I expect? I'm a miserable cow.

We pile into a large club, it's called Ringos or Dingos or something like that, I'm not sure. Despite it still being daylight outside, it's quite dark inside the club. After some shouting at the bar by Carol-Anne and Kerri's cousin, we're shown to a long table and everyone stumbles and giggles as they take their seats.

Bottles of wine are already on the table and fortunately so are bottles of water, both still and sparkling. I make myself a white wine spritzer and when I top it up later, I only use sparkling water. Dinner isn't especially memorable but is served quickly and efficiently. It's obvious that this club has this procedure down to a tee. I wonder how many hen parties and stag groups they cater for in a week?

I feel like the biggest party pooper in the world

and I find myself comparing last night's dinner with this one. My meeting with Roger and Sue seems a lifetime away. Maybe it is. A new little life.

Once dinner is over, the wine bottles that aren't empty are grabbed – I grab a sparkling water – and we decamp to the disco at the back. It's loud. I thought the dining area was loud but here the music is thumping into the walls, the floors, the chairs and tables. More drinks appear, including shots, and then the dancing starts.

I am such a party pooper that I'm already planning my escape and have seated myself as close to the door as possible. That way when I do go it won't be so noticeable. As well as being loud it's also very hot in here but thankfully there's a little burst of cooler air every time the door is opened.

Even though I offered to look after the handbags, I'm soon dragged up for a dance. Someone laughed in my face when I made my offer, jangling her tiny handbag which was attached to her wrist. Oh well. I slide my bottle of sparkling water down onto the floor and tuck it under my seat before getting up.

I like dancing, even when I'm not drunk and everyone else is. Inevitable someone falls down and is hauled up by the others. Carol-Anne is suddenly in possession of several blow-up pink hammers which she distributes around the group. I don't get one but I do get a bonk on the head which, of course, doesn't hurt but does annoy me. Party pooper.

I use this as an excuse to slink back to the table and retrieve my water from under my seat. Some of the others slump back down next to me and then I spot a group of, what should I call them, boys? Men? Lads. Definitely lads, heading our way.

'Dance, dance,' they seem to roar collectively. Soon everyone is pulled up onto the dance floor, everyone except me. Now would be a good time to make my escape.

Except it wouldn't because there's a spare man for me. He's just standing there looking at me, trying not to stare at my pink, criss-crossed boobs. He's older than the rest of his group. Maybe *he's* the party pooper in *their* midst.

'May I?' he asks, gesturing towards the seat next to me.

'Sure.' I shrug, then remember where I am and smile.

'Is that water?' he shouts, because only shouted conversation can take place in here.

'Sparkling.' I yell back.

'Could I have some?' He yanks a clean glass from the middle of the table and waits for me to pour some of my precious water into it.

I half fill it.

'Thank you.' Even shouting, his voice sounds nice. 'I'm too old for this shit.'

I laugh before yelling, 'Tell me about it.'

'Shall we go somewhere quieter?'

Four

We've navigated our way to a table in the corner of the front bar. It's much quieter and it's near the door, the street door; I'm still anticipating my early escape.

He gets another bottle of sparkling water from the bar before sitting opposite me. We have a table for two, nice and cosy, and no space for anyone else. He's just pouring me a glass when Kerri and her cousin appear at the bar.

'Hoi hoi,' Kerri yells. 'Didn't take you long.'

I nod and smile, though it's more of a grimace. I wish I'd just slinked out of the door.

'Your bride,' he asks?

'Yep.'

'My groom is more intoxicated than your bride.' He smiles then, it's a nice smile. 'I'm Matthew, by the way,' he says. 'Most call me Matt.' He holds out his hand for me to shake. It seems weird in these surroundings but I do.

'Esme,' I say. 'Most call me Esme.' Then we both laugh.

The light is better here than it was in the disco

and I can see his face well. He's bald and brown-eyed. Pleasant faced though not what you'd called great looking but certainly not ugly. Attractive, I suppose, yes attractive, but he looks tired.

'You're not drinking?' he asks.

'No, no.' I don't elaborate.

'Me neither. I need to leave early and get back to work in the morning.'

''Oh, was it worth coming? I mean did you have to come far?'

'Far enough. And no, it wasn't worth coming really. But I'm the last-minute stand-in best man so…' He nods his head a little.

'What happened to the best man?'

'Broke his leg skiing day before yesterday. Stuck over in Switzerland somewhere.' He rolls his eyes theatrically. It makes me smile. 'To be honest I'm a bit old for all this, well, mentally anyway.'

'Yeah, me too.'

'You don't look it.'

'I'll take that compliment, thank you.'

'You're more than welcome. So what's your story?'

'My story?'

'I mean why are you not necking back the shots like your friends?'

'Like I said, I've kind of grown out of all this. I do wonder why I even came.'

'Yeah,' he says, with a sigh.

'Listen to the old party poopers.' I laugh when I say it and he joins in. He seems nice. Really nice.

Then we have a long conversation about not

drinking. He's been teetotal for two years now and he feels so much better for it. The way he tells it, it sounds as though he had a bit of a drink problem.

'You think I was an alcoholic,' he says, reading my mind. Are my thoughts really so obvious on my face?

'No, no. Not at all.'

'I wasn't but it was probably only a matter of time. I've seen the destruction alcohol dependency can cause, so I thought, enough's enough. I did dry January and felt so much better, just carried on. What about you?'

'I'm not teetotal. I'm just being careful. I can't stand the hangovers.' None of which is untrue, it's just not the whole truth. I'm hardly going to tell a stranger that I might be pregnant. Especially when I might not be.

Sue had said to me that Roger was willing and able to give it as many goes as it took if it wasn't successful first time and I still wanted to. Much as I liked Sue and Roger I don't want this turning into a long, drawn-out saga. I want a baby and I want it now.

'Penny for them,' he says.

'What?'

'Your thoughts. You zoned right out there.'

'Oh, um, sorry. Just tired. Been really busy lately. Work and stuff.'

'Yeah, I know what you mean.'

Right then a big cheer goes up from the bar. We turn and look. 'M-A-T-T, M-A-T-T,' is being chanted and fingers are being pointed at us.

Matt gives them a sheepish wave and fortunately they soon lose interest in us as the barman is now serving them.

'Sorry,' Matt says.

'Your groom?'

'No, some of his juvenile mates.'

'They seem to know you well.'

'Yeah, don't know why. I couldn't name one of them, not one.'

'I suppose it's because you're the new best man.'

He grimaces.

'Don't you want to do it?'

'No, not at all. But I must. And I'll have to do it justice, do a proper job. I've already had to wangle the day off at work which didn't go down well. But I'll do my best, as best man.' He smiles a little smile and his eyes crinkle which accentuates the dark circles under his eyes.

'Couldn't he get anyone else?'

'Well,' he grins, 'You've seen the best of the rest.'

We laugh together then.

'I wish they would hurry up and go back to the dancing, I was planning on making a speedy escape.'

'Me too,' I say. 'I don't think anyone is going to miss me either.' Then I bore him with the hotel room mix up, if mix up is the right word.

'I can't believe it,' he says, shaking his head. 'I'm the same, staying in a different hotel because I didn't want to share and I needed to leave early. Though unlike you I was never booked to come in the first place.'

'Your groom sounds desperate.'

'Like I said, you've seen the pool he had to pick from. I went to school with his big brother, was always round their house, so I've known him for years. Odd choice, I thought, but then…' He jerks his head towards the lads at the bar, they're still trying to organise their drinks and the barman looks bored out of his head. I bet he has to put up with this shit all the time.

Finally, amid a lot of clattering and shouting, they leave the bar area with several trays of drinks and head back to the disco. Sadly they're soon replaced by another group of rowdies, this time girls, fortunately not Kerri and co.

We sigh simultaneously, then laugh. It's horrible being a party pooper.

'Couldn't his brother do best man duties?'

'He *was* the best man. He's the idiot with the broken leg.'

'Oh, that's even worse. Will he make it back for the wedding? When is it?'

'Next weekend. And frankly, I doubt it. He's had fairly major surgery on it and even if they got him back to the UK in time, which I don't think is doable, he'll be in no fit state to be going anywhere.'

'Sounds grim. Poor man. I've never been skiing.'

'Me neither. Never appealed. Too cold, too dangerous.' He looks at his watch. It's an expensive looking Tag Heuer. I know this brand because Gary wanted one for Christmas, he seriously expected me to buy it too. The most expensive thing I was prepared to get him was a decent hairdryer. He never got that either.

'Nice watch,' I say. 'Do you use all those dials and things?'

He glances at the watch again. 'Sometimes, in my job. Sorry, rude of me to keep looking at it. I was wondering how long I should stay before I sneak off.'

'Why don't we go now. We've finished the bottle of water and I don't feel like fighting at the bar for another one, do you?'

'No.'

Without further discussion we up and leave.

Outside the air is cool and clean. I gulp down a lungful.

'Does feel a bit like that, doesn't it?' he says, doing the same. 'I'll get you a taxi.' He leaps out into the road and hails one. After it coasts into the kerb alongside us, he holds the door open for me. 'Where are you going?' I tell him the name of my hotel and he smiles. 'Me too,' he says. 'Can I cadge a ride with you?'

He insists on paying for the cab and we're soon going through the door of our hotel. It's so sedate and peaceful, quiet muzak, which I would normally hate, is playing and after the noise and rowdiness of the club it's very calming.

'Fancy a nightcap?' He nods towards the bar, gleaming and tidy, with no other customers in sight.

'Okay. Do you think they do coffee?'

'Let's ask.'

When we ask, a menu is proffered. I see exactly what I want and it's not coffee.

'Hot chocolate for me, please.'

'With marshmallows?'

'Yes, please.' Suddenly it feels like Christmas. Weird that. It's not Christmas.

'Are you local?' he asks.

'No, no, not at all. What about you?'

'Ditto.'

And that's the only conversation we have about where we live. Maybe we intend to go back to it, but we never do.

We chat about nonsense really, our top ten best films; he, as might be expected, likes action movies. For me it's romcoms. He smiles when I admit this.

'Do you think they reflect real life?' he asks, his face earnest.

I think about my life of late, sneaky Gary and the never-never wedding. I really don't understand why he proposed in the first place. Long term he spoiled a good thing; sex with him was always great and then we went our separate ways. I don't really understand what motivated him to ask me to marry him.

'Not really,' I admit. 'But I live in hope.' Spinning the question back on him I say, 'Do you think action movies reflect real life?'

He grins at me. 'Fucking hope not.' We both laugh, it's funny how casual, occasional swearing makes people laugh, it shouldn't, but it does. 'Because if it does any minute now a ten-tonne truck is going to come crashing through that window.' We both wince at the prospect. 'And no one will be injured.'

'Apart from a bit player, a minor actor, who you'll be able to pick out way before it happens.'

'But in a romcom it'll be the quiet guy who wins the girl,' he says, countering my ribbing.

'Not always. Anyway, even if he is quiet, he'll be shit hot.'

'Oh yeah, I forgot that. He'll have abs, pecks, triceps, biceps, quads, the lot that can only be attained with anabolic steroids but he'll never go to a gym even though he'd need to be there five hours a day to look like that.'

'Stop it, you're shitting on my favourite films.'

'You shit on mine.'

'I didn't, you did.'

We giggle together. This evening has turned out far better than I imagined. I really didn't expect to have a laugh this evening; I was expecting a headache.

'I'm going to have a brandy,' he says, standing up. 'I find it helps me sleep. What about you?'

I think for a moment or two. One brandy wouldn't hurt, would it? I imagine the warm liquid flowing down and making me sleepy, and my potential baby.

'Go on then, just the one.'

He calls the barman, who seems to have been polishing glasses the entire time we've been sitting here, and orders two brandies. He asks for a specific brand and when informed the hotel doesn't have it, quickly moves onto another, then another.

'You know your brandies,' I quip. 'Not exactly teetotal or dry.'

'No. You've caught me out. My only vice. Don't drink as such, don't smoke or do drugs, so brandy, yeah, but only ever one.'

'A large one,' I say, as the glasses are put on the table.

'Yeah, they are.' He frowns but picks up his glass and takes a sip. 'Best place you've ever been on holiday,' he says, holding up his glass to the light like a connoisseur.

'Norway. For the fjords.'

'Good choice.'

'Is yours Thailand?' I think of Dad Dan.

'No, though I have been there, as a student. Nice enough.'

'So?'

'Australia. Spent my gap year there. Wide open spaces, fantastic beaches, great weather.'

'Great weather, yeah. All that sun. Would you live there?'

'No. All that sun and all that skin cancer.'

'Oh, that's dampened the mood.'

'Sorry.' He looks into the bottom of his glass before taking another sip.

I have to admit that I'm enjoying the brandy too, it's smooth, warm, thick, almost syrupy. 'It's quite sweet this.'

I expect him to start telling me about its provenance or whatever it is, but he doesn't, just smiles at me before finally saying, 'Like you.'

'Ha, ha, I've never been described as sweet. I'm a strong, independent woman I'll have you know.'

'I don't doubt it. I'm a strong, independent man.'

I frown. What a weird thing to say.

'What?' he says, reading my face.

'Just sounds weird that, from a man.'

'But okay from a woman? Isn't that a bit sexist?' He looks at me but I can see a glint in his eye, the sides of his mouth twitching.

'No. Men are always those things even when they're not. Women aren't.'

'Even in this day and age.' He raises his eyebrows – not just one, which is what would happen in one of my romcom films. I don't think many men – people – can actually do that.

'Fuck off,' I mutter, but he hears it and roars with laughter.

'Seriously,' he says. 'I admire strong, independent women.'

'Gee, thanks,' I say, squeaky voiced and coquettish.

'Any time.'

We've finished our drinks now and if he were to offer me another, I'd take it, even though my rational brain is screaming no. But he doesn't. He stands up instead and I follow him.

'Floor?' he asks, as we step into the lift.

'Four.'

'Me too.'

'Well, this is me,' he says, stopping outside a room. 'Thank you for a lovely evening. Much, much better than I was expecting, I'm glad to say.'

'Me too. Thanks for the escape too.'

We giggle. Then he leans in to kiss me goodnight as though we're old friends. He wraps his left arm around my back, pats my shoulder. This feels like the most natural thing in the world. As we part, we both pull away, our eyes meet.

Then our lips do. It's good. Too good. I know where this is going and I don't want to stop it. That brandy has gone straight to my head, and my loins, and before I know what I'm doing I'm inviting him to my room.

'You sure?' he questions.

'Absolutely.'

What follows is frenzied and, on my part at least, desperate. Despite Jeremy's kind offer I haven't been with a man since Gary left. And now I come to think of it we weren't especially active in the run up to his leaving, probably too busy using himself up on her, the child.

'I really needed that,' I hear myself say afterwards. I hadn't meant to say it out loud. We're lying side by side on top of my bed and staring at the ceiling.

'Me too,' he says. 'Thank you.'

'Oh my God, did we use a condom?' Because if we did, I wasn't aware of it.

He sits up, turns and smiles at me, a little cheeky smile. 'Yes, I did.'

'Ah, good. You came prepared then?' I feel a little insulted, no a lot, like a notch on a headboard even if the headboard is mine.

'Not usually. But part of my best man duties was to ensure that everyone was protected.'

'What?'

'I had to buy the condoms and dole them out, bought a bumper box and after sharing them out there were two left, so I stuffed them in my wallet. They were spares for if anyone else needed them.'

'Two?'

'Yes.'

'So you still have one left?'

'I do.'

'And no way of giving it to one of those lads now you've left the party?'

'That's right.'

'Seems a shame to waste it.'

He laughs, it's a deep throaty laugh and I like it, very much. 'But can we get into bed and under the duvet first because I'm freezing,' he says.

'You go ahead, I'm going to the bathroom.'

I take off the rest of my clothes, clean my teeth, and clean all the makeup off my face. Matt probably won't recognise me when I go back into the room.

But when I creep back in under cover of semi-darkness he's snuggled up in my bed and sound asleep. His clothes, and mine, have been picked up from the floor and laid neatly over the chair in the corner. Gary never did that.

I climb in, careful not to wake him up then lie on my back rigid, unmoving. This is a strange turn of events, very strange. It dawns on me that I know nothing about this man, this man who's now lying in my bed. He could be an axe murderer. But he seems so normal, so nice, my rational brain says. Don't they always, my irrational brain screeches back.

I'm so glad I'm not staying in the other hotel with the rest of them. This would never have happened and I enjoyed it. But more than that, no one ever needs to know.

I just hope this doesn't make my potential

pregnancy any less viable. I feel a little flood of guilt, then bizarrely after this, I don't feel anything else because I fall asleep.

I don't know what time it is when I wake up, it's still dark and quiet. Matt is in the bathroom. He comes out and stands silhouetted in the doorway, illuminated only by the light from the smoke alarm in the ceiling. I like what I can see. He looks smooth, trim, fit but not over-muscled.

'Sorry,' he says, shivering a little he climbs back into bed. 'Did I wake you?'

'I don't think so.'

'Do you want me to go?'

'No, why?'

'Well, I don't want to outstay my welcome, inflict myself on you.'

'Don't say that; you're spoiling it now.'

'Sorry.' He leans over and kisses me softly on the cheek.

And that's how it starts again, and it's better this time, no frenzy.

Afterwards I'm staring up at the ceiling again, smiling to myself and watching the little green light flashing on and off. 'I always imagine that's a camera,' I say.

'Really?'

'Yeah. I think a lot of women do.'

'It must see some great sights then.' He laughs.

I slap his arm playfully and he pulls me to him and I fall asleep in his arms. Now that's a first.

The hateful sound of a phone alarm wakes me with

a start. It's truly horrible; I was sound asleep. I'm sure I never set my alarm. It's not my alarm.

'Sorry,' he says, reaching for his phone and silencing it. 'Really sorry.' He sits up and so do I.

'It's okay. You did say you were leaving early.'

'Yeah.' He yawns, then climbs out of bed and starts putting his clothes back on, just his jeans and t-shirt. 'I'd love to spend the day with you but duty calls.' He balls up his socks and underpants in his hands and picks up his jacket and shoes. 'I'm going to shower and change, then I'm going down to breakfast, about eight. Would you like to join me?'

'Um,' I mumble.

'No pressure. I'll be by the lift at eight. If you don't come I'll understand. I expect you want to go back to sleep. I know I do.' With that he leaves my room quietly and without fuss.

I lie back and think about it. Then I hunt around for my bag to retrieve my phone and see that I've got half-an-hour if I want to join him. Half-an-hour to shower, dress, do my hair and makeup so that I don't look like a witch who's been out on the lash the night before, even if I have, although I haven't, not really. He has no hair so I don't suppose it takes him long to get ready. And he doesn't have to bother with makeup, does he?

I turn on my side and snuggle down fully intending to go back to sleep, but I can't. Yet I must have because when I look at my phone again it's quarter-past-eight and I've missed my chance if I did want to see him again.

But I'm hungry now and really thirsty. Despite

this being a pricier hotel than the one across the road, unlike that one this has no tea or coffee making facilities in the room.

I get up. In the bathroom I run the cold tap and fill the toothmug, but the water tastes nasty. So I have a shower; I might as well get up and get dressed now, then I can go for breakfast and he will be long gone.

Once ready and feeling very hungry and thirsty, I grab my bag to leave. That's when I see the note that's been pushed underneath my door. My heart sinks a little as I pick it up. Then, as I open it and see his name and mine, my sneaky stomach does a little flip.

Hi Esme
Sorry I missed you. Knocked on my way back from breakfast hoping to catch you and say a proper goodbye. Obviously, you've either left or are sound asleep and sadly I must leave. Anyway, came back with this note. Thank you for a lovely evening (and night). I realise that we never exchanged phone numbers. I don't even know your last name. My number's below if you ever feel like a catch up.
Kind regards
Matt x

I was in the shower, I think, feeling a little disappointed that I missed him, but also relieved. The last thing I need at the moment is complications. I really enjoyed last night but with my baby plans progressing I don't want to be embarking on a relationship with a man who lives far away and might turn out to be just like Gary.

It's almost ten by the time I wander back from breakfast. I've had a pleasant time on my own. I've wondered how breakfast with Matt might have been, possibly embarrassing. I did rather like him. He did have a nice sense of humour and he was a grown up. This hen party, or specifically last night, has made me fully realise that I'm making the right decisions, moving on and planning a family. I'm done with all this drinking and partying. That phase of my life is over, no matter what happens.

Back in my room I check the itinerary on WhatsApp. We have a dance class at eleven. That should be entertaining; I expect they're all hanging badly. So glad I'm not.

The theme for the dance is Bollywood. Not sure why this was picked but I'm sure it'll be fun. I do enjoy a Bollywood romcom after all; what could be better, romance, comedy usually in the form of misunderstandings, and dancing to great music.

As predicted there are a lot of green faces at the dance class. Two have not even turned up and Carol-Anne is fuming about that. She also tells me that Kerri and her cousin had a big fall out last night so Kerri's cousin came and slept in with Carol-Anne. All I can think is what a lucky escape I had, I imagine playing musical beds in the middle of the night. Urgh. Anyway, I had better things to do.

'And,' Carol-Anne says, 'She had the cheek to complain about me snoring. I don't snore loud and nasty. My husband says it's cute.' She looks most indignant and hurt. Definitely a lucky escape for me. 'What did you get up to? You disappeared early. Kerri said you were with some man.'

'Oh, no,' I say, feeling shy, sneaky, embarrassed and ridiculous. 'I went back to my hotel and went to bed.' It's the truth, just not the whole truth.

Right on cue Kerri saunters over, she definitely doesn't look too good this morning. Her cousin is with her, the pair have obviously made up because they're linking arms. Or it could be that they just need to hang onto each other to stay upright.

'Where did you go last night?' she says, a little accusatory tone to her voice.

'To bed,' I say, looking around the room and wondering when the class will start. 'I don't have the stamina of you young 'uns.' I laugh, trying to make a joke of it, but I just come off sounding like an ancient old biddy.

'We missed you,' Kerri's cousin says and I realise that I still don't know her name. Do I care? Probably not, so I just nod.

'Yeah, you missed the stripper. You'd have loved it. Hot guy, dressed as a fireman. We all thought the place was on fire when he walked in wielding his hose.' Kerri giggles as she says it and her cousin, Carol-Anne and I all join in.

'Shame, I'd have enjoyed that.' I wouldn't particularly, not now I'm a proper, responsible grown-up.

'Don't know what Garth will think, but expect he's had similar.' She titters again and we all nod sagely. Thinking about the doling out of condoms on Matt's stag night, I suspect more was planned, but I could well be wrong.

'Have you noticed Sherri and Elle aren't here?'

I didn't know who was missing, but nod my agreement.

'Copped off,' Kerri's cousin says. 'Not very ladylike, is it? And they're both in relationships. Hope it doesn't get back. What do you think, Esme?'

'No, oh. Well, what happens in Cardiff stays in Cardiff, doesn't it?'

I hope.

I'm so glad I moved hotel.

Five

It's four weeks since my meeting with Roger and Sue. And six weeks since my last period. Which means I'm six weeks pregnant, apparently.

Definitely pregnant. I've wee'd on so many sticks because I cannot believe my luck. Roger has lived up to expectations and more. Sue did say on our video call that he was super fertile with a high sperm count and high motility. Lucky me. Roger and Sue are thrilled for me, urging me to keep them posted. They even want to come and visit once the baby is born.

I've been online and sent them a luxury hamper from Fortnum and Mason. It's the least I can do. It cost an arm and a leg but is worth every penny and a lot cheaper than further fertility treatment. I'm hoping for a bit of a refund from the clinic.

But now I'm scared. I've woken in the middle of the night worried about what I've done. I have to keep reminding myself that it's what I wanted, yearned for, in fact. But it doesn't stop me being scared.

It's going to be fine.

I'm telling Mum and Tim today.

'What a lovely surprise,' Tim says, when he opens the door. He hugs me right on the doorstep. See, a much better dad than my biological one. 'Come in, come in.'

Mum comes out of the kitchen to hug me in the hall. I haven't even got my jacket off and they're all over me. 'Everything okay?' Mum asks.

'Yeah, great. Can't I just pop round and see my old parents any time I like?' I laugh.

'Less of the old,' Tim says. 'Just because we've retired now doesn't mean we're past it. Early retirement, we're still young.'

Tim retired two weeks ago, and Mum's last day was four weeks ago. Actually, it would have been the day of my meeting with Roger and Sue. There's a nice little coincidence.

'Cup of tea?' Mum asks, rushing back into the kitchen, grabbing the kettle and filling it.

'Yes, lovely.'

'I was going to call you so you coming here is even better. We have some news.'

'News?' Suddenly I feel concerned.

'Good news,' Tim says, patting my shoulder. 'Very good news.'

'Well?'

'Let's get our tea first.'

We're soon sitting in the living room sipping tea. I find myself nibbling on a rich tea biscuit, something I never do because I like to keep an eye on my weight and I always view biscuits as wasted calories. But lately I've been feeling a little nauseous sometimes and nibbling dry things helps.

'So?' I say, desperate to hear their news before I tell them mine.

'We've booked a cruise.'

'Wow. That's nice.' Not earth shattering though, they've been on several before.

'Yes, very nice. It's a big one.'

'Round the world,' Tim says.

'Wow, that's something else. When?'

Tim pulls a brochure out of the coffee table drawer and hands it to me, it's folded back on the appropriate page. It does look amazing, so many countries, so many ports. They're going all the way down to Australia and back again.

'Travelling through the Suez Canal and the Panama. We're so excited, we're like a couple of little kids. We've spent weeks poring over the brochures, spent two hours in the travel agents, but now we're booked. Holiday of a lifetime,' Tim says, waiting for me to be suitably impressed. I am impressed, then I spot the date. They won't be back until a week after my due date. My heart drops.

'What's wrong?' Mum says, concern in her voice.

'Nothing, no, it's fabulous, you'll have an amazing time.'

'But?' Mum says. You can't really fool my mum.

'Well,' I start, taking a deep breath. 'I have some news too.' I take another breath and they wait, both still and silent. 'I'm having a baby.'

Tim grins and Mum jumps up and grabs hold of me, hugging me tight. 'That's wonderful, wonderful news. When's it due?'

'Before you come back,' I say. 'But only just and maybe I'll go over, so it'll be fine.'

'Oh.' Mum visibly deflates, shrinking back down into her seat.

'Maybe we could change the date, put it off for a year,' Tim offers.

'No, no, you can't do that.'

'I'll ring the travel agent.' He gets up and goes straight off to do it. 'No, you can't do that. This is your treat, your retirement treat, you've looked forward to it, no don't change it,' I yell, but Tim closes the door behind him.

'So, who's the lucky father?' Mum says, smiling again. 'Are you back with Gary?'

'God no. And don't pretend you'd be happy if I was; you never really liked him, did you?'

Mum tries to keep her face passive, because if there's one thing she does well it is not interfering. But I'm pretty sure she didn't especially like Gary, although she never said a word.

'It's not that I don't like him, he's affable enough. It's just that I don't think he's good enough for you.' She pauses. 'Especially after cheating on you. I think that proved my point. Sorry.'

'It's okay. I was going to dump him anyway. Finding out he was cheating just made it easier all round. Made it happen quicker, which suited me very well. I didn't tell you the gory details, Mum, but I threw him out the day I found out.'

Mum looks taken aback.

'I never realised.'

'No, well, it wasn't very dignified and my pride was hurt, but he was going anyway.'

'Okay, so who is the father?'

Before I can answer Tim comes back into the room. He looks pale.

I glance at him but it's Mum who says, 'Well?'

'Yes, we can postpone until next year.' He smiles softly then sits down.

'Couldn't you go later this year?'

'No, they only go in January for world cruises. It's okay, we can wait.'

'No problems then? Just transfer our deposit over and everything.' Mum looks so happy.

'No, no. We'll lose the deposit, but that's okay.' He doesn't look as though it's okay, but he's too kind and generous to make a fuss.

'Have you done it?'

'Nearly. She said to go away and think it over, ring back later. She said it's a lot of money to lose.'

'How much have you paid?' I'm thinking I can make up the difference; it's the least I can do.

Tim shakes his head, not wanting to tell me. I snatch up the brochure and look for myself. He, or Mum, has circled the cruise and cabin they've booked. Beside it in small print it says twenty-five-percent deposit required. The sum is thousands of pounds each. I imagined a deposit of hundreds; I can't offer thousands, not now.

'You cannot cancel that. You cannot lose all that money. You're going. I'll be fine. You can video call me. Frequently,' I add, forcing a smile.

'But what about the baby? I want to be around

when it's born.' Mum's voice sounds tearful.

'Mum, you're due back a week after it's due. I'll just cross my legs. Tim, go and ring the agent and tell her you're definitely going.'

Tim looks from me to Mum several times.

'I mean it. Anyway, I haven't had this officially confirmed by a doctor, so I might even have the date wrong.'

Mum nods and Tim goes off to make his phone call.

'I feel sick,' Mum says. 'I'm so sorry the dates clash.'

'You weren't to know. I didn't tell anyone my plans, why should you? Anyway, you've always said you wanted to do a big cruise once you retired. It's going to be fine. Absolutely fine.' I'm not convinced but I'm not telling Mum that. I wanted her with me. I wanted her to be my birthing partner, holding my hand, mopping my brow and encouraging me.

'When are we going to meet the father?' Tim says, coming back in and looking relieved.

'Ah, well, you're not.'

'Oh. Right,' he says, looking affronted.

'I'm going it alone. This baby was planned and conceived via artificial insemination.'

Both my parents' mouths drop open before Tim finally speaks. 'I wish I'd known that before I uncancelled the cruise because you're going to be on your own, completely.'

'I'm a strong, independent woman,' I say, laughing and trying to make light of it.

'Of course you are but well, everyone needs

support when they have a baby.' Mum reaches over and grips my hands.

'You did it on your own,' I counter.

'I didn't give birth on my own. Your father, feckless as he is, did manage to show up for the event and even helped a tiny bit afterwards.'

'Look, don't panic. I have lots of friends who can help, lots of friends who've had several babies.' And most of them are sooo busy they haven't got time to worry about me. But just my saying I have suitable friends seems to soothe Mum and Tim. 'Anyway, you'll soon be back, coming round to do my washing and cleaning,' I add, smirking. 'It'll keep you busy now you're retired.'

Mum and Tim smile. They're convinced but perhaps not totally.

Me neither. I wish I'd know their plans because I could have waited another month before I conceived. Although, to be honest, after the IVF failure I didn't expect to hit the jackpot so soon.

'How does it work then?' Tim starts, 'With the father, I mean.'

'Donor,' I correct. 'We've signed a contract, he has no legal rights, won't be named on the birth certificate and isn't liable financially. He and his wife would like to come and visit though, once the baby's born.'

'He and his wife?' Mum screws up her face.

'Yes, he's donated a few times.' Mum's face drops when I say this. 'But he's keeping it strictly to a limit. They have four children themselves and two grandchildren. They're a lovely couple.'

Tim frowns. Then he shakes his head. I know what he's thinking.

'It was not a threesome,' I tell him.

'Thank God,' Mum says, as Tim nods his agreement.

'Anyway, I won't be telling anyone else for while because obviously it's very early days and well, you know, heaven forbid and all that, so don't tell anyone, will you?'

They both nod.

'How old is this donor then? You said he had grandchildren?'

'Fiftyish,' I say, knocking a couple of years off his age.

'Not as old as us then,' Mum says, sighing with what I think is relief.

Now it all feels a bit flat. I feel as though I've ruined their news and my own, which, on repeating sounds a little sordid. It's not, I remind myself. So, after half an hour I make my excuses and leave. I tell them I'm meeting the girls, which is true, but not until this evening.

Have I done the right thing going it alone with the baby plan?

Too late now.

Kerri has a tan, she looks amazing. Next to her Carol-Anne and I look pasty and wan. We're at the bar buying our drinks and the lighting is awful so it could be that, but no, I'm kidding myself. We've all ordered soft drinks because we're all detoxing. That's the story I'm sticking to, anyway.

'How was your honeymoon?' I ask, as we find ourselves a table. She didn't go until a few weeks ago, they got a much better deal than if they'd gone the day after the wedding.

'Fan-bloody-tastic.' She grins from ear to ear. 'I just love Barbados. All that rum, all that sun, all that…' She grins. 'Lovely sea.'

We laugh. 'When did you get back?' I ask.

'Been back a week now.' She pulls her mouth down into a sad face. 'Been back at stinky work too.' She groans. We all know that Kerri hates her job even though she trained for ages to do it. She's a dental hygienist, well more than that, because she can do fillings too and extract baby teeth.

'How was that?' Carol-Anne asks, looking slightly bored. There are only so many horror stories about teeth you can hear without feeling sorry or guilty.

'Usual old cabbage mouths.' Kerri rolls her eyes. She really is in the wrong job. 'Shouldn't say it really, but know I'm among friends here, but had a stinky woman in this week who had bits in her teeth, as so many do, but also was farting for England the whole time I was scaling her teeth, and not quietly or discreetly either. Then she burped in my face. Thank God I had a mask on but even with the mask, honestly it made my eyes water. I really thought I was going to be sick. I had to excuse myself and skip out of the room. Stood out in the corridor gasping for air. Then had to go back in, and explain I was having a sneezing fit. I'm the one apologising when it should have been her. I hate people.'

We laugh, how can we not? Neither of us goes to

Kerri's practice, and we're both grateful for that.

'Did you see my pics?' she says, pulling out her phone and flicking through to her gallery.

'Only the few hundred you posted on Facebook,' I say, with a smile. 'Got any more?'

'Yes, actually, this was on the last day and I didn't dare post it.' She pushes the phone across the table so Carol-Anne and I can look together.

'Is that a Covid test?' Carol-Anne says, mischief in her voice.

'No, no. Look again. It's a pregnancy test. I'm having a baby.'

Mouths drop open, not least of all mine. 'Wow,' I say. 'That's amazing. Congratulations'. I feel such a liar, I cannot tell her my news, I've promised myself I won't tell anyone else until after my twelve-week scan because you just never can tell, especially at my age.

Carol-Anne hasn't said anything but her face is quite ashen.

'You okay, Caz?' Kerri asks. Only Kerri is allowed to call Carol-Anne Caz and only on special occasions. This is definitely one of those.

'Yeah, I'm great. Well done you. Congratulations. I'm delighted for you, really delighted. Especially as I have some news too.'

We both turn and look at her. I hope she isn't getting a divorce or something, she's not been married long herself.

'I'm pregnant too. About eight weeks. I wasn't going to say anything because I know that you, Esme, are sort of trying yourself and I didn't want to rub salt in the wound and all that.' She looks at me sadly. She feels sorry for me. I should put her out of her agony but I can't.

'No problem,' I mutter.

'I'm so sorry,' she says, tears in her eyes.

'Don't be. Really, it's fine.' I smile, hoping that will do the trick.

'Oh yeah, I forgot about you, Es,' Kerri says. 'Sorry.'

'Don't worry about me. How many weeks are *you*, Kerri?'

'Oh, only about three, so keeping it to ourselves. Only told me mum and dad, and Garth's mum and dad. You can't be too careful, can you?'

I shake my head slowly.

'We haven't even told our parents yet. We're a bit scared. I wouldn't have told you today except it would have been a bit weird sitting here knowing that I was after you said you were. Bit sneaky too, don't you think? We weren't even trying. So I'm a bit worried after all the drinking at your hen party. I didn't drink at the wedding though,' she says, sounding a bit brighter. 'Because I did suspect by then.'

Oh God. That's exactly what I'm doing. I'm sitting here and being weird and duplicitous. I can't do it.

'I have a confession,' I say.

They both stop and look at me.

'What?' Kerri says. 'What have you done?'

'I'm pregnant too.'

They screech and squeal and someone on the

other side of the bar shushes us.

'Fuck off,' Kerri whispers between us and we all squeal again.

'I can't believe it.' Carol-Anne prods me in the arm. 'When? How? Who?'

'Was it that guy we hooked you up with on Facebook? Jeremy something.' Kerri waits for an answer.

'Oh yeah, the sperminator,' Carol-Anne adds.

'The what?'

'The sperminator, that's what he calls himself.'

'Yuk, no. It was most definitely not him.' I then tell them the full story of Jeremy's visit while they squeal and laugh throughout.

'Sitting on your drive wanking,' Kerri says. 'That's disgusting. And probably illegal. You should have rung the police. That's like dogging or something, isn't it?'

'Eww,' Carol-Anne says. 'Not sure if it's that exactly but definitely illegal, sex act in public and all that. What if one of your neighbours had seen? Your drive is really open, isn't it?'

'Yes. I was mortified. I just wanted him gone. He didn't seem to think there was anything wrong with it.'

'And to think that turkey baster has been up other women's vaggies before yours?' Kerri mock gags.

'It didn't go up mine,' I remind her. 'But I had to wash it out before I gave it back.'

'We should post something about him on Facebook. Let's find him on that group. Give me your phone, Es.' Kerri holds out her hand.

'No. Definitely not. Don't want to stir up that can of worms.'

'Can of sperms more like.' Carol-Anne nearly falls off her chair laughing at her own joke.

'No. Stop it. I don't want to talk about Jeremy the sperminator. Not now, not ever again.'

'So, who is the father?'

'IVF at the clinic,' I lie. Having just spent the last ten minutes laughing and gagging about Jeremy the sperminator, I am most certainly not telling them about Roger and Sue. Somehow, even though it absolutely was not, they'll turn it into something sordid.

'You sure about that? What about that guy we saw you with at the hen do? You looked very cosy with him.' Kerri eyes me.

'Oh yeah, I only caught a glimpse of him, no hair, tall, looked kind of cool.'

'No,' I shake my head. 'We were just chatting. I told you IVF, all nice and clean and tidy and no man involved.'

'Not strictly true. Just because you didn't meet him doesn't mean a man wasn't involved, does it? Because a man definitely was involved.'

'Stop splitting hairs, you know what I mean.'

'No dirty business,' Kerri says, before she and Carol-Anne launch into another session of squealing with laughter.

'You two,' I say, shaking my head.

'We'll have to find you someone nice. Someone who won't mind you having a baby. What apps have you got on your phone?'

'None. And I don't want a man, I've told you. I had one and I'm glad to be shot of him.'

'Not every man is like Gary.' Kerri drains her drink. 'Shall I get another round of baby-drinks?'

We all agree it's a good idea and especially so if it takes the attention off me, my pregnancy and my love life.

But it doesn't.

'How did you meet Gary?' Kerri starts, once we all have fresh drinks.

'Via an app. And look how that turned out.'

'Yeah, I know about app men,' Carol-Anne says. 'I met some right stinkers before I struck gold with my darling husband. And I didn't even meet him on an app, my mum worked with him. Doesn't now though,' she adds, grimacing. 'Thank God.'

'That would be weird, your husband working with his mother-in-law.' I try to imagine Gary working with my mum. Despite her non-interference policy I think even she might have given him some advice on treating me properly. Maybe it might have worked.

'Unless it's a family firm. That might work,' Kerri says, pondering.

Carol-Anne and I nod our agreement.

'I think the best way to meet the best men is to meet them through friends or family,' Carol-Anne returns to her favourite subject, namely finding me a partner.

I don't say anything, but Kerri does, 'Yeah, I met Garth at football, but it was one of my friends who introduced us. It wasn't a setup, it was a chance thing, but my friend knew him. So I suppose that sort of counts.'

Carol-Anne nods. I just smile. Who knows, who cares? Not me.

'I once chatted with a guy online who said he liked curvy girls with a thigh gap,' Kerri says.

'Very specific.' And picky, I think.

'Yeah, so I replied that I was a curvy girl but that I didn't have a thigh gap and was that a problem? The arse came back and said that it was a deal-breaker for him, then he blocked me. I mean, I don't know any curvy girls with thigh gaps, none.'

'I've got a thigh gap,' I say.

'I'm sure you do but you're not a curvy girl, are you?' Carol-Anne says while Kerri sniggers.

I glance down at my breasts, definitely not insignificant.

'No, *they* don't make you a curvy girl. You're tall and slim with big boobs, not the same at all.'

Maybe they're right, maybe not. I don't really care. 'Well, I'm sure I'm going to be a curvy girl in the relatively near future; we all are.' I'm getting tired now, and I'm seriously thinking about going home.

'I wonder if you'll keep that thigh gap?' Carol-Anne ponders. 'Hey, maybe we should track him down, he might be perfect for you. You'll have what he wants.'

We all laugh. Not that I find it funny, at all.

'Seriously,' she continues. 'I think he might be worth a go. Which app was he on, Kerri?'

'Carol-Anne,' Kerri says, her voice whiny. 'That was years ago, wasn't it. He's probably married with two kids now, or something.'

'No, he's probably still looking for that illusive creature with a deal-breaker thigh gap.'

'You called him an arse, he sounds like an arse, why would I want him?' I need to bring this ludicrous conversation to an end.

'Yes, you're right. We need to find you someone nice. Apps are out. You can't trust what men put on apps. How did Gary describe himself? Did he match up to his own description?'

'I can't remember,' I lie. I can, he said he was tall, solvent and had his own teeth. All were true. The last one was a bit of a joke; he said that a lot of women put that in their wants list. I suggested he'd been on the wrong apps because no one our age even thought of that.

Soon we're all yawning – glad it's not just me.

Growing another human is tiring work.

Six

We went for the three-month scan today. Mum came with me.

I drank the requisite pint of water beforehand, as instructed. Then we were delayed, appointments were running late. I was desperate for the loo but couldn't go. I've heard about this before, I think a lot of pregnant women tell this tale. I just never thought it would happen to me. I asked Mum what happened when she went for a scan. She laughed before telling me that they weren't invented then. They were, but just not for everyone.

Anyway, we finally got in there and I was so dying for the loo that I couldn't give my full attention to the scan. I was so annoyed later. When the sonographer slapped that ice cold gel on me and then pressed down I thought I was going to disgrace myself on her table.

'I don't think I can wait,' I yelped. 'I need the loo.'

The woman, who looked older than Mum and thoroughly pissed off into the bargain gave me such a withering look. 'If you go to the toilet before the scan is completed, you'll have to fill up again and sit out there until I can fit you in. Frankly that could be hours. So do you think you can hold it?'

I nodded meekly which isn't like me at all.

It's odd how being pregnant is making me weak and compliant.

Anyway, I lay there gritting my teeth and trying to focus on the scan and the baby. Finally, she asked, rather snappily Mum later recalled, if we wanted photos.

Of course we did.

It seems the baby is the right size for my dates and the due date was confirmed as being before Mum and Tim comeback from their cruise. We felt a bit flat after that.

Once the sonographer said I could go, I dashed out of there without even wiping all that gel off me and ran for the toilet. I've never felt such relief. Then we went for a drink and a snack in the hospital café because it was lunch time by then. After we'd both had burnt paninis, Mum said that we would find somewhere better next time.

We're back now, just arriving at Mum's.

'Tim, Tim,' Mum calls as we burst through the front door. Come and see.

Tim hops out of the kitchen. 'I've put the kettle on,' he says, then cautiously, 'Everything all right?'

'Yes. Yes. Lovely.' Mum flops down on the sofa and pats the seat for me to join her.

'Did you get a photo?'

'Several,' I say, pulling a strip from my bag.

We all study the photos carefully, Mum pointing

out the baby's head, hands and legs to Tim who's struggling to make sense of it.

'Date's right,' Mum says, with a sigh. 'We won't be back in time.'

'You might if I'm overdue. Were you overdue with me?'

'Yes, of course. But I was a lot younger than you. And it was different then. Doctors and midwives didn't believe you when you told them your dates. No scans then.'

'What's age got to do with it?'

'I don't think, because you'll be forty, that they'll let you go much over.'

'How do you know that?' I can't remember being told that. Did the sonographer say something?

'Dr Google,' Tim says, scathingly.

'Oh right. Well no one's said that to me so…'

'Tea?' Tim asks.

'No thanks,' Mum and I chorus.

'We had something in the hospital café.'

Tim grimaces.

'Yes,' Mum says.

Tim goes off and comes back with his iPad. 'Can I take a few pictures of the baby photos? Then I can blow them up for a better look.'

'Good idea.' I lay them out.

We study the results ten minutes later. 'Do you think the baby's got big lips?' I don't have big lips myself and I'm trying to remember what Roger's lips were like.

'Probably pouting,' Mum says. 'They do that.'

'Do they?'

'Oh yes,' Tim agrees. 'Saw it on Facebook.'

'Right. Don't go posting any of these on Facebook, will you? I haven't told anyone at work yet. I might not for a few more weeks yet.'

Mum and Tim nod furiously.

I do wonder if that was the plan. Showing off. And who can blame them?

I want to be posting everywhere too, shouting from the highest rooftop, telling everyone, but I also want to be cautious.

I'm going to have to think carefully about my strategy at work. I've seen other women side-lined once they've announced a pregnancy. As head of HR I've had too many women in my office complaining about it over the years. I always sympathised with them and in some cases, where it was so patently obvious it was painful, I was able to stop it. But other managers were a lot sneakier. Often these managers were men and had families of their own and I wondered what they were like at home because at work they could be the most unaccommodating arseholes ever. But, to be fair sometimes they were women. And sometimes there were no problems at all. Either that or the pregnant women just wanted to focus on their babies and stay the hell out of there until their maternity leave was over. Then came other problems.

My director, David, is a bit of an unknown quantity where this is concerned. I had to go to him once where blatant bullying was going on by a female manager of a pregnant woman. Said woman was the best salesperson in the department. Made the most sales, made the most bonuses for herself, and of course, made the most bonuses for her manager. I could see how angry the manager was when I spoke to her. But she was adamant that she wasn't discriminating, she wasn't bullying. I couldn't make her see sense. I took the matter to David, hoping that if he intervened the manager would calm down and be reasonable. His response was for me to handle it, said it came better from a woman and that I was the HR expert. I remember his smile when he said that. I told myself he was old school, he's well over sixty although he acts a lot older, and younger sometimes. He can be incredibly immature at times. But even so, he was the director, it was his job to sort out the unsortable.

In the end I told the manager that David had given me complete autonomy on the situation and his one-hundred percent backing – which was sort of true, I think. I also told her if she didn't stop it then I would be opening a disciplinary case against her. I didn't hear any more after that. It went ominously quiet. The manager shunned me in the corridor – which was fine. The woman having the baby left after her maternity leave finished and went to work somewhere else, earning more apparently. So that manager really shot herself in the foot, alienating her best salesperson, but she still shuns me. Probably all *my* fault, not hers.

That was five years ago. David is still my director. He's coasting his way to retirement but, as he has pointed out in the past, there is no hard and fast retirement age anymore. No one can be forced out against their will. He's right and I wouldn't dare even think of it. But I suspect the other directors want him gone; there are even rumours that he sometimes dozes off in the middle of long board meetings. I don't know how true that is.

So for now I'm keeping quiet. No one is going to side-line me until it suits my convenience.

'This is much better,' Tim says, bringing me back to the here and now.

'What's that?'

'Look, you can almost count the toes.' He uses his iPad stylus and counts them on one foot. I'm not completely convinced but if it makes him happy.

'We could go for one of those 3D scans,' Mum says. 'I've been looking them up, you can get videos too. What do you think?'

'Yes, why not. It would be great. How many people can come along?' Surely if you're paying it must be more than the one allowed with the NHS.

'As many as you like, I think, within reason.'

'Great. Tim, you can come to that. Mum, do you want to book it? Fit it in around yourselves, any day is good for me except Wednesdays.' Wednesdays are when I meet with David and I don't want to arouse any suspicion by having a *medical* appointment then.

'I've been thinking,' Tim says, sounding hesitant. Then he stops.

'Yeah?' I encourage.

'Do you mind if the baby calls me Grandad?'

'What do you mean? What else is it going to call you?' Then it dawns on me, in all the time Mum and Tim have been together I've never called him Dad.

I was fourteen when he came into our lives and although at that point I'd never actually met my biological dad, it still felt wrong to think of Tim as my dad. Throughout all the years since, including my difficult teenage years it has been Tim who has performed the dad duties. It was Tim who drove up and down the motorway with a car load of my junk when I went to university, of course Mum was there but it was Tim negotiating the weird one-way systems of an unknown city. It was Tim who picked me up late from nightclubs, it was Tim who took me out in the car when I was learning to drive. Like I keep saying, he's been more of a dad to me than my real one ever has. Is now the time to say all this? I chicken out, instead saying, 'Unless you fancy Grandpa, or Pops or something different. What about you, Mum, what do you want to be called?'

'Granny,' she says, giving me the impression she's considered this already. 'Definitely Granny.'

'Tim?'

He looks a little embarrassed. 'Grandad, I prefer Grandad.'

The girls are round tonight. They're desperate to see my scan photos and Carol-Anne is bringing hers. Kerri has a few more weeks to wait for her scan appointment; no doubt we'll be comparing pictures again then. It's good to have my friends on the same journey as me, except it's not quite the same but nearly, sort of.

'Garth says he's videoing the birth,' Kerri tells us, as she tucks into the family size bag of *Doritos* which she brought with her. 'Anyone want one?' She asks but we both refuse. Just the smell of them is making me feel nauseous.

'I'm not sure I would like that. What's he going to do with it afterwards, post it on TikTok?' Carol-Anne is wearing a face of disapproval.

'Urgh, no. Better not.' Kerri giggles before almost climbing into her *Doritos* bag to get the last few crumbs out.

'Maybe just put it on for friends and family when they come round. It'll look good on your fifty-five-inch TV.' Carol-Anne is really going for it.

'God, yes, wouldn't put it past him. I'll make sure he keeps away from the business end.'

'Yes, better to just focus on your sweaty, puce head than your sweaty, puce…'

'Another drink anyone?' I cut in. Carol-Anne seems to be in quite a gritty mood tonight.

'Milk for me,' Kerri says. 'I just can't get enough of the stuff, used to hate it. I have sooo many cravings. Do either of you?'

'No,' Carol-Anne says.

'I do wake up in the night hungry sometimes, not like me at all,' I say, hoping to jolly the conversation along. 'I even cooked myself some fish fingers at three am the other day.'

'Fish fingers. You have fish fingers in your house?'

'Yes. Bought them about two weeks ago. Saw them and just had to have them. Bought a thirty-six pack so I wouldn't run out. Only eaten about eight so far.'

'Are you worried about getting fat?' Carol-Anne asks.

'That's going to happen anyway, isn't it.' I laugh.

'I've put on six pounds. Six pounds. It's far too soon to be porking up yet.' Her face says it all and explains why she's so grumpy. 'How much have you put on, Kerri?'

'Nothing. Lost weight in fact.'

'But you're always stuffing yourself.'

'Yes, but I'm also always being sick. Every damn morning I vomit for England, then have a shower and get back to eating again.' She stops for a moment. 'Do you think I've got bulimia?'

'No, you're pregnant. I'm not being sick anymore, still feel it with certain smells but I haven't been sick for over a week. And I never vomited a lot.'

'I've haven't been sick once. And I have no cravings. In fact, if I hadn't seen my baby jiggling about on the scanner I wouldn't even think I was pregnant, just fat.'

Kerri catches my eye then rolls her own.

'I don't suppose you've put an ounce on, Esme, have you?'

'Of course I have. Five pounds. My work skirts and trousers are horribly tight. I've had to go and buy a couple of loose fitting dresses just so it doesn't look too obvious.'

'It doesn't show on you because you're tall.'

'I think a lot of it has gone on my boobs. I'm sure I saw one of the IT guys staring at them this morning. Fortunately the dresses will hide them too.'

'Have you still not told work yet?'

'No. I'm biding my time.'

'I've told work,' Kerri says, grinning. Also told them that standing up for long periods makes me feel sick and dizzy. They're having to make adjustments for me.' She grins again. Kerri will do anything to skive off work. 'Mind you it would be poetic justice if I puked in one of those old dear's cabbage gobs, wouldn't it?'

'Kerri,' Carol-Anne and I chorus. She really is the worst.

'I suppose you'll be having the baby sleep in your room,' Carol-Anne says, changing the subject, her voice sounding wistful.

'Um, yes, I suppose so.' I really hadn't even thought about it. Funnily enough Mum asked me when we went for the scan which room I'd be decorating for the baby. Again, I hadn't even thought about it which is bloody ridiculous. Have I got baby brain or am I just self-centred and thoughtless. Mum says Tim is keen to help if redecorating is required. She also said I should give the baby the bigger of my two spare rooms so then I won't have to move him or her later when they get bigger.

'Olly doesn't want the baby sleeping in with us,' Carol-Anne says, her voice trembling.

'Oh. Why not?'

'Doesn't want his sleep disturbed, doesn't want our room to smell of mouldy milk and baby shit.' I assume she's quoting him now.

Neither Kerri nor I say anything. Kerri picks up the empty Doritos bag and rustles it, checking it's definitely empty.

'So I told him to slink his hook just like you did Gary,' Carol-Anne says.

'Oh. Right.' I'm useless in such situations. 'Olly isn't Gary.'

'What did he say to that?' Kerri screws up the Doritos bag and hurls it onto my fire, which is gas with fake coals.

We all watch as it catches light and melts itself onto the fake coals. The smell and fumes are so bad that I jump up and open the window, even though it's cold outside.

'I've always thought that was real,' Kerri says. 'It's a good fake, isn't it?'

'It was,' I mutter.

'It'll be fine. Just let it burn off.'

'And in the meantime, we'll all be gassed or toxic fumed or something.' Carol-Anne sounds close to tears. 'Just think what this is doing to our poor little babies.'

I turn the fire off but the bag continues to smoke.

'I think we should go,' Kerri says, getting up. 'It's not healthy here for us.'

'What about me? I live here.'

'Keep the window open. Or maybe go stay at your mum's for a while.'

Before they leave I open the patio doors too to create a bit of a draught. After they've gone I message Mum and she says that Tim will be round as soon as he can to sort it out. Which he does very quickly, taking all the coals away, wiping down the grate and hearth and finally closing the windows.

'I can get some more of these online,' he says, holding up the bag of coals. See, he's the best dad. 'Is your friend a bit dim?'

'I'm beginning to wonder.'

I've just got out of the shower, my hair wrapped in an old towel, and after drying myself I pull on my favourite pair of leggings. They are tight. I'm sure they weren't this tight last week. But it isn't around my waist that they are tight, it's on my thighs. Thighs. Who knew that being pregnant meant your thighs expanded. I'm going to lose my thigh gap, so that guy Carol-Anne was on about certainly won't be interested in me now. I laugh to myself. Who cares.

The doorbell goes and I grab my thick jumper pulling it over my head as I dash down the stairs. Inevitably the hair towel half falls off just as I answer the door.

The hottest man in England is standing on my doorstep. Tousled blond hair, a soft tan and abs to die for prominently displayed under a very tight t-shirt.

'Esme Haste?' he asks in an Australian accent, his teeth gleaming white as he speaks.

'Er, yes,' I say, fighting with the hair towel that is determined to leap to the floor.

'For you.' He hands over a beautiful bouquet of flowers. I hadn't even noticed he was holding them because I was so blinded by his beauty.

'Thanks,' I say, having to use both hands to take them, so letting go of the wet towel which hits the hall floor with a plop.

He grins and jogs back to his delivery van.

I stand and watch as he drives away. I'm not sure why.

Finally I step back inside and, juggling the flowers, close the door. In the kitchen I read the card.

*Garth says I'm a stupid b****h for not realising your fire was gas. He says I could have killed us all. Bit melo-d but you know what he's like. Anyway, wanted to say sorry. Silly me, baby brain, lol. Hope I haven't caused any permanent damage. Love Kerri xx*

Well, other than a thank you text there's not much I can say to that. I certainly didn't expect flowers. No one buys me flowers.

Gary certainly never did.

Seven

I'm running late this morning. I slept in. I never sleep in. I'm a lark not a night owl. It's going to be one of those days. You know when you wake up and nothing goes quite right. Not majorly wrong, not tragedy, but minor things, one after another. Very minor things really.

My electric toothbrush ran out of charge. A really minor thing but I've recently bought a new one, it's great, has a timer and everything and the super sensitive brush heads which I like. But, and this is a big but, it runs out of charge with no warning at all. My old one used to flash red for a while before it ran out so you knew that at least you could finish brushing your teeth before charging. This one just dies, mid-mouth, bonk, gone. So I had to clean my teeth with a dead electric toothbrush, neither easy nor effective.

I have a check-up this morning, not for my teeth, for my baby. So I need to take a urine sample with me. I've already learnt that you wee in a jug – I have a special plastic one I keep in the bathroom – then pour it into the tiny little tube they give you. Yet I struggled to pour it, my hand kept shaking and inevitably the wee slopped onto the outside of the tube, soaking the label and smudging my name in the process. So I get the hairdryer out to dry the label which melts the glue and makes it move then dries it on skewwhiff. It really doesn't matter but now, what with the smudging too, I think it's obvious I've wee'd on it. Oh, this must happen all the time. It seems to be a theme with me.

Then the kettle played up. And I was down to the last drop of milk, bad planning on my part. So I only managed half a cup of tea.

Minor things. Really minor, but they start to add up.

Now I'm sitting in the doctor's waiting room. I'm not seeing a doctor; I'm seeing a nurse or she might be a midwife. I never know. They're keeping a closer eye on me because of my age and something or other they want to keep an eye on in my urine. I've already been told it's nothing major, minor really.

So I'm sitting here waiting, which is annoying because I didn't have breakfast so I could get here on time and now I'm waiting. And my stomach is growling. I've got a cereal bar in my bag and I'm tempted to take a bite, but I know that the minute I do my name will be called and I'll have a mouthful of chewy cereal smeared all over my teeth.

It's fairly early, I like an early appointment although it hasn't gone so well today, anyway, it's early which means it's not too busy. Then someone bursts into the surgery banging the outside door against the wall so loud that the few of us waiting all jump. I look up and see it's Gary. Oh no. Minor things really.

He lumbers over to the screen and books himself in. Except he doesn't because there's a problem so I slyly watch him burst through another door and into the receptionist's area – they like to keep themselves well away from the public – to sort out the problem. I'm grateful for this because then my name is called and I slip past him without his seeing me.

Gary is the past and I don't want him tainting my future.

'Did this get wet?' Nurse Tilley asks, probably grateful that she's wearing gloves.

'Mmm,' I mutter.

'You need to wee in a plastic cup first then decant…'

'I know,' I cut in. 'Shaky hand.'

Her head twitches. 'Shaky? Is that normal for you?' She flicks to her computer screen. 'It's not in your notes.'

'No, it's just been one of those mornings.' I give a little half-laugh. 'You know, toothbrush ran out of charge, kettle playing up…' I let the words trail away because she's giving me the stink eye, as though I'm mad while simultaneously popping a test stick into my sample before comparing it against a chart.

'Looks okay, bit borderline, we'll still keep an eye on that. Cut down on the sugary snacks, okay?'

Then she decides it's blood taking time. I'm not squeamish, really, I'm not, but the last time she took blood it took her four attempts. I can already feel my veins contracting as she rips off her gloves, washes her hands and then fetches the tray with the blood test kit in it.

'Which arm?' she says.

I want to ask if it matters after the last time when she started in one and finally finished in the other, but offer my left arm first, as this was the successful one last time.

Fortunately, it all goes well. The relieve I feel is ludicrous but I'm glad to be out of there and in the fresh air of the car park.

'I thought that was you,' Gary's voice says from close up behind me just as I'm opening my car door.

'Oh hi.' I put my leg in to make it obvious we won't be chatting.

'I thought I saw you in the waiting room, then you were gone.'

What can I say to that? 'Yeah.'

'Everything all right?' He scrutinises me in a way I don't like.

'Yeah, fine. You?'

'Got a bit of a sore throat, turns out it might be an allergy, had it for weeks.'

'Hope you get it sorted soon,' I say, turning my shoulder and making it obvious I'm getting into my car right now.

'Not been hitting the gym lately?' I can hear the smirk in his voice.

'You know I don't do the gym.'

'Maybe you should. You've blown up a bit since we split.' He's proper smirking now and it infuriates me.

'I'm pregnant, you idiot.' That wipes the smirk off his face. In fact he goes quite ashen.

'Shit, really.' I can see the cogs whirring. 'Is it mine?'

Now I smirk. Then I wait for just long enough to give him a scare. 'No, of course not.' He never was much good at maths; or am I *that* large? I climb into my car, slam the door, start the car and drive off and Gary just stands in the car park staring at my retreating form. Idiot. And to think I wanted a life with him. Whatever was I thinking?

I sidle into the department at work and try not to make too much fuss. My intention is to nod my hellos, get into my office and hide away. But it's not to be.

David, my director, is perched on one of my colleague's desks, he's laughing and joking with the whole team and they're lapping it up, except for one, Pearl. He jumps up when I walk past as though he's been caught out.

'Esme, I was wondering where you were. Not like you to be late.'

'Medical appointment,' I say as I continue towards my desk, shrugging off my coat and putting down my handbag. 'It's in my diary.'

'Oh, you know, I never look at those.'

'Pam, your PA does though. Didn't she tell you?'

He shakes his head just as I come to my senses and realise that I can't talk to him like this; he isn't Gary. I've seethed all the way here after my altercation with Gary in the doctors' car park.

Because he called me fat, because I couldn't bear it and told him the cause he now knows I'm pregnant. And now that he knows it's only a matter of time before it becomes common knowledge. Because Gary is many things but discreet isn't one of them. I'm going to have to come clean, I'm going to have to tell David, then everyone else.

I was hoping to wait until after my twenty-week scan next week. After that it would become increasingly more obvious anyway. I'd also know the sex of the baby after the scan. Even though Mum and I went for a 3D scan several weeks ago we still don't know as he or she was lying awkwardly in my womb. Mum asked me why I wanted to wait until after twenty weeks to go public and I couldn't really explain why. It's just something I've fixated on. I find I'm fixating a lot lately. I assume it's a pregnancy thing.

I feel a bit annoyed about the 3D scan because Kerri, who's several weeks behind me already knows the sex of her baby from that scan. We meet regularly together with Carol-Anne and compare notes. She's already been for her twenty-week NHS scan and she's having a boy. Kerri is having a girl. And I have no idea.

'Can I help you with anything, David?' I ask, remembering who I am, and moreover who he is.

'No, not really. Just, you know, checking on the troops.'

I smile at the same time thinking, you've checked, we're all present and correct now, so push off. I hope he can't read the truth behind my smile.

'Would you like a coffee?' I ask him, heading towards the door. 'I can get one from the vending machine.'

I see a look of horror pass over his face; in his office he has a proper espresso machine and his PA fusses around him like a mother hen, making him two-hourly coffees. I think the idea is to make sure he doesn't nod off in any board meetings, although that's not always successful.

'No, thanks,' he says, just as I knew he would.

I close my office door before he can escape. 'Actually, I was going to come and see you for a chat. Why don't you take a seat.'

'Oh, right. We could go to my office instead. You could have a decent coffee,' he says, trying to tempt me. Of course he doesn't know that I rarely drink coffee now and certainly not anything as strong as espresso.

'Okay, but I'll pass on the coffee.' I smile, so does he.

'Nice dress by the way, very feminine.'

I just nod at that. I don't like that he's commenting on my clothes and I really object to the feminine comment. I could probably haul him over the coals for that. I'm sure in the HR manual there's a rule against such a personal comment. But what's the point? He's not saying he likes my boobs, is he? He is, sadly, just old school, and he can't see anything wrong with, what he considers to be, his compliment. I could comment on how his paunch is straining his expensive shirt, but I don't, do I?

I open my office door again and we trot off

together. The rest of the team watch us while trying to make it look as though they're not watching us. No one will ask why we've gone off together but they'll all assume I'm in for a telling off, because why else would we leave my office and go to his? It would never occur to them that coffee is the answer.

'Sure I can't tempt you?' David asks, as Pam fusses around making him his coffee.

'No, really, thank you.'

'Pam could get you something else,' he offers. He nods at Pam who nods back. There's a smutty joke in the business that David and Pam are having an affair. I think nothing could be further from the truth. I've met David's wife, she younger and more glamorous than Pam who, despite being younger than David, acts more like his mother. I've even seen her sorting out his cufflinks when he was struggling. No, no affair there. Anyway Pam's husband is the love of her life, she's tells anyone who'll listen.

'No, I'm fine. Really.'

David gives up and sinks into his seat. I sit down opposite him.

'What did you want to chat about?' he asks, while Pam continues to fuss around with the coffee.

She brings his over but then goes back and plays with the machine. I know she's hovering so that she can hear what I'm going to say, but I'm not, not in front of her. She's the world's worse gossip and she'll know soon enough, when everyone else does.

With a quick glance in her direction I say, 'Well, I wanted to talk about staff retention…'

I see David suppress a sigh. Staff retention is

most certainly not his favourite subject. Nor mine either. Realising there's no juicy gossip here Pam slinks out of the office, closing the door quietly behind her.

'Actually, that can wait. What I really wanted to say is, to tell you, is that I'm having a baby.'

David, who has just picked up his coffee cup nearly drops it. 'You?' he says, staring at me. There really is no need to make his shock so obvious. 'You? You're having a baby?'

'Yes, me. Why not me?'

'Well, I thought you were a career girl. I heard you'd split up with your boyfriend and had declared men off the menu.' I know where he's got that from. Pam.

'I've always wanted a family and now I'm going to have one.' I smile; I'm almost enjoying this.

'Yes, well, yes. Congratulations.' It sounds as though he's in pain as he says this.

'Thank you.'

'So when err…' He nods at my middle. 'Only I was thinking about retiring in the next year or so and I don't know how that's going to work with you likely not being here.' He really looks quite pained.

I don't know and I don't care. I really don't. I'm surprised how little I care about work. I will have to come back because I'll need the money but worrying about David's plans for his future is definitely not on my agenda. He's long overdue retirement, not so much from an age perspective but from an attitude perspective. He's actually quite a dinosaur which isn't a good look on an HR director. His other directorship is finance and he's definitely better suited to that. Although we've always clashed on his penchant for cutting the staff training budget to save money.

As I start to outline my plans, when the baby is due, when I'll be going on maternity leave, I watch as the pompous wind is knocked right out of him.

'What will we do without you?' His voice has taken on a whiny tone.

'I'll be back,' I say, standing up to leave.

'Wait, before you go. Who else knows?'

'Here? No one.'

'Could we keep it that way until after the board meeting later this week? I'd like the other directors to know before it goes public.'

Is the man mad? I don't think the other directors will give a damn although Mike Cohen, the CEO, might be vaguely interested but only because we've both worked here for so long. It's been a kind of little joke between us.

'That's fine,' I say. 'I'll wait until next week. But I'll have to start telling people soon because I'm starting to show.' I'm actually more than starting to show, my little bump has 'popped' out recently and soon no amount of subtle dressing is going to hide it.

'Yes. Thank you.' His voice sounds almost robotic. Why do I feel as though I've burst his bubble?

'Maybe he was going to suggest you as his replacement,' Mum says, when I tell her about it later.

'No, never. He's far too old school to think a mere woman is up to such an exalted job. Anyway, they'll do what they did when he was appointed, get a finance bod and then just slap the HR bit on top. David knows nothing, and I do mean nothing, about HR. He totally relies on me.'

'That's why he's not happy about it,' Tim says, with a laugh.

'Aww, what a shame,' Mum says, and we all laugh together.

'Oh, they'll just get an interim in to cover me. I'll have to start organising that once I go public at work. We need someone qualified and available and that won't be an easy task. Anyway, I'm far more interested in the twenty-week scan. So excited.'

Later in the week David sends me through an email telling me it's fine to go public with my news. That's mighty big of him. Now I can tell people, I feel shy and embarrassed. I could just send Pam an email and let the rumour monger do her work. But that wouldn't be a good look on me. So I wander out into the main HR office to tell my team myself, then I chicken out and slink along to the toilets. I don't want to go at all, I just needed a destination after I'd come out of my office and loitered without intent.

I go back and schedule a meeting for this afternoon with the team. This needs to be done properly. I make notes. I feel weirdly disconnected from my own wonderful news.

The meeting acceptances come bouncing back

immediately.

'So,' I begin, after everyone has got themselves a drink and settled down around the table. They all have their notebooks and pens poised too, except Pearl who likes to make notes on her iPad. 'I expect you're wondering why I've called this meeting.'

A few nod, some look down. There are only seven in our department including me so we're quite close knit really but despite our business being human resources, therefore people, there are some introverts among us. Well one person who is very introverted, Pearl, who was forcibly transferred into the department by David and the IT director a few years ago. I wasn't happy about it at all. She doesn't like interacting with people yet has gone on to gain all the relevant qualifications and certificates and has more knowledge about industrial tribunals than anyone else – not that we have too many of those, thankfully. She's a brilliant data gatherer and despite her forced arrival is an essential member of the team. Technically, she's the departmental expert even if she does sit in the corner keeping her interaction to a minimum.

'Well,' I start, taking a breath. 'I have some news. Some personal news. I'm having a baby.'

Smiles sweep around the table, which is nice.

'How lovely,' someone says.

'Oh congratulations,' someone else says.

'We already knew that,' Pearl says, looking not at all surprised.

'Did you?'

'Well yes. Look at you. You are either pregnant or

have a serious glandular problem.'

'Pearl,' someone admonishes before asking me, 'When's it due?'

I give them the details and tell them when I'll be going on maternity leave. I'm following the pattern most women do, working until the last minute so I can have the whole year off with the baby. Fortunately I do have a month's holiday due to me so I'll be finishing a whole month before my due date. The prospect of waddling around this place at eight months pregnant is daunting enough, never mind nine.

'What will happen when you're not here?' Pearl asks the question on everyone else's lips.

'There'll be an interim providing cover for my maternity leave. Probably someone from outside.'

'What about someone from inside?' Pearl again.

'Well, it'll be advertised so anyone can apply.'

Pearl nods and I wonder if that's her plan? She's certainly qualified enough on paper but interpersonal skills? I don't think so. But we'll cross that bridge when we have to. If we have to.

'For now though, it's business as usual.' I stand up, signally the end of the meeting.

I detour to the toilet on my way back, and just as I'm leaving I bump into Pam. She looks me up and down.

'Well that was a bit of a shocker,' she says. Does she mean me and my news?

'What was?'

'You. Of course. What else?'

'Why?' I thought she'd probably already have

guessed but maybe not.

'Thought you were a career girl. I imagined you taking over from David when he retired. Although you have put a spanner in the works so to speak as regards his plans.' She arches her eyebrows.

'Have I?'

'Obviously. He's going to have to wait it out with your replacement, train them up, get them up to speed.'

'Train them?'

'Of course.'

'But, Pam, he knows nothing about HR.' I could bite my tongue out but it's said now, no way of retracting it.

She arches her eyebrows again and stomps off towards his office, no doubt to report back.

I spend the rest of the day waiting for a summons to his office for a ticking off about defaming him, but it never comes. And by the end of the day I've decided that I don't care. It's the truth, he does know nothing about HR, he doesn't even pretend to be interested most of the time. HR was only tagged onto his finance director duties because no one else wanted it; it's like a poison chalice, more hassle that it's worth. I don't care what poison Pam feeds David and I don't care how David reacts.

Eight

It's scan day again and we're on our way to the hospital. Mum's driving, having picked me up from work, and I'm swigging from a bottle of water to ensure my bladder is full. I hope we don't have to wait too long.

We're both beyond excited. Today we should find out the sex of the baby, even though, according to the scan appointment letter, that is not the purpose of the scan.

'Boy or girl?' Mum says, as she parks the car. 'I'm going girl. What do you think?'

'I really have no idea. Last week I dreamt it was a girl, last night a boy.'

She grips my hand as we walk across the car park. It's exciting and just a little bit scary.

'Supposing they find something wrong,' I voice my concern out loud.

Mum's response is to grip my hand harder while I cross the fingers on my other hand. It's not likely, this will be my third scan including the private one which in the end Tim couldn't attend. Still, he enjoys the photos.

Inevitably we go past the time of my appointment; I do hope it's not going to be a repeat of last time. Then, suddenly, we're called. We go through the name checking, date checking, climbing on the table and enjoying, or not, the cold gel slapped onto my bump followed by the pressing down of the scanner head – if that's what it's called.

We watch on the screen as the sonographer clicks and measures everything.

'All looking fine,' she says. 'Do you want to know the sex?'

'Yes please,' Mum and I chorus.

After our dismal visit to the hospital restaurant last time we've elected to stop off at the nearest pub and have lunch before I go back to work. The car park is quite full and I wonder if we should have booked, or gone somewhere else.

As we go inside it's busy, and a lot of the customers are hospital staff.

'Comes recommended,' Mum says. 'My friend works at the hospital in the fracture clinic, she says this is where everyone comes if they want a decent meal at a decent price.'

'And for celebrations,' I add, nodding over at a table decorated with balloons.

We find a table in the corner, choose our food, order on the app, which I have to download, and wait. It doesn't take long for our drinks to come although obviously there's no alcohol to celebrate our news that everything is okay. I have all the scan photos tucked safely away in my bag and this time the baby does actually look like a baby, and that pouty lip is still there.

'A boy,' Mum says, the biggest grin on her face. 'So exciting, so novel, for me.'

'And me.' I laugh.

'When I had you I was friends with other mums with babies your age and we all had girls, every one of us. I don't think I've ever even held a baby boy.'

'Me neither.' Truth is I've never held a baby at all. When the opportunity has arisen, I usually decline, laughingly saying I'm no good with babies. That is going to have to change.

'Have you thought of any names?'

'Toying with Aaron.'

For a moment Mum doesn't say anything, then forces her face into a smile and says, 'That's different.'

'Is it? You don't like it, do you?'

'Oh, it's nothing to do with me. He's your baby, your son.'

'I'd like you to like his name though.'

'I'll grow to like it.'

'I haven't decided yet. Have you any ideas?'

'Matthew's a nice name. All the Matthews I've met have been nice men, kind.'

'Yeah, me too.' I'm instantly transported back to Cardiff and Kerri's hen party and Matt, my unintentional, unplanned, and rather sensational one-night stand.

Funny, I've haven't given him a second thought since that night, actually that's not strictly true. I gave him a lot of thought in the immediate aftermath, then I forced myself to forget him because a long-distance romance with me having someone else's baby was never going to work. Anyway I've been so preoccupied with getting pregnant, staying pregnant, being pregnant, that I've no time for anything else, least of all a new relationship. Recently I came across his note, complete with phone number, stuffed into the bottom of one of my going out handbags. I toyed with throwing it away, but in the end I left it there as a memento. I won't be using that handbag again for a long, long time. The memory will bring a smile to my face when I do.

'Tom's nice, or John, or David,' Mum's running names by me but I've not been fully listening.

'Not David,' I say, suddenly paying attention. 'That's my boss's name and he's a bit of an old, sexist dinosaur.'

'Oh dear. How old?'

'Older than you, Mum.'

'Poor sod. He must love his job to keep on working when there's a whole big wide world out there to explore when you're not tied down by the nine-to-five.'

'Loves the money, Mum. Although he says he's planning on retiring in the near future but my absence might scupper his plans.'

'He doesn't want to leave, otherwise nothing would stop him. Ignore that bit of emotional blackmail. I can see why you dislike that name, strike it off.'

We're still laughing when our food arrives.

'We'll have to get one of those baby name books,' Mum says.

'Already ordered one. Did it last night. I thought once I know the sex I'm going to need it.'

'Bring it with you next time you come round.'

The food is great and I can see why this pub is so popular with hospital staff. The time flies and soon I must go.

'Lovely as this is, I have to get back to work.' I start to pull on my coat, hunt down my scarf because it's cold outside now. Winter is definitely on its way. I wrap the scarf around my neck and pull it up like a mask.

We're weaving our way out of the pub, there are so many people here, some leaving, some arriving. This place really is popular. I grab the door, another hand takes the handle at the same time, yanks it open, a male voice says, 'after you,' I mutter my thanks and push through, Mum close behind me. A little tingle runs down my spine. The voice sounded warm, nice. I try to turn around to see whose it was but it's so crowded, especially by the door and all I can see is a hand, gripping the door, no longer on the handle. He's wearing a watch, a Tag Heuer. Another tingle runs down my spine, makes me raise my shoulders and shudder a little. We push on out through the door and I manage to turn just as the owner of the hand, the watch, moves across in front of me on his way to the men's toilets. He turns and looks at me, the bottom half of his face obscured by someone's head. For a fleeting moment our eyes meet; his brown, mine blue. He has a shock of springy, fair hair that catches my attention. Then he's gone and Mum and I are out in the cold and wind, with rain threatening.

'Urgh, winter's well and truly on its way,' Mum says, as she clicks the remote to open the car doors.

'Yeah.' I glance back but of course all there is to see now is the closed pub door.

The mind is a funny thing, playing tricks on you when you least expect it. That watch, that voice, even those eyes, they reminded me so much of Matt from the Cardiff hen do. But not the hair. Matt was bald, completely bald. I know men can have transplants but I don't think they work that quickly. I smile to myself as Mum drives me back to work. All that talk about baby names, Mum suggesting Matthew, then my mind just conjured someone up who looks a bit like him.

Weird.

Actually, it's months since I met him, and we spent an intense time together but it was only one evening, one night. I'm not even sure I could pick him out of a crowd of three now.

I'm mad busy at work; since I told David the news he's been in full on panic mode. This afternoon I'm finalising the details for my maternity cover replacement before the advert goes out to the two recruitment agencies we use. It also has to be posted internally which means giving it to Pearl to put on our company intranet. I'm not anticipating any internal applicants since no one in the department has shown any interest at all, not that I expected any.

But it's always possible that someone in the business has a friend who might be suitable. It would save us a fortune if that happened because the recruitment agencies cost a bomb and David is already moaning about the effect of that on his budgets.

No sooner has Pearl posted the advert internally than I receive an email from her. She's applying. I'm shocked. On paper she's more than qualified but well, I don't know what to think. She's obviously been busy because this application is comprehensive, she's just been waiting for the opportunity to send it in. I ping back a reply to say thank you, then forward it to David.

After a quick visit to the loo, I grab a drink before trotting round to his office to find him perched on the corner of Pam's desk drinking coffee. They're talking about films on *Netflix*, hardly work, so I don't feel bothered about interrupting.

'We've had an application,' I say.

'Yeah, we were just looking at it.'

I don't like that. I don't think Pam should be involved in this, even though I know she will be. And they couldn't have looked for long because they were chatting about films when I arrived.

'Good candidate, we think,' Pam says.

I nod, I want to snap at her to mind her own business, but I don't. 'Shall we discuss it in your office,' I say to David, ignoring Pam.

'I'm very impressed by her CV,' David says once we're seated in his office.

'Yes, she has all the knowledge and all the paper qualifications…'

Before I get a chance to carry on, he butts in, 'And we'll save money on recruitment fees.'

I knew it would be all about the money. 'She has no interpersonal skills.' It sounds harsh when I say it. I know David won't understand what I'm saying. He's one of those people who schmooze their way through life, a charming charmer who doesn't even notice when others lack his charisma because he's so focused on himself.

'I've always found her fine,' he says, his tone so dismissive that I decide not to engage in arguing with him. There is no point.

'Be interesting to see what the agencies find,' I say, getting up and heading for the door. 'I'll send any over as soon as they come in.' Realistically that could be a week or more before the first one even arrives.

I don't know why I care so much; I won't be here to suffer the chaos. No, but I will have to come back after maternity leave and sort it out. I wonder how much I'll want to come back, much less work extra hard sorting out any issues I'll inherit.

I've woken up early this morning, it's still dark outside; it's Saturday and I'd much rather have slept in. I can feel the baby, my boy, wriggling around inside me, but that's not what woke me up. It's work. I must have been dreaming, or at least thinking, about it. I've come to a decision; work is not the be all and end all of my existence. I'll do my best with regards to my temporary replacement but I am not stressing over it. There is no point. What happens when I'm away on maternity leave is neither my responsibility nor my problem. David can grow a pair and deal with it himself, after all, he's the one earning the big salary.

I'm meeting Mum later and we're going Christmas shopping. It's only five weeks until Christmas and Mum is keen to get all hers done now. She also wants to dress shop, cruise dress shop that is. I'm meeting her in town and I'm going to go a little early so that I can have a quick look around the baby shop that's replaced the now shut down Mothercare, a shop I know well from my many past visits to buy presents for other people's babies. I hope this shop is as good as Mothercare.

I'm just coming out of the baby shop carrying a bag of goodies, yes I couldn't resist. I have blue vests, blue sleepsuits, blue mittens and hats, blue everything. I know it's a cliché, but hey. I feel so happy, so excited, so thrilled. And scared. I'm always a little scared.

'Woomph.' I have the wind taken out of me.

'Sorry, so sorry,' the voice says. 'Oh, it's you.' It's Gary. The idiot.

'Watch where you're walking.' I pull myself up to my full height and take a breath.

'Are you okay, I mean you didn't hurt anything, did you?'

'If anything is hurt it's you who's done it, not me.' This sounds so familiar, so reminiscent of the rows we used to have. Anything bad that happened in our relationship was always about blame. It was so toxic and it's taken me a long time to realise. The baby extends a foot, or maybe an arm, inside me. He's probably been woken up by my idiot ex, but at least he's active.

Gary decides not to engage in an argument with me, which is just as well. Instead he changes tack. 'How are you anyway? You've grown a bit since I last saw you.'

I resent that comment after what he said about me being fat but he's right, it may only be a few weeks since we last met but my bump has truly popped out and there's no hiding it now.

'I'm fine.' I sound curt, too curt. 'How are you?'

'Okay, okay. Not bad. You know. My back's been playing up a bit.' Probably from giving his little girlfriend piggy back rides. Even in my head that is super bitchy, so glad I didn't say it out loud. 'I really miss our bed, haven't had as good a night's sleep since I left it.'

'My bed,' I correct him.

'Yeah, I suppose it is now.'

'It always was. I paid for it.' We were supposed to split the cost but somehow that never happened even though it was bought at his insistence. I was quite happy with my standard double, but he wanted a super-king size. I'm appreciating it now though, and no doubt will do even more after the baby's born.

'Did you?' He knows full well I did. 'I really miss that mattress.'

'Oh yeah. Rock hard.' At his insistence, it used to make my bones ache, it was like sleeping on a pebbly table top. 'I got rid of it, changed to a softer one.'

'Did you? Have you still got the old one? Did you put it in the garage or something?'

'No. It went down the tip.'

'Shit, no. It was only a year old.'

'I know, but it was tainted, wasn't it? You and your little schoolgirl friend had soiled it.' I smile and turn to walk away.

'We didn't, we were careful.'

I turn back and face him. Other than the hairdryer I had no real evidence that they'd been up to no good in my bed. And I hadn't said stained, but that's obviously what he thought I meant. 'You're unbelievable,' I say.

''She's not a schoolgirl either; we're getting married soon.'

I raise my eyebrows in question at him because I'm lost for words. He probably told anyone who'd listen that *we* were getting married soon too, but we weren't. Idiot.

'Christmas Eve,' he says. 'In case you're interested.' He thinks he's got one over on me. Well, I suppose he has.

'Hope it goes well. And don't keep her up too late or she'll find out Santa isn't real.' With that I turn and march away, if he says any more I can't, and don't, want to hear it.

I'm still seething when I meet Mum who insists on tea and biscuits to calm me down. It does the trick because we're soon laughing about Gary and the mattress.

'Did you really take it down the tip? It was almost brand new.'

'No, I got the charity shop, you know the one that likes furniture donations, to take it. There wasn't a mark on it, after all as Gary said, they'd been careful.' I shudder as I imagine them in my bed. I stripped it off the minute he'd gone and threw away that bedding, which I'd never liked anyway. But I never slept in it, electing to sleep in the spare room on my old double bed until I bought a new mattress.

'You should have told him which one, he could have tried to buy it back.' Mum has a mischievous twinkle in her eyes.

'No, I like to think of him sleeping on his old lumpy mattress at his flat, I slept there once or twice and it was horrible. Maybe the schoolgirl has insisted on a new one, if so, he'd have had to foot the bill because I doubt her Saturday job could fund that.' Ooo, that feels better.

'Miaow,' Mum says, laughing. 'You don't need him.'

'Never did.' And that's the truth. I don't know why I ever allowed myself to be persuaded otherwise. 'I don't need any man, Mum,' I add, grinning.

'Do you still want Tim to decorate the baby's room?' Mum asks, grinning. The fact is it was Tim's idea, not mine.

'Yes, absolutely.'

'Then we need to choose what you want because he's keen to get it done soon. We'll be leaving on the fifth of January don't forget.'

I'm really saddened by that, sad that Mum will miss my expansion, probably miss the birth too.

'Oh, exciting. We'd better get on with the shopping then.'

By the time we get back to Mum's I'm so exhausted that I can hardly keep my eyes open. Fortunately, Tim is on hand with cups of weak tea and a lovely meal for us. I put my feet up and let him run around looking after me, which he seems to thoroughly enjoy.

Mum has bought all her Christmas presents except for the few she's ordering online. She's bought two cruise dresses, or cocktail dresses as she called them. And we've been to B&Q and bought wallpaper, paint and a new rug for the baby's room. We've agreed it should be the big room not the smaller one, so Tim is going to dismantle the bed and move it. It should just about fit. There's nothing in that room now, Gary used to keep his crap in there, his golf clubs, his gym kit, some old CDs that he couldn't bear to part with.

'I'll give the carpet a good vacuum before you move the bed,' I say, yawning.

'Don't worry, we'll do that. You shouldn't be doing heavy manual work in your condition.' Bless Tim.

'Okay.' I'm not going to argue with that.

Nine

Christmas

Just the three of us for Christmas, Mum, Tim and me. Last year Gary joined us and to be honest he ruined it, he wanted the TV on too much, wouldn't play the silly games we like and was generally a pain in the arse. Looking back I can see the writing was on the wall then, but I was too blind to see it at the time. Or I was in denial.

We've eaten dinner, cleared up – the dishwasher is on for the second time today – and now we're sitting around eating sweets. Mum has dived into a tub of Quality Street. Tim is eating peanut brittle because he wants to break some teeth while there are no dentists available for over a week – but, as Mum says, he won't be told. And I'm sucking on Newbury Fruits, sucking the liquid centre out before chewing on the sugar-coated jelly outer. I love these, they're my Christmas treat, Mum buys them every year, making me take them home with me, and I usually eek them out, maximum two or three a day. But I've already eaten seven. What a little piggy I am, but hey, if you can't enjoy your treats when you're pregnant, when can you?

'I feel a bit sick,' I say, pushing the box away from me, then snatching another one. 'Please, someone, take them away.'

'Not like you to be a piggy.' Mum picks the box up and puts it on the sideboard. It's far enough away that I won't be tempted. Probably.

'I know, but I'm a hungry horse these days.' And greedy, definitely greedy.

'I'm taking these away too,' she says, grabbing Tim's peanut brittle from his hands.

'No,' he yells through a mouthful of the stuff.

'Yes, while you still have some teeth. I don't know why I let you make me buy this stuff every year.'

'Because you love me.'

'I love you with teeth.' She takes the nut brittle out to the kitchen and hides it somewhere.

'I'll find it,' Tim calls after her.

I sit and watch this performance and smile, remembering that this relationship is exactly what I wanted with Gary. How foolish I was. Well, that's a ship that's well and truly sailed. Gary got married yesterday to his child bride, not that I care, good riddance I say. Poor girl, I hope she knows what she's let herself in for. Maybe he'll treat her better than he treated me, after all, he did actually marry her.

'Charades?' Mum asks, coming back in with a tray of drinks. I'm on sparkling water, I have a real craving for it. It also helps with indigestion. Though, according to Tim, it creates indigestion.

'Yeah, why not.' I haul myself up. 'I'll start.'

We're soon playing the same silly game, using the same clues, as we do every year. Except last year, because Gary sulked so much he spoiled it and we stopped playing. I never understood why he was so anti. It's just a game, a daft one that we play badly. Maybe he felt left out.

Not that it matters now.

After that we play a game of Monopoly, until it gets nasty. It always gets nasty. Tim, who hates losing always loses. He insists that me and Mum gang up on him. We don't. Well, not deliberately anyway. We've played this every year since Tim met Mum. It started on the first Christmas as an icebreaker, now it's both a tradition and a war of attrition. Usually either Mum or I win. I cannot remember Tim ever winning.

By nine pm I'm flagging. I start hunting round for my presents, which we opened immediately after Christmas dinner, before me and Tim fell asleep.

'The bed's made, you can stay here,' Mum says.

'No, I'm better off in my own bed.' I'm really appreciating the size of that bed now, especially with its lovely new, soft mattress. I hug her goodbye, then hug Tim, who still smells of peanut brittle. Despite having passed the morning sickness stage certain smells make me nauseous, apparently peanut brittle is one of them.

Tim goes out and scrapes the ice off my car, running the engine to warm it up, before loading all my bags in. He's a great dad. The best.

A thought strikes me: should I try to contact my biological dad and tell him about the baby? Maybe not; he can't be bothered with me, never mind my son.

Once home I just dump everything and go to bed. I never imagined pregnancy could be so tiring.

It's that weird time between Christmas and New Year and I meet up with Kerri and Carol-Anne. They are both as rotund as me. Our due dates are within a month of each other with me in the middle. It's going to be a busy time.

'Garth says I'm a killjoy now,' Kerri says, sighing.

'Why?'

'I've gone off sex.'

'Sex? What's that?' I say, laughing.

'I can't get enough of it,' Carol-Anne says. 'It's bloody exhausting. We're at it more now than ever, even more than we were when we first got together.'

'Don't tell Garth, please.' Kerri rolls her eyes.

'Oh, we're making the most of it, we both know I'll be too tired and won't be interested once the baby arrives.'

'Has anyone settled on names yet?' I'm changing the subject.

'No. Still arguing.'

'Us too,' Kerri says. 'What about you?'

'No, can't decide. Got a book but not been inspired. My mum likes Matthew.'

'That's nice.'

'It is, but…'

'What?'

'Nothing. I'm not sure.' I'm not going to tell them about Hen Do Matt and Cardiff. They'll put two and two together and make five, or ten probably in Kerri's case. The truth is that since seeing that guy in the pub near the hospital, I've thought about Matt more than I would like too. I'm sure it's just the weird raging hormones of pregnancy doing it. Or maybe I'm lonely. Who knows?

'Hey, Esme, Garth has a friend who's back on the market.' She makes him sound like a house. 'Was married for like ten years, two children, but divorced last year, now getting out there. Good with children, obviously, lots of experience…' she giggles and I want to reach over and gag her. 'He's up for it if you are.'

'What, you've told him about me?'

'Yes. He was round ours last week, saying what shit the apps are, how all the women want is either a stud for a night or a meal ticket. He wants to settle down.'

'Thought he'd have had enough of that,' Carol-Anne says.

'No. Not at all. Yes, it didn't work out or last forever but he says they had some very good years and he has his children, so looks on it as a success, which I think is a very healthy way to look at it, don't you?' She looks straight at me. 'Because if you spent ten years in the same job then left to go somewhere else, you wouldn't call that a failure, would you? That's how he's framing it and I think I agree with him.'

'Fair point.' And it is and I've never thought of it

like that, not that I've been married or even with someone for ten years, not even two years. 'Good for him. I'm not interested. I don't need a man.'

'They're useful for doing things around the house, if nothing else.' Carol-Anne giggles now. 'Olly built the cot, crib and wardrobe last week.

I just smile. I have Tim for that. 'I'm fine,' I say. 'All done.'

'Garth hasn't done ours yet. We're still arguing about which room the baby is going in. He says smallest room, but that's only because he doesn't want to give up his man cave. I've told him, move out to the shed or the back of the garage like normal men do.'

We all laugh. Garth always makes me laugh, he has a lathe in their second bedroom, makes some wonderful things but the dust and noise must be horrendous. 'Will he even be able to do that indoors with a new baby in the house?'

'That's exactly what I've said. And the answer is no, of course not. He's definitely moving out to the shed; he just hasn't accepted it yet.'

We all laugh because we all know that Garth will be moving out to the shed or the garage sooner rather than later.

'Garth is still going on about videoing the birth.'

'Eww.' Carol-Anne grimaces. 'Are you going to let him?'

'Can't decide. I mean, I don't want it posting online or anything like that and he said that was not his plan, but I'm sort of warming to the idea. Be something nice to look back on, though not immediately. And we do love our wedding video, even the bit where the camera seems to focus on the hairs up Garth's nose.'

'It won't be his hairy nose it focuses on for the birth, it'll be your hairy minge.'

'I don't have a hairy minge, thank you very much.' Kerri throws Carol-Anne a look that could kill before she changes the subject. 'Is your mum being your birth partner, Es?' She smiles at me in that pointed way that says, this smile is not for you, Carol-Anne.

'Well, yes, that's the plan. I just don't know if she'll be back from her big cruise by then. I'm hoping I go overdue.'

'Tough timing that,' Carol-Anne says. 'Is there no one else? I'd offer but I suspect I might let you down at the last minute if I go into labour myself.'

'Same here,' Kerri says. 'But I'm due after you so if I haven't had mine and your mum's not back, you can count on me, unless you've already got a back-up?' Her face says she's hoping I have, says it so clearly that I let her off.

'I probably have, but thank you.' I haven't, all my other friends, the ones my age are far too wrapped up in their own families, most of them I haven't seen in months, years in some cases. 'I've got a hospital appointment the week after next.'

'Have you, Es? I don't have one booked at all, it's all my GP surgery seeing the nurse or midwife.' Kerri offers me a little smile; it might be gratitude because I haven't pinned her down to be my birth partner.

'I think it's because of my age. I'm an elderly primigravida apparently.'

'A what?' Carol-Anne frowns.

'Over thirty-five,' I mumble.

'Oh yeah. I always forget how old you are. Isn't it your birthday soon? Aren't you forty?'

'Thanks for reminding me. New Year's Eve.'

'That's a great time to have a birthday, everyone's always out celebrating anyway. I bet you've had some great parties in the past.' Kerri makes me sound ancient.

'Yeah.'

'What are you doing this year? Not having a party? Because if you are I missed my invitation.'

'Not having a party. Mum and Tim are taking me out for lunch.'

'Not dinner?'

'No. Too late, too rowdy.'

'Yeah, know what you mean, I can't stay awake much past nine these days.' Kerri sighs, wistful for times gone by that will never return.

We chat some more, mostly about stretch marks, aching backs and the best support bras. We talk about the pros and cons of breastfeeding and we all moan about never being slim again. It seems amazing to think that only six months ago we would have known nothing about these things, much less discuss them.

We finish our evening early, we're all too tired, except Carol-Anne who tells us she's feeling randy again.

'Eww, TMI, Carol-Anne,' Kerri says, pulling on

her coat.

We're sitting in the restaurant on my birthday finishing our coffee, well sparkling water for me, with lemon, when I glance outside. 'It's starting to snow.'

Mum looks alarmed. 'I hope it comes to nothing; I don't want our cruise delayed.'

'It won't delay our cruise,' Tim says, smiling at her. 'Might delay our journey down, that's all. We'll be fine.'

'But it's a worry. I don't like snow. Lovely to look at but so dangerous.'

I've offered to drive them down, I can easily get the time off work, it's only a day, but they've refused. They're off in three days' time and then I'll be on my own. I'm worrying again that going it alone with motherhood isn't such a good idea. I never realised how much I depend on my parents for support and advice. Mum, ever vigilant, picks up on my concern.

'We'll make sure we get internet access as soon as we get on the ship,' she says. 'So we can keep in touch with you.'

'Yes, we will. But be aware that reception can be patchy at sea, and the weather definitely affects it.' Tim's trying to let me down gently. The last cruise they went on they rarely had internet access and relied on waiting until they were in port. Not that it mattered, I wasn't talking to them every day, it was just that Mum wanted to post nice photos on her Instagram page. And they were only away three weeks. And I wasn't pregnant then either.

'I hope we don't have to do that.' Tim is staring out of the window.

'What?' We all turn to look. Two men are pushing a car away from the kerb but it's slipping and sliding about. They're laughing as they push and shove the car, finally it's where it should be and they run round to get back in. Just before they do, one turns and faces us, probably not seeing us as we see him. He looks just like that guy from the pub near the hospital. The Matt lookalike, but with hair. I shake the thoughts out of my head.

'Are you all right?' Mum asks.

'Yeah, just hoping we don't have to do that too.'

Ten

Mum and Tim have been gone almost a week now. Last I heard from them they were in Madeira. Since then there's been radio silence, possibly because they're in the middle of the Atlantic.

I've had a video call with Roger and Sue, followed by a phone call with Sue now. I'm telling her about my predicament, possibly, well no, probably, not having a birthing partner.

'I could come,' she says. 'If you get stuck, that's if you want me to. Roger would drive down with me but he wouldn't want to be with us. He's really quite squeamish. He actually fainted when I gave birth to our first. I was so bloody angry with him, I screamed that there wouldn't be any more children. He pulled himself together after that, but I wouldn't trust him after all these years.'

I'm glad to hear it. The last person I'd want in the room with me would be Roger even though this is his baby. 'I'd love that,' I tell her.

'Excellent, I have your due date already in the diary, so we'll see how it goes nearer the time.'

'Are you sure? I mean it's a long way to come.'

'Not a problem. Although we have got a two-week holiday booked touring Scotland earlier that month, so don't go into labour early.' She gives a nervous little laugh.

'I won't,' I say. 'Obviously I'll pay your petrol and the cost of a hotel. I wouldn't want you being out of pocket.'

'Okay,' she says, sounding embarrassed.

I feel a bit happier about the birth now, at least I'll have a friendly face with me if Mum doesn't get back in time.

I have my hospital appointment this afternoon. I'm a little bit worried, although no one has said anything is wrong. I try to take my mind off it by going through the applications for my maternity cover that the agencies have sent in. David is still keen on, to use his words, 'giving Pearl a go.' I have explained to him that's all very well but what if Pearl doesn't work out? He just shrugged and wandered off, smiling and charming and with his head in the clouds and muttering something about the bottom line and budgets. It's always about the money with David.

Pearl hasn't asked me about her application, she knows the closing date is another week or so away. She watches me like a hawk. I'm not sure what she's expecting me to do or not do, but I do feel very observed. She will definitely get an interview, I wouldn't dream of not doing that, but even if I did David would override me. As far as he's concerned she's got the job. From what I've seen of the applications so far, hers is definitely the strongest, on paper. Apart from the complete lack of experience and interpersonal skills.

At the hospital I have to provide a urine sample, a fresh one done right there and then in their toilets. Oh no, it'll be the tiny tube again. Happily, it's not. A plastic cup, the sort we get coffee in out of the vending machine at work, is thrust into my hands.

'That looks fine,' the midwife says, after testing it. 'How do you feel?'

'Emotional, tired,' I say, without thinking.

'Hormones,' she says. 'Shall we weigh you?'

After telling me I've put on a little more than I should – not that I needed her to tell me – it's all those Newbury Fruits and other sweet treats, checking my blood pressure and poking my stomach, she announces that I don't need to see a doctor.

'Good, so everything's fine?'

'Absolutely. But we'll see you again in four weeks or so.'

'Why do I have to come up here? I mean, my friends just go to their GP surgery.'

'How old are your friends?' she says, giving me a bit of a pitying look.

I shrug.

'Younger than you.' She's interpreted my shrug correctly. 'It's your age; this is your first baby. Better safe than sorry. Any problems and we have the experts right here, no waiting for another appointment.' She smiles. 'Do you have your birth plan?'

'No.'

'Did you forget it? Bring it next time.'

'I haven't made a birth plan. From what I hear there's not a lot of point.' I've heard enough horror stories from friends my age who had their first babies ten or more years ago. They all said the same, once the action starts all plans for a drug-free birth are thrown out of the window. I'm not even going to pretend I want a 'natural' birth if it means drug free. I want every painkiller going; I'm not into playing the heroic martyr.

She frowns at me. 'Make a birth plan and bring it next time.'

'Okay,' I say, smiling at her. Like hell I will.

I leave the room feeling faintly cheated. I've come all this way for nothing. I have to remind myself that this is very good news. I don't want any need to see a doctor.

Despite just having a wee I need to use the loo again. I nip in and out quickly and am walking down the corridor when I notice toilet paper stuck to the heel of my boot and trailing behind me. Oh for pity's sake. I'm doing a little dance trying to get it off with my other foot, at the same time thinking that even when it's loose, I don't want to touch it, never mind pick it up, but of course I'll have to.

'Can I help?' a voice says.

A man in scrubs is bending down to my foot. He whips a surgical glove from his pocket and uses it to pick the toilet roll off my boot and off the floor and then throws the lot into the bin, glove included.

'Thank you,' I say, feeling mortified. 'Thank you

so much.'

'No problem.' He turns and looks at me. Like everyone in medical settings post-pandemic, he's wearing a mask, as am I. A pair of dark brown eyes crinkle suggesting he's smiling. Then he frowns.

My stomach grips and my heart misses a beat. It's him, the man with the springy hair, the man that reminds me of Hen Do Matt. How can that be? Is he following me around?

'Thanks again,' I mutter, before getting myself out of there as fast as possible.

Out in the cold air of the car park I pull myself together, try to be logical. He reminds me of Hen Do Matt because he has brown eyes; lots of people have brown eyes. It is quite likely he's the same man I saw in the pub because that pub is popular with hospital staff. And he'd never be interested in me anyway, not in a hundred years. I also think he's the same one that was pushing the car in the snow, but so what; it's a small world and actually a small town.

I take myself straight home from the hospital. Yes, I'm skiving. There's still another hour of work but I just don't want to go back. I'd much rather put my feet up and finish off the bar of chocolate I bought last night. I promise myself it will be the last one because I don't want to put on more weight than necessary. It'll be all the harder to get it off afterwards.

Once home I rummage around and find the birth plan form. Then I fill it out; it doesn't take long. I write: *Deliver my baby safe and sound, whatever it takes and don't kill me in the process*. I stuff it back into my folder and forget about it. Of course I won't hand it in, it's far too sarcastic. I'll just say I've forgotten it again. That's if anyone even asks.

The four weeks until my next appointment whizz by. I buy more baby items – soon my house will be overrun by them, but that's what I wanted, isn't it? I manage to have a couple of conversations with Mum and Tim, video call Sue and Roger who are getting excited about their forthcoming holiday touring Scotland. I don't say anything to them but I do wonder at the wisdom of touring Scotland in the early spring, which is the equivalent of winter up there. However, Sue pre-empts me – has this question been asked of them before? She tells me that they're hoping for snow as they have booked a dog sledding ride and while it still takes place in dry weather it would be so much more fun in snow. I can almost see the charm in that.

'Don't go falling off and breaking anything,' I joke.

Roger rolls his eyes at that and Sue gives a nervous giggle. Then Roger says, 'Wouldn't be the first time.'

It transpires that Sue is a bit of a thrill seeker and broke her leg ten years ago while snowboarding.

I don't know whether to laugh or cry. I hope nothing happens to her both for her and, selfishly, for me.

At work we've finally interviewed candidates for my maternity cover. Four people so far, Pearl will be last. David is nit picking over the salaries two of the others are expecting and is already moaning about the agency fees. I feel like giving up and just telling him to give it to Pearl. Why do I care? It won't be me who has to sort out the problems when I'm not here. Sort them out when I return yes, but that's a year away.

We interviewed Pearl this morning. It went very well. She's obviously done her homework. In the interview as well as on paper she seems like the best candidate, except I know she has no experience. I'm now sitting in David's office waiting to discuss it. We need to make a decision this week as whoever gets the job needs to come in and shadow me. David and Pam are fannying around with his coffee machine, yet again. I wouldn't be so bothered if I wasn't going to the hospital soon. I have my appointment in just over an hour and I need to factor in getting there and parking.

Eventually he comes and sits down, without his coffee.

'Machine's playing up,' he says, sighing as Pam picks up the coffee machine and takes it away. 'Pam's going to bring it back when she's sorted it out.'

I nod at him. I really don't care. Selfishly I hope she doesn't sort it out before I leave because lately I've found the smell of coffee nauseating. I haven't actually been sick over it, but feeling sick is bad enough.

'I don't have long,' I remind him, otherwise he'll

sit and whinge on about his coffee machine.

'Of course. What did you think of Pearl? I thought she did very well, very well indeed. I was impressed. I know you said she had no interpersonal skills but I thought she came across very well. And her qualifications are excellent.'

He's already made up his mind. The fact that Pearl will be cheap too is also in her favour. Who am I kidding? It's the primary factor.

'Pearl did come across well,' I agree, because the last thing I want to do is badmouth her. 'And on paper she's excellent, but she has no practical experience at all.'

He grins at me. It's unnerving and I don't like it.

'Well, she's really very clever, she was telling me she's a member of Mensa.' He sits back and watches me. I don't know when she told him that but it certainly wasn't in her interview.

'Wow,' I say.

'Yes, I was impressed.'

He was meant to be and maybe Pearl isn't so inexperienced after all; she's playing him.

'Knowing the theory isn't the same as experiencing the actual job.'

'How did you get your experience?' he asks.

I smile at him as I consider my answer. I had a feeling this might come up because I know he pulled my personal file. I know this because the keeper of all data, Pearl, told me.

'I worked in HR for years, climbed my way up through various jobs and promotions.'

'Pearl has worked in HR for years.' He grins at me

again.

Right then the baby sticks his foot under my ribcage and pushes. It's not exactly painful but it's definitely uncomfortable and I lift myself slightly off the chair to relief the pressure.

'Are you okay? Not going into labour, are you?' He gives a nervous little laugh.

'Fine, fine and of course not.'

'Only me.' Pam bursts into the room carrying David's steaming coffee. She's also put two biscuits on his saucer, yes David drinks his coffee from a cup and saucer, the dinosaur. The aroma of coffee wafts towards me and I suppress a gag. Oh God, can we just get on with this.

'Are you all right?' Pam asks, sensing my distress. 'Can I get you a glass of water?'

'Yes please, Pam. And could I have one of those biscuits.'

'Ah, tin is empty. Sorry. David has the last two. I'll get you that water.'

I eye David's biscuits. He has two, I only want one. He sees me eyeing them and pulls his cup and saucer closer. Mean git. He should give the biscuits a miss anyway, his belly isn't much smaller than mine. Well, if I'm sick in his office it's entirely his fault for drinking coffee and being so mean and greedy.

'What were we saying?' He picks up a biscuit, dunks it in his coffee then puts the whole thing in his cavernous mouth. Greedy dinosaur.

'You were saying that Pearl has worked in HR for years. I was about to answer that sitting in the corner, not really interacting with her colleagues, crunching biscuits, I mean numbers and posting job vacancies on the company intranet doesn't really count as experience. Or at least, not the kind of experience she'll need to do my job. Imagine her at an industrial tribunal.'

He swallows his mouthful of biscuit down quickly before saying, 'Oh gawd, we haven't got another one, have we?'

'No, no, not that I'm aware of. But there's bound to be one during the time I'm off.'

He picks up the second biscuit, greedy dinosaur, and dunks it too. At least his actions are making the biscuit very unappealing although those same actions increase the stench of coffee wafting my way.

'I can support her if that situation arises,' he says, before again wedging the whole biscuit in his mouth.

I have to look away, the sight of soggy biscuit churning around in his gob is making me gag. I just need to get out of here. I really do. Yet a part of me wants to laugh in his face. He knows nothing about HR procedures; he relies on me for all knowledge. He even makes me take the lead role in tribunals saying that he, as a director, is just there for support and to show that the company takes this very seriously.

I surreptitiously glance at his wall clock, time is ticking away and I need to go.

'You seem set on Pearl.' I smile my brightest smile.

'I think we should give her a go.'

'Okay.' Be it on your head. 'Pearl certainly has all the knowledge.' Committed to her brain like a computer, but hey ho. 'I'll sort out the paperwork and stand the recruitment agencies down.' I start to haul myself off the chair.

He beams back at me. I know that he couldn't really give a toss about HR, and I can see his *ka-ching* eyes flashing in delight. 'Thank you, I knew we'd make a good choice together.'

Oh no. I slide back down into my seat. 'For the record,' I start. 'I'm not agreeing with your choice. Pearl, for all her attributes, is most certainly not my choice.'

He sits and stares at me for a little too long, his brain whirring away as he balances the pound signs against common sense, not that he has a lot of that.

'I still think she's a good choice.' He picks up his coffee and takes several sips. I hope it's full of soggy biscuit and he chokes on a bit.

I get up. 'I'll do that paperwork,' I say. 'Oh, and remember, I'm at the hospital this afternoon.'

'Well, I'll let Pearl know this afternoon, if that's okay.' He smiles up at me and I nod in agreement. The arse will do it anyway because he wants the glory, he wants to be the benevolent boss.

Eleven

It's a long wait at the hospital. Annoyingly long.

But to be fair I'm in that kind of mood. Thanks to the arse that is David. Well, he's making his bed and he can enjoy lying in it. That amuses me and I snigger to myself. I cannot for the life of me imagine Pearl agreeing to lie in any bed with David. I don't know her well enough – I don't think anyone does – to know what her preferences are, male or female, but I'd bet my job that David isn't one of them.

I wonder if he thinks he is?

Unconsciously I shake my head to dismiss the idea. He wouldn't be so low as to employ someone just so he could get inside their knickers, would he? No. Definitely not. He doesn't need to anyway, he has a lovely wife, I've seen her. No, he wants Pearl because she's cheap, to employ, that is.

Maybe I should warn Pearl. No, far too hurtful.

Just as I'm thinking these really unkind thoughts – what the hell is the matter with me – I get an email on my work phone. It's from David. I could just ignore it. Legitimately I could. I open it.

Esme
Great news, Pearl has accepted the job. She can start shadowing you next week.
Regards
David

I don't reply because there is nothing I can say that won't sound sarcastic. Not for one second or even micro-second was there any chance that Pearl would refuse the job.

'Esme Haste,' a voice says, pulling me back to the maternity outpatients waiting room.

I jump up and smile, stuffing my work phone back into my handbag as I follow her.

'Do you have your sample?' she asks.

I hand it over. I'm getting good at this now; I haven't even wet the label. 'Can I have another tube for next time?' I ask, before she forgets and they make me wee in a cup again.

She wanders over to a drawer, yanks it open, and pulls one out. 'There you go.'

Twenty minutes later I'm out of there with the knowledge that the baby seems fine but that he's large for dates. And that I've put on too much weight. They've taken a few blood samples. My blood is probably pure sugar as I just crave sweet treats. I've stopped with the Newbury Fruits mainly because it's not so easy to find them in the shops now Christmas is long gone – although I did look online. I stopped myself though, that's a step too far. I'm trying to eat fresh fruit instead but it's not the same, is it? I'm desperate to get out and get home because now all I can think about is eating something nice. There's a strawberry flan in the fridge, I made it last night from Mum's recipe; it's one of her specialities.

I've almost made my escape when I come face to face with Gary and his schoolgirl wife. We both stop dead in our tracks. Shame I didn't pretend I didn't recognise him with his surgical face mask on. She's wearing one with a cartoon mouth on it, making her look scary and freakish. Her forehead is a bit spotty. Shame, but that's teenage acne for you.

'You're blooming,' Gary says, grinning.

'Thanks,' I say, whether he meant it as a compliment or not. Then it dawns on me, this is the maternity unit.

'You haven't met Cherry, have you? This is Esme,' he tells Cherry, who doesn't even bother looking at me. 'We'd better go, we're here for our first scan,' he says. Then they scuttle off leaving me standing in the corridor looking like a complete idiot. I stand there working out the dates; it's only a couple of months since they got married. She was already pregnant. But only just. Does that mean they got married because she was pregnant or started trying as soon as they decided to get married?

I shake my head. What the hell do I care? Gary is old news to me. Discarded. Done with. He'll be a feckless father. And even if he isn't I don't care. I'm happy as I am, I don't need him. Never did.

I'm out of the door and heading for the car parking pay station, fumbling in my bag for the ticket as I dash along. Found it. I'm wondering how much that long wait and then bumping into Gary will have cost me. Too much.

'Excuse me, hey,' someone is calling. But it can't be me they're calling because I'm on my own, so I ignore the voice.

'You can certainly leg it for someone who's so pregnant,' the voice says.

I turn and it's him, him again of the blond hair and brown eyes. Is he stalking me? He's conveniently wearing a surgical mask, and scrubs, so I won't be able to describe him to the police. Except for the eyes, maybe.

'You dropped this,' he says, handing over my work mobile.

'Did I? Did I really?' My tone screams that I don't believe him. Surely, I would have noticed. Did he snatch it out of my bag? My stalker.

'Yeah, really. You're welcome.' He turns and jogs back into the hospital and I just stand staring at his retreating form.

I yank my mask off before yelling, 'Thank you.' I doubt he can hear me now but he raises a hand in acknowledgement or he could just be waving to a friend.

I'm disconcerted now. It takes me a lot of fumbling to pay for my car parking and it costs me five-pounds-fifty. Bloody expensive afternoon. But it could have been worse; it could have cost me my work phone and that would have been more hassle than it was worth.

At home I settle down with half the strawberry flan and a big dollop of ice cream. It's so good. I've got another six weeks to go so I need to curb this eating because if I carry on at this rate I'll burst. I suspect that I won't be one of those who whizzes back down to their pre-pregnancy weight two weeks after giving birth.

I bet Gary's child bride does.

I'm almost impressed; I didn't think he had it in him.

Well, he didn't for me.

'I saw Gary yesterday,' I tell the girls as they bustle into my house. It's cold outside and they bring the smell of cold air with them. I sniff heavily because I really like it. 'You smell cold,' I say.

'Bloody cold,' Kerri mutters, pulling off her coat and dumping it on my stairs. 'It should be warming up by now.'

'What was that about Gary?' Carol-Anne asks.

'I saw him yesterday. The child bride is pregnant.'

'What the f….' Kerri starts.

'I know.'

'You're so well rid of him. What a scumbag. How old is she?' Kerri sounds more bothered than I am.

'Twelve,' I say, and we all giggle.

We're all looking rotund but I am most certainly the most rotund of the three of us. I'm taller than either Kerri or Carol-Anne and at the beginning I was slimmer, but not now.

We start comparing notes, and weights, or rather how much we've gained. I win that one easily.

'Yep,' Kerri says, sipping on a glass of orange squash which she says she is addicted to and brings with her everywhere she goes, 'You are definitely curvy now, but what I want to know is, do you still have a thigh gap?'

We roll about laughing.

'No idea,' I say. 'I haven't seen my thighs for months.'

'My toes have disappeared.' Carol-Anne demonstrates trying to look over her belly to see her feet. 'See, nothing there.'

'My belly button has disappeared. I mean, not just out of sight but gone completely. My belly is smooth and buttonless.' Kerri rubs her baby bump.

'Me too,' I say. 'It's normal apparently and will come back later.'

'But what will it look like?'

'Stretched then puckered,' Kerri says, before we all laugh again. 'Or should that be puckered then stretched?' You have to laugh, don't you? 'I've given up shaving my legs,' she adds. 'I probably look like a Shetland pony but really, life is too short.'

'I've given up shaving too and not just my legs,' I confess.

The girls roar with laughter.

'Olly's doing mine but…' she pauses for effect. 'He nicked me last time; I bled like fury. It wasn't nice. He was using that stick thing that he uses to stop the bleeding when he cuts himself shaving. It stung and I was swearing a lot. I should never have allowed him to do it because he's always cutting his face and he goes through those stick things like they're going out of fashion.'

'But he has a stubble beard,' Kerri says, frowning.

'Yes, but every Friday night he shaves it smooth then lets it grow until the following Friday. And he always cuts himself.'

'What stick thing anyway? I might need that after the baby's born.' Kerri's already planning ahead.

'Stopdic or something like that.'

'Styptic pencil,' I correct.

'Yeah, stopdic is something else, isn't it?'

Monday morning and Pearl's first day of shadowing me. I don't really know what we're going to do. Go through my emails I suppose. Since I've become pregnant I've not been very proactive with work. The truth is that while I have loved my job and especially the money and financial independence it has brought me, I'm tired by it now. What a confession, though not one I'd voice aloud.

Pearl has drastically changed her appearance over the weekend. So much so that we all gasp when she walks in. She's on time but later than the rest of us and very late for her. She's always first in, tucked into her corner seat, usually has earbuds in and it's as much as she can do to say good morning. But not today. She's making an entrance. Normally she wears shapeless trousers and baggy tops. She pulls her hair into a tight high ponytail and spends most of the day pushing her loose glasses up her nose. But not today.

'Woah,' calls a colleague. 'Where's Pearl?'

Pearl giggles, yes giggles. That's a first.

'Give us a twirl then,' someone else says.

She doesn't but she does do a little bow before

heading into my office. I have to admit that her appearance is quite gobsmacking. She's had a haircut, a chic chin length bob that I know from experience will require a lot of blow drying – hence my lovely (though now tainted) hairdryer. Gone are the old glasses, and in their place a pair that are strikingly similar to my own, which I only wear for computer work. She's wearing makeup, the first time I've ever seen her do that. She's also wearing a suit that is almost a replica of my favourite suit, not that I can get it anywhere near me at the moment.

'Wow, Pearl. I almost didn't recognise you.' Is that tactless? Too late. I soften it a little. 'You look fantastic.'

'My friends restyled me over the weekend. I thought I'd better look the part.'

'You look amazing.' She really does. No longer the little mouse that sits in the corner peering over her sloppy specs and watching everyone.

Maybe I've misjudged her. I don't believe that appearances are everything, in fact I find the way women have to assert themselves in the workplace by dressing a certain way rather annoying when men are mostly dressed by their wives, especially when it comes to ensuring everything is clean and pressed. Well, that was my experience with Gary anyway, and I know that Mum is the laundry queen in their house. But Pearl has definitely come out fighting and I admire her for that.

'I'm afraid it's not going to be very exciting this morning,' I say, sounding as apologetic as I feel. 'It'll just be going through my email inbox.' And hoping there are no problems there because I don't have the energy for it even if Pearl needs the experience. That's just too selfish of me, I know.

We spend the morning sifting through tedious stuff. I am going to have to up my game here if Pearl is going to stand a chance when I'm off on maternity leave. But really, sometimes HR is just bloody boring, sometimes it's firefighting and sometimes it's exciting, but mostly it's boring. Process and tedium is the name of the game.

Fortunately, Pearl's going to continue her own job in the afternoons which means I can put my feet up after lunch, metaphorically at least.

Pearl disappears for lunch and when she comes back she's wearing her old clothes, even swopping her glasses and has her lovely, shiny bob scooped up again. I do a double take.

'Where's this morning's Pearl gone?' Bit tactless but too late now.

'I feel I need to differentiate between my old job and my new. I'm just one of the team now, not the boss.' With that she puts her head down, taps furiously on her computer and ignores me standing by her desk like a spare part. Definitely back to old Pearl.

Weird. I did say she was weird.

Day two of Pearl's education is led by her. 'I think,' she starts, as soon as she arrives in my office; today she's wearing a different power suit and it looks as though it's straight out of the 80s or 90s. Weirdly it suits her and it does seem to give her some power, at least over me. 'That we should concentrate on getting a replacement for my old job. We should advertise internally because I'm sure there's a geek or two in IT who'd love to work in a nice soft job.'

'Morning, Pearl,' I say, getting up and closing the door. 'First off we don't call staff geeks.' I'm sure I've referred to her as a geek but hopefully only in my head.

'Not to their faces,' Pearl says, looking at me earnestly as though she knows that I think she's a geek.

'Ideally not at all.' I arch my eyebrows at her but she just stares at me blankly. 'But I do think your idea for a replacement is a good one.' It'll keep her occupied as well because there's so much tedious paperwork and budget sign-off to go through before you can even post a vacancy on the intranet which is the only bit she usually sees.

By the end of the morning I think she's pleased to go back to her old job for the afternoon. And, just like yesterday, she changes her clothes and takes up her old seat. This odd demarcation line obviously works for her.

The week progresses and by the end of it we're having a meeting with David to sign off the budget for Pearl's replacement, turgid as usual but also rather entertaining. In choosing Pearl because she would be cheap, he hadn't factored in finding a replacement for the vacancy created by her moving up. I'm obviously not on top of my game either because it would have been a good argument for not choosing her. Then we could just have had an external, experienced person shadowing me for two weeks instead of the month or more that Pearl is.

'Can't you do both jobs?' David asks.

Pearl's face is earnest when she replies. 'No,' without any explanation.

'But you are now.' He sits back rather pleased with himself.

'I'm only shadowing Esme for half a day. The other half of the day I am indeed doing my old job. However, I am working extremely hard and while I'm prepared to do that short term, long term it is not sustainable.' She blinks at him several times. It reminds me of a snake or lizard just before it darts its tongue out and reels in its prey. 'David,' she continues. 'Could you do two full-time jobs indefinitely?'

Of course he couldn't, he barely does his one job himself, Pam does a lot of the grunt work for him. I'm sure she influences his decisions too. In fact, given what Pam knows I suspect she could do his job just as well as he does.

'Um, well, probably not.' He sighs. She's caught him out.

It's ironic, to me at least, that his long-gone predecessor could have replied honestly that yes, she could. But she moved on to better things and we got lumbered with David the dinosaur.

By the time we leave his office he looks exhausted, Pearl looks triumphant, I am highly entertained though trying not to show it on my face and Pearl is clutching the signed paperwork in her hand. Yes, everything has to be on paper.

‘Have you ever thought of automating this process?’ she asks once we’re back in my office with the door firmly shut.

‘Oh yes. Many times. But David won’t sign off the budget for a new system, says they’re far too expensive.’

‘But there are little budget decisions going on like this all the time, aren’t there? All over the company, I mean.’

‘Yes, I assume there are.’ I don’t work in finance so it’s not my issue, but she does have a point.

‘It would save so much time, so much energy, so much paper. Financially companywide it’s a no brainer.’

‘Mmm,’ I say, smiling. Good luck with that. ‘It’s not really an HR decision.’

‘But David is the finance director too, isn’t he?’

‘Yes.’ I smile, because that’s the problem.

‘I’ll talk to some of the ge.. guys in IT, see if we can build something simple in-house. It doesn’t have to be complicated or expensive. It’s just a simple workflow…’ She carries on talking, thinking aloud but it sounds like geek-speak to me and I’ve lost interest so I zone out. ‘I’ll present it to David as a fait accompli,’ she says, just as I zone back in. ‘He won’t be able to resist.’

‘No. Very good.’ Maybe she can persuade the old dinosaur.

After that she goes back to her other job, changing her clothes over lunchtime, and her persona. While I still don’t think she has the right kind of soft skills for this job she certainly has the measure of David. I almost wish I could be a fly on the wall in a few months' time.

The weeks fly away and other than the odd little update on progress which is little more than a sentence, I hear no more about it. Pearl is mastering all the technical skills required to do my job. But typically, we haven't had a proper, meaty HR issue since she started shadowing me. I mean, where are the wrongful dismissal, clash of personalities problems that HR are good at sorting out?

'I'm ready to present my solution to David,' she announces one morning. 'I've spoken to Pam and she's squeezing us in later this morning.'

'Wow. That's great.' I don't really care.

I feel so heavy and lethargic these days. I go off on maternity leave next week and I can't wait. I just want to relax. Four glorious weeks and no work; I'm so looking forward to it. I received a *WhatsApp* message from Sue this morning, a photo of yet another loch with their beaming faces photobombing it. She's sent me something most days, although she always says she hopes I get it as mobile reception isn't too good. Seems okay so far. Every time I see one of their photos – there've been several feet up in front of a roaring fire ones – I feel envious, not because I want to go to Scotland but because I want to put my feet up. Being pregnant at forty isn't quite as easy as I thought it would be.

We trundle into David's office late morning. Pearl is bouncing and full of energy, I flop down into my chair and there is an audible hiss as the seat cushion protests. David gives me a look bordering on disgust. That's rich coming from the fat bellied dinosaur over there. Then my stomach rumbles. I'm hungry despite nibbling on rich tea biscuits all morning. But I also feel a little sick, probably all those biscuits.

This is coming cold to David; he knows nothing about it. Pearl's decision. I did warn her that we should feed the idea to him in little bits, get him used to it, but she was adamant. I decided not to pull rank, not because I want Pearl to fail – I don't – but because after this week I won't be here to make those decisions for her. I warned her, she decided.

And I'm too tired to care that much. There, that's the truth.

'What's this about then, ladies?' he asks. At least he didn't call us girls.

'I've been working on an idea to improve efficiencies across the company,' Pearl says, her voice strong and confident. She's already mastered the art of management bullshit speak.

David moves his shoulders back and raises his eyebrows. He doesn't like it when anyone, least of all a subordinate, implies the company isn't efficient.

Pearl then outlines the paper process we currently have for signing off budget items. David looks bored. I'm not exactly bored, just a bit preoccupied because I have this feeling in the base of my spine; a little like someone gripping too tightly and then letting go. An agony and relief cycle. It's not too frequent and now I think about it I think it started early this morning, but now it seems to be increasing in frequency and intensity. I wriggle around on my chair; I'm probably sitting on a nerve.

But the wriggling seems to make it worse.

'What do you think of all this, Esme?' David asks, sounding a little annoyed, which I did predict.

'It's a great idea.' I smile then glance over at Pearl to show solidarity. The truth is I haven't been listening but I assume she's told him about her new system. I'm sure it's a great idea.

'And how much is it going to cost?'

'Nothing. The work is done. In house.' Pearl allows herself a self-congratulatory smile.

'In house. When? And by whom?'

'By me and some of the IT team.'

David leans back again. He's pulling his face into a that smug, fat toad look that he favours.

'Then there is a cost, isn't there? Because if you and the IT team have been working on this unauthorised project you've obviously been neglecting your proper work.' He's so pleased with himself. He doesn't care about improving anything, or saving money unless it's him who's orchestrating the saving. And that's usually by cutting someone else's budget.

Pearl opens her mouth to speak then closes it again. The wind has been well and truly taken out of her sails. Bastard dinosaur.

Oh well, nothing ventured and all that shit. 'They did it in their own time, didn't you Pearl?'

Pearl glances at me, colours slightly, then speaks. 'Yes, we did.'

I have no idea if what I've just said is true but I'm not going to let David ruin this just to score points.

He swallows hard. 'Very commendable. What are the next steps?' He looks up at the ceiling in a dismissive, bored way. The arse.

Pearl then talks about how it needs to be live trialled; they've tested it of course but that's not the same…. Her voice fades away as the pain in my back really grips me.

'Woah,' I say, leaning forward.

'Are you okay?' Pearl looks at me, her earnest little face showing genuine concern.

'I think I'll just stand up for a second,' I say.

And as I do, the gush from between my legs is unmistakeable. The chair is soaked, my legs are soaked, my dress is soaked, my tights and my shoes are soaked.

Oh God.

'Don't worry, Esme,' Pearl says. 'I can handle this.'

Twelve

The journey in Pearl's car is both frightening and exciting. She's made me sit on a black bin liner – I can't imagine why she keeps a roll in her car. Anyway, I don't think I can make it any worse because her car is a tip. It's ancient, a bit grubby, and sounds like it's about to take off at any moment, except it crawls along.

I actually feel a lot better since my waters broke, assuming that's what it is and I haven't just wet myself. The pressure on my back has eased and I don't feel so sick now. I'm all for going home but Pearl won't hear of it. And, since she's driving, I don't have much say.

'You'll be able to afford a better car once you officially take over my job.' Why don't I just mind my own business?

'I can afford a better car now if I want, but I don't want. There is nothing wrong with this. It runs well, it's very economical and I believe you should use your car up until you can't.'

'Right.'

'If I got a new car what do you think would happen to this?' It's a rhetorical question because she answers it before I get a chance. 'It would be scrapped, that's what. What a waste. I will drive this car until I can't, until it won't drive any longer.'

'Okay.' Now shut up. 'Do you think we could just detour to my house to pick up my hospital bag?' All I have is my coat and my handbag and she didn't really want me to grab those, but she needed her own so it was hard to stop me from going back to my office.

'No, Esme, I don't.'

'Look, I'm not going to have the baby right now, am I?' Least of all in your filthy old car. I shudder at the thought of it.

'A detour is out of the question. If you give me your keys and tell me where it is I'll go and bring it up for you after I've dropped you off.'

'But…'

'No buts,' she roars. My oh my, where is the little mouse in the corner now? I really misjudged Pearl. She's a lion, not a mouse.

We screech up outside the maternity wing and, parking in the ambulance bay, Pearl abandons the car and runs inside the building. I sit there praying that no more ambulances appear. This is stressing me out more than my waters breaking.

Suddenly Pearl reappears, she has a porter with a wheelchair in tow.

'Really not necessary,' I say, as I haul myself out of the car. 'I can walk.'

'Well, it's here now so you might as well.' Pearl

points to the chair and the porter and I exchange a look. So I sit in it. At least it has a wipe down seat.

'I'll take her through but you'll have to move the car,' he says. Then adds, 'Before you come and find your partner.'

'I'm not her partner,' Pearl spits. 'I'm her colleague. Please wait a moment.' Then she turns to me. 'Give me your keys and address and I'll go and fetch your hospital bag. Where exactly is it in your house?'

After I tell her she roars off in her crappy old car. It's only after she's gone that I realise I never even thanked her properly. What an ungrateful cow I am. But I'm going to cut myself some slack, I'm on hormone overdrive, I'm not rational.

Now I feel abandoned. Alone. Scared.

The porter wheels me up to the desk where I answer a series of questions before he wheels me round to a cubicle. He waits while I get out of the wheelchair and plonk myself in a chair. Then he nods before disappearing behind the curtain he's just pulled around me.

I sit there for quite a while listening to the sounds around me, mostly the heating and distant footsteps. It seems very quiet here, not what I was expecting at all. I imagined chaos and people running around, women screaming. This calm is good, I tell myself.

Calm before the storm.

I get my phone out and send a long *WhatsApp* to Mum and Tim. I haven't heard from them for a couple of days so who knows when they'll get this. Then I copy and paste the message into a text, covering all bases. Then I do the same to Sue, whom I also haven't heard from for a few days. I cross my fingers and hope that Sue is on her way back home now so the journey to get here won't be so long.

A young midwife comes in. She tells me her name but it passes me by as right then, just as she's speaking, my entire body is gripped by a spasm of pain. I leap up off the chair and rub my back.

She waits until I calm down then asks a few questions, the same questions that they asked at the desk. Then she helps me take some of my clothes off and wraps a gown around me. It's not the best fit, gaping at the back. You'd think that they'd have bigger gowns in the maternity wing, wouldn't you? It's not as though rotund stomachs are unusual here.

She has a ferret around; I use this phrase because it's what my mum said the midwife who she had when she gave birth to me used to say. And me and Mum laughed so much that I've adopted it. In private. In my head.

'Yes, waters have definitely broken. And you're starting to dilate.'

'Starting to dilate? But he's not due for another four weeks or more. I don't even finish work until next Tuesday and I was so looking forward to the rest.'

The midwife I suspect, despite her youth, must have heard this a dozen times. She just smiles and pats my hand. 'We'll get you up on the labour ward,' she says. 'It might be some time.'

'Will he be born today?'

'Possibly. Maybe tomorrow. We'll just have to see

how it goes. This is your first baby so it might take a while. Put your dressing gown on and if you're up to the walk I can take you straight there, they have a bed.'

'I don't have a dressing gown,' I say, feeling close to tears.

'Oh, didn't you pack one in your bag?'

'I don't have my bag. My colleague has gone to collect it for me.'

'How long will she be?'

'I don't know?' I say, remembering how slow that car moved.

She glances around the cubicle. 'Why not put your coat on, that'll do the job.' She picks it up and holds it out for me. Thank God it's cold outside and my coat is substantial. She glances at my now discarded clothes piled on the chair. 'I'll get a bag for those,' she says.

So here I am strolling, or should that be rolling, down the corridor towards the labour ward, my coat over a gaping hospital gown, my clothes, including my damp knickers, tights, dress, the lot in a transparent plastic bag. I have my feet in my slightly damp shoes. Not very dignified or comfortable.

The labour ward has four beds and I'm the only person here. I think that's a good thing, nothing worse than going through this with an audience.

Twenty minutes later I'm thinking otherwise. I'm bored. And lonely. And apart from when the spasms grip me, which isn't often enough, I have absolutely nothing to do. Neither Mum nor Sue have seen my messages, in fact, according to *WhatsApp* they haven't even been delivered. And there's no sign of Pearl.

I get my work phone out and text her work phone – no *WhatsApp* on work phones. I sit watching the phone, willing her to reply but she doesn't. Then I start imagining all sorts. What if she's been in an accident because she was rushing to get my bag. What if she's been seriously injured or killed. That car would definitely not come off well in a collision. What if she got to my house and it's flooded or on fire and she's dealing with that. What if, what if…

I'm crying. I'm actually crying over my imagination.

'We'll get you something for the pain,' a sweet little voice says. Another midwife, a student according to her badge which also displays her name, Anji is standing in front of me looking concerned.

'No,' I manage between snivels, 'It's not that. My colleague is getting my bag and she drives an old wreck of a car for eco reasons, I think, and she might have killed herself in an accident or my house might have burned down…'

She rests a hand on my arm. 'Have these things really happened?'

'I don't know. Nobody's answering my messages. And my mum's on the other side of the world and Sue isn't here either. And I'm not supposed to be having my baby yet. It's too soon.'

'Let's get you a nice cup of tea and would you like a biscuit? You've missed lunch now. And I can definitely get you some painkillers.'

'I really don't think I need them yet, but thank you. And yes to the tea, two sugars please, but I don't need a biscuit just yet. Thank you.' I'm not going to own up to the half a packet of rich teas I've already eaten. Still, they'll keep me going for hours.

An hour later and I'm still on my own in this ward. After all the excitement of my rant over imaginary happenings I'm starting to feel tired. I've also accepted some painkillers because the last spasm I had, although technically I've been told to refer to them as labour pains – I prefer spasms – was quite a horror. I'm glad they're not too often.

I'm in bed. Yes, actually inside the bed, covers over me and I'm lying back. It's almost pleasant. What would make it even more pleasant would be a nice bit of Netflix. I wonder if I can get it on my phone?

I grab it and start searching. Yes, success, I quickly find it, but then I don't know the login and password details, it's written down somewhere at home but I don't know where. Then it dawns on me that even if I did know I couldn't use it as I only pay for the one device subscription. Maybe there's something on YouTube or iPlayer or any of the catch-up services. Why aren't there any TVs in here? I know from visiting Tim when he had an operation on his foot a couple of years ago that the other wards have those personal TVs and phones. Okay not many people used the phone but the TV, even though expensive, got plenty of use. It would be a good distraction I think as another spasm grips me.

I fumble around on iPlayer but I can't concentrate enough to choose something and rest my phone down while I sigh.

'All right?' a voice says. It's Anji again.

'Yeah, just had another one.'

She glances at the clock on the wall and smiles. 'Shall we have a quick look at you?'

It's not really a question, is it? More a statement. She pulls the curtains around my bed and lifts the covers. She soon has her head up between my legs. I have to admit I do not like it. Where is the dignity? Apparently, according to Carol-Anne it has to be left on the doorstep on the way in and you can pick it up on the way back out, providing you can carry it but as you'll have so much baby paraphernalia, as well as baby, you'll probably forget anyway.

She prods my stomach then pulls the covers loosely back over me. 'Don't move,' she says. 'I'm just going to check your notes.' A few minutes later she's back and with her head between my legs again. 'Yes, you have dilated quite a bit more. Well done. How are the painkillers working? Do you think you need anything stronger?'

'Not yet,' I say.

'Well don't leave it too long if you want an epidural. What did you put on your birth plan?'

'Can't remember,' I mutter, cringing at the memory of the midwife finding it and insisting that she log it. Yes, despite my best intentions I forgot to remove it from my folder before going for my appointment.

'Did you bring it with you?'

'No.' I don't say that it went in the bin immediately after that hospital appointment.

'Not to worry. Can you remember what it said?'

'No.' I shake my head.

She frowns a little. I can't be the only woman not to have brought her birth plan with her, can I?

'I'll just check if we've got it on the system.' She skips off again.

I want to tell her not to bother.

She's soon back and trying to hide the little smirk on her face. I don't ask if she found it because I know full well that she did. 'So,' she says. 'It says do anything to get the baby out.'

'Does it?' I affect nonchalance.

'Would you like an epidural? Because if you do I'll need to book the anaesthetist sooner rather than later because she's pretty busy at the moment.'

'Really? But it's boringly empty here.'

'Yes, this ward is empty but the other labour ward, which has six beds, is full. They all came in together first thing this morning to be induced. It's starting to work and one mum has already gone down to the delivery suite.'

'Oh, right.'

'There's a spare bed in there now if you want me to move you.'

I don't give it much thought before saying, 'No, thank you.' I'd rather have Netflix.

'Shall I book the anaesthetist for that epidural?'

Right then, right on cue, another spasm grips me. I gasp for breath. If this is a taste of things to come then the answer is, 'Yes. Please.'

I settle back down then and wait for the next one. I Google epidural. I've read all the books so I know roughly what it is, but I don't know the exact details because I didn't want to know. Kerri and Carol-Anne had been quite prescriptive about their birth plans, what they wanted, when they wanted it, they even had a playlist. I just thought it was over the top. My plan was to see how it went and hope for the best. And take any drugs offered if I needed them.

And I definitely will be needing them.

I check to see if Mum or Sue have received my messages. They haven't. Then I get my work phone out and check to see if Pearl has replied. She hasn't. I'm annoyed with her, assuming that she hasn't crashed her car and killed herself, she should have been back here hours ago. I've got lots of nice goodies in my bag, my dressing gown for a start off. A couple of soft long t-shirt style nightdresses for the actual birth. Some sucky-sweets because someone had suggested them. I do quite fancy one now. And a book to read, a novel. I could definitely do with that. And a glossy magazine I've been saving.

'Come on, Pearl. Where the hell are you?'

Then I doze off. I think. I can't really remember but I'm soon awoken by a great big spasm. As it wears off I notice that my work phone is flashing. Yay, at last, Pearl.

Sorry for the delay. Issue at work. Nothing for you to worry about. I should be with you about six.

Six. Six. That's hours away. I'll probably have had the baby by then. I fire off a quick *WhatsApp* message to Kerri and Carol-Anne. We have a group and Kerri called it Baby Babes. We don't say very much in it really, mostly moaning about our fatness, cravings and tiredness. We do share our scans though and that's nice. I look at the last one I shared; those little lips are still puckered. I hope he doesn't have a weird mouth. I wasn't going to message the girls until after the baby was born, I wanted to make it look easy, for their sakes rather than mine as they have all this to look forward to. Except they won't be waiting it out on their own, they'll have their husbands to hold their hands. Even if Garth will be documenting everything on his phone.

I pace around the ward in an attempt to get comfortable, because I'm starting to feel most uncomfortable. After pacing for a while I lie back on the bed. Nowhere is good, nowhere is comfortable. The next hour drags along, interspersed by spasms that almost lift me off the bed. I never expected it to be like this. There's no sign of this epidural and I'm thinking I could definitely do with it now. On the plus side it's almost four and that means that Pearl will be here in two hours with my bag.

Two hours. I'll have had the baby by then. I fire off a quick text to her telling her I'm currently on the labour ward but I might be in the delivery suite by the time she arrives. She replies back not to worry and that she will make sure my bag gets to me.

Around five the anaesthetist arrives; she looks harried and tired. She gives me a quick smile and waits while Anji gets me into the correct position. Another not very dignified process. And it's not painless, or maybe I'm a wimp. Right in the middle of the process I have another spasm and it grips me from head to toe. I wish she'd done this ten minutes earlier.

'All done,' she says, scurrying away. 'Who's next?'

'I don't know,' I say, stupidly. Of course she's not asking me, I know that.

After the epidural takes effect, I feel a lot more comfortable. I manage another doze until the Anji comes to check on me. She has another rummage and says I'm progressing nicely. I'm still aware of the spasms but they don't seem so intense and they're definitely not painful. But I'm tired now. Really tired. Perhaps I'm pressing the epidural plunger too often.

'Cup of tea before I go off shift?' Anji asks.

'No, thank you.' I've had so many cups of weak, milky tea I feel as though I'm sloshing around in it. 'I'm hungry though. Have I missed the meal time?'

'Ah, no. Well, yes. You can't have a big meal because you might give birth and it's not advised.' She gives me a sympathetic smile.

I know this. I know why I can't eat. In case something goes horribly wrong and they have to intervene, operate on me. But I've had an epidural so surely I'd be fine. They do caesareans with just an epidural. Does she think they're going to intervene?

'Am I doing okay?' I ask.

'Yes, absolutely. You've got a while to go, but you are progressing nicely. Don't worry. Really. When is baby's daddy arriving?'

I let out a little half laugh. 'He's not.'

'Oh, sorry. Well, I'm off now. So good luck and

hopefully when I'm back tomorrow this will all be a memory.'

'Hopefully.' I watch her leave, no doubt off to fill in my notes before she goes.

I wish I could get up and go. I've already been helped to the toilet twice and that isn't very dignified either.

It's ten past six and there's no sign of Pearl. I'm feeling unreasonably annoyed with her. She's totally unreliable. She should have made bringing my bag up here a priority. Work and whatever has happened – and I suspect it's nothing – could have waited. If I had those sucky sweets I'd feel a lot less hungry and all that sugar would give me a bit more energy. And why hasn't Sue replied? Unlike Mum she's not on the other side of the world. Surely Scotland isn't that remote. Everyone is letting me down. Maybe I could ring Kerri or Carol-Anne and ask them to come up and cheer me up. Maybe not. Not really fair on them.

I'm not even allowed to march around the ward anymore because I've had the epidural. The only good thing is that I'm being checked regularly so at least I get a bit of company then. Otherwise, I'm bored and lonely. So very alone.

It's nearly quarter-to-seven when Pearl finally shows up. She marches purposefully towards me and heaves my bag onto the bed.

'Hi,' she says, looking me up and down. 'How's it going? I went to the delivery suite first, I thought you'd probably had the baby by now.'

'No such luck,' I say, sounding begrudging. Then I remind myself she doesn't have to do this for me.

'Thank you for bringing my bag up. And thank you for bringing me to hospital earlier. I didn't get a chance to say a proper thank you.'

'No problems,' she says, glancing around her, spotting the chair and dragging it closer to the bed before plonking herself down in it.

'So what's been happening at work?' I don't care that much but if it keeps Pearl here and keeping me company and distracting me, that's good.

'There was a fight,' she says. 'A proper physical fight.'

Thirteen

'Time for a quick check,' a voice says. A new midwife, Beth, who's a lot older than the previous one. 'Are you staying for this?' she asks Pearl.

'Absolutely not, no.' Pearl struggles to hide the disgust on her face.

The midwife, unperturbed, shrugs while Pearl beats a hasty retreat.

'Wait, Pearl,' I call after her. 'I want to know all about the fight.'

'Okay. I'm just going to find a coffee then I'll come back.'

'Goodness me,' Beth says, after her ferret around. 'You're almost fully dilated. Have you felt the urge to push?'

'No. Should I?'

'Mmm. We'll have to see about getting you down to delivery. Don't go anywhere.' She gives a little light laugh but I don't find it funny. Right then, of course, a great big spasm engulfs my body, but I'm only aware of it because I can see my bare belly gripping. That epidural is doing its job bloody well.

I cover myself up as I hear Pearl clomping back into the ward; despite her snazzy business suits she still favours heavy soled shoes.

'Everything okay?' she asks.

I decide not to tell her. 'Yeah, fine. What about the fight?'

She sits back down and sighs. 'You won't believe it. I can hardly believe it and I witnessed it.' Then she stops speaking, her eyes flicking right and left as she remembers.

'So?'

'After I dropped you off I went straight to your place for your bag. By the way, it weighs a tonne, what's in it?'

'Just baby stuff,' I say. 'The fight?' I'm urging her on because any minute now they could come and cart me down to delivery and Pearl won't want to be part of that.

'I was going to come straight back, obviously, as I knew you were waiting for your bag. But I got a text from David telling me to get back to the office immediately. When I asked why he didn't reply.'

'That would have been Pam sending that.'

'Yes, it was. I didn't realise quite what a luddite David is.' She rolls her eyes. 'He really needs to get with the programme, doesn't he?'

'Oh yes. But what about the fight?'

'Well, back in the office the atmosphere was tense to say the least. Harshad was sitting doing his work, head down as per, then I noticed his ears were red.'

'Someone had hit him?'

'No, no. Red from embarrassment. You know

he's quite shy really.'

I just thought he was wet and nerdy, especially for a man in his mid-thirties, but he's good at the job, just as Pearl was. I'm impressed at how quickly she not only managed to recruit him but also got him straight into the work.

'No, it was two of our colleagues, they had been arguing over him.'

'Over him? What do you mean?'

'They both liked him and somehow, and I haven't got to the bottom of it yet, they both thought they should have a relationship with him.'

'What did he say about that?'

'Nothing. He decided not to engage with them. I think he thought it was a joke. It might even have started out as a joke. But by the time I arrived David had been in, said a few choice words then skipped out of there. Then, somehow there was pushing and shoving and hairpulling. A fight.'

'In the HR office?' I cannot believe it.

'Quite. Not what anyone would expect.'

'What did you do?'

'I sent them home and told them we'd discuss it tomorrow.'

'Is Harshad okay?'

'Absolutely fine. Obviously he doesn't like the attention focused on him like that, but fine.' She sighs. 'I suppose we'll have to come clean now and tell everyone we're an item.'

'You're a what?'

'Together. Me and Harshad.'

'Were you together when you appointed him?'

'No. But all those afternoons huddled together over my desk while I showed him the job, well…'

'There'll probably be another fight,' I say, thinking aloud.

'Not if they want to keep their jobs there won't. Anyway, that's why I didn't come straight back and why I couldn't even message you because I was preoccupied with that.'

'What a start to your new job. Sounds like you're handling it just fine. I can't say I've ever experienced a fight in the work place… Oh my God I want to push….' I suddenly have this urge. It seems to have come from nowhere and, even though I thought it shouldn't, it hurts.

'I'll get someone.' Pearl jumps up and runs off.

It didn't take long for me to be transferred to the delivery suite. Pearl is here with me. Not planned, not expected. But I wouldn't let go of her hand and now she's here. She's not complaining about it but she looks wide-eyed and scared. Why do I want her here? Because she's a distraction, that's why. When she was telling me the fight story I was so lost in it I didn't notice anything.

Also, I need someone. And Pearl, bless her, is that unfortunate someone.

We've been here nearly an hour and I've been pushing and I thought the baby would have been here by now but he's not. The pain is tolerable because the anaesthetist came in and did something and I think she's increased the drug or something, because it's okay, especially when I remember to push the plunger. But I'm starting to get worried now because Beth the midwife looks worried and she pressed the button and someone else came in. Now they're both down there ferreting away.

'Push,' Beth says, 'Push.'

I do. I really do. But I'm so tired, so bloody exhausted. I'm gripping Pearl's hand and making noises like a grunting pig.

'What's going on?' Pearl mumbles in my ear. 'What's with the conflab?'

'What?'

'Them.' She nods at the two midwifes at the end of the bed, their heads together, their voices whispers.

'Just going to get a doctor,' Beth says, her voice sing-songy.

A few minutes later a doctor appears. He's wearing scrubs, as do most of the medical staff, he's masked up, but everyone is masked up, even Pearl. I'm the only one who's not. The doctor is even wearing a hat, if that's the right word. He joins the conflab, as Pearl called it, then turns his attention to me. He introduces himself but it coincides with another spasm so I miss what he says. Now's he's ferreting about between my legs. I don't care anymore; I just want my baby born. And I'm starting to get worried.

'Everything okay?' I ask, my voice sounding meeker than I expected.

'Just going to take this monitor off,' Beth says, undoing the belt that they strapped around my baby bump when we first came down here.

The doctor steps forward. He has kind eyes, though they look tired. I hope he isn't too tired to get my baby out.

He starts talking, his voice is calm and soft. Nice. He introduces himself again but his name washes over me. I'm so tired I find it hard to concentrate on what he is saying but the words deliver baby, forceps and ventouse are mentioned.

'Yeah, just get him out safe and sound,' I mumble. See, that birth plan was spot on.

'Just going to empty your bladder first,' he says.

I put my free hand over my face. God, the indignity. But I don't feel a thing.

'Just going to make an incision,' he says.

I don't feel anything but the thought makes me cringe inwardly. 'Is it too late to change my mind?'

'Yes,' Pearl answers.

I hadn't realised I'd said that out loud.

'Okay, forceps,' he says, but he's not talking to me. 'Get ready for a contraction.'

Beth places her hands around my baby bump and then urges me to push. I feel a pulling sensation but little else.

There's some mumbling from between my legs then some fumbling. I'm glad I can't really feel much of this, I'm aware of sensation but not pain. I look up at Pearl, her face is white. I wonder what she can see.

'Is my baby all right?'

'Fine,' Beth says. 'Let's just concentrate on getting him out.'

I don't really like the sound of that. And the room

is filling up with people. What am I? A freak show.

I hear the word ventouse again then Beth is urging me to push and pressing down on my bump.

'Push, push, push,' she says. 'Really try.'

Pearl stands up. I'm still gripping her hands. I grunt and push. Then I yell, because it helps with the push.

'Stop pushing. Take a breath.'

'Now push,' the doctor says.

I wish they'd make up their minds.

There's a horrible popping sound then I feel a warm gush between my legs. Is that him? Is he finally here?

Pearl flops back down in her seat.

A hot little body is lifted onto my now empty bump. I look down and see the top of his head; he has hair. He's not moving and he's not crying. Suddenly he's whisked away to the corner of the room.

'He's fine,' the doctor says. 'Don't worry. They're just checking him over.'

I can't see what they're doing but it feels like a lot of activity. Then he cries. Then I feel something else slither out from between my legs. Is that another one?

'Placenta delivered,' the doctor says. Then he stands up, ripping off his gloves as he goes to see the baby. My baby. I see him nod.

Then the little bundle is brought to me. He's loosely wrapped and still bloody. His little brow is furrowed. He's crying. It's loud. Then he stops. His little lips are puckered. He looks just like he did on the scans. Pearl stands up and peeks at him. She's rubbing her hand.

'He's amazing,' she says.

'Thank you. And thank you for being here. I know it can't have been easy for you. Sorry about your hand.'

'No worries. It was an honour,' she says. I think she means the birth, not my squeezing her hand so hard.

I stare down at him. My baby boy. He's managed to get his hands free and they're flapping around aimlessly. Then his mouth finds his thumb.

'Ahh,' Pearl and I chorus, then laugh.

The doctor's back in the room. All the other people have left except Beth.

'You need a few stitches,' she says, then turns to Pearl. 'Would you like to hold your baby while we do this?'

Pearl looks aghast. 'He's nothing to do with me,' she says. 'I'm just a colleague.'

'Oh. Right. Sorry. But would you like to hold him now? We need to lie Esme down for a while.'

'Go on,' I say to Pearl. 'Sit down.'

The midwife lifts my baby from my arms and places him in Pearl's.

'Let me know if you feel any pain,' the doctor says, as the bedhead is lowered. 'Might take a while, quite a few stitches. Sorry.'

'That's fine. Thank you,' I say, mechanically. It's not fine, it's really not.

He seems to be down there for ages but it is painless, I do feel tugging and I dread to think what it must be like down there. Like some old patchwork quilt. Then I glance over at my boy contentedly sucking his thumb in Pearl's arms and I don't care.

'Have you got a name for him yet?' Beth smiles at me.

I think of my Mum, miles away and missing all this. She will be so disappointed. 'My mum likes Matthew,' I say. 'So probably that.'

The doctor stops mid-motion.

Beth gives a little laugh. 'That's his name too,' she says.

I close my eyes. I'm overcome by so many emotions: elation, relief, sorrow about Mum missing this. Concern about what's to come. How the hell am I going to manage when I get home?

After what seems like ages the doctor has finally finished. He nods at me and smiles, or at least I think he does because his eyes crinkle up, obviously I can't see his face. He has brown eyes, nice, kind.

I thank him again then wish he would go away. Now.

'Are you hungry?' Beth asks, sitting the bed back up as the doctor sidles out of the room.

'Starving and thirsty.'

'Toast and tea?' she asks.

'Such a cliché,' Pearl mutters.

But I just say, 'Yes please.' After Beth has gone and I have my sleeping baby back in my arms I ask Pearl what she means.

'It's what they always do, isn't it? In films, on TV, give the new mother toast and tea. You'd think they'd be a bit more imaginative.'

I laugh. Who cares? I certainly don't. 'Thank you, Pearl. For being here with me. I know I sort of forced you but I am really grateful. I don't think I could have done it on my own.'

She blushes. 'Of course you did it on your own, with a bit of help from the dishy doc of course.'

'Was he?'

'Was he? Are you joking? Those eyes. And they seemed to be focussing on you.' Above her mask she arches her eyebrows.

'Of course he was focussing on me, he was getting my baby out or stitching me up. Where else would he be focussing?' I laugh, because it really is laughable, isn't it?

She gives a little shrug, then yawns. Even behind the mask I can see it. 'All I know is that every time I looked at him he was staring at you, your face not your fanny.'

'I don't think so. Look, you've been great. Thank you so much. Why don't you go home now. Is Harshad waiting for you?'

'He was waiting in the car but he's gone home now. I'll message him to come and get me.'

'He's keen.'

'Yes, he is. We both are. Even if others have their eyes on him.'

Pearl holds my baby, this time more enthusiastically, while I eat my toast. I've never tasted anything so good. Who knew that toasted cheap white bread and butter could be so delicious?

She hands him back when I finish and checks her phone. 'Oh, Harshad is outside. I'd better go.'

I thank her again, though I can never thank her enough, and she's gone. Now it's just me and the baby which is scary. I've made a person and now I'm responsible for keeping him alive.

'Are you breastfeeding?' Beth asks, as she comes through the door.

'God, um, not sure. He doesn't seem hungry. He's been asleep the whole time since he was born.'

'The epidural probably. We should wake him and put him to the breast, let him have a go.' She unravels the hospital blanket he's wrapped in and flicks his feet. He kicks but doesn't wake. 'I've got his card here,' she says, handing it to me.

Baby Haste weight 6lbs 2oz apparently.

'Good weight for a premature baby. He'd have been a bouncer if he'd gone full term.'

'He felt like a bouncer when you were getting him out.' I'm glad that's all over and I don't ever have to do that again because one thing is for sure, there won't be any more babies for me. I'm already panicking about how I'm going to cope with this one.

'Where's your phone? I can take some pics for you to send to your friends and family.' She locates my bag and I pull out my phone. She takes a few snaps for me.

There's a WhatsApp message from Mum. She's just got my message and hopes I'm okay. I send back a photo. There's a long wait and I wonder if Mum has got it. Then she messages back.

Tried to ring you but the phone network and the internet are not cooperating. He looks gorgeous. So tiny. Are you okay?

I reply to tell her that he didn't feel tiny coming out and that yes, I'm fine.

For the first time I start to cry. Silly really after all I've been through. Beth hands me a tissue.

'Let's try to wake him again.' She flicks his feet. Poor little man.

He cries out then starts turning his head.

'Ah, he's rooting,' she says. 'Let's try him at the breast.'

Inside I'm wondering if I really want to. Throughout my entire pregnancy I've been a bit ambivalent about breastfeeding, saying things like I'll give it a go, I'll see how it goes, I'll see how I feel. Now, I don't know how I feel. But it seems to be out of my control now because Beth is pulling aside the hideous, crumpled, sweaty hospital gown and my boy latches on and starts sucking. It makes we wince.

'Ouch.'

'Yes, might be a bit like that initially, but it'll get better.'

'I bloody hope so. And he still hasn't woken up. Look his eyes are still closed.'

After trying him on the other side, more wincing on my part, Beth brings in a bowl of warm water. I assume it's for Matthew – I've decided that's definitely his name, he looks like a Matthew – but it's not, it's for me. Soon I'm clean and tidy and in my own clothes, one of the lovely soft, baggy t-shirts that I planned to give birth in. I brush my hair and feel almost human again. Then together we dress Matthew and throughout all this he doesn't wake up.

'Just waiting for the porter to come and take you up to the ward,' Beth says. 'I'll come with you to make sure you're settled. He seems really contented there in your arms,' she says, stroking his cheek.

'I expect he'll wake up when I doze off.'

'Probably. Do you want some painkillers?' That epidural will be wearing off with a vengeance soon.'

'Yes please.'

'I'll just go and check on the porter.' She leaves and I lay back on the pillows. I feel weird. Elated. Excited. Scared. My heart bursting with love for this tiny little bundle.

A bed is brought down and I'm transferred into it. I'm feeling the effects of the birth now and the waning epidural. Everything is sore or aching. Then I'm wheeled through the maternity wing to a ward. It's late at night so the main lights are off and the curtains around each bed are closed but nightlights are on and there's the sound of activity, babies mewling, mothers reassuring. I'm clutching Matthew. He's still asleep.

'Is he okay?' I ask Beth as she settles me in.

'Fine. He's just as exhausted as you. Shall we put him in his crib now so you can get some rest?'

I nod, although I'm quite reluctant to let go of him. But I am also very tired and I can't bear to think what would happen if I fell asleep with him in my arms.

I give him a quick kiss on the forehead and suddenly his eyes pop open.

'I've woken him.'

Beth laughs. 'So cute.'

'His eyes are dark?' I feel alarmed.

'They are. Lovely, dark brown eyes. And underneath that gunk I think his hair is probably blond.'

'But I thought all babies are born with blue eyes.'

'No.'

'But I have blue eyes. So does his father.' Although calling Roger his father seems very wrong. But I don't know what else to say and it's not as though he doesn't have a father, he wouldn't exist otherwise.

'Throwback,' Beth says, smiling as she takes him from me and places him in the Perspex crib. He flails around for a few seconds before settling down, closing those very dark eyes.

Fourteen

Despite being exhausted I do not sleep well. I need help to get out of bed and go to the toilet. I need help when Matthew decides to yell the ward down in the middle of the night waking all the other babies in the process.

Sue finally messages me. They're still in Scotland, in some remote highland place but she can come down as soon as possible. She might take the train although she thinks it'll be cheaper and quicker to fly.

I message her back with a photo of Matthew and me, one of the ones that Beth took immediately after he was born. She sends me back half a dozen heart emojis and asks if I'd still like her to come down.

I hesitate before I reply. The truth is I would but that's so totally selfish of me. Her holiday has another three days to run, she tells me. It seems a shame to curtail it. I say no and thank you. Then I wonder if I've done the right thing.

She messages back. *I'm back at work immediately after I get back from Scotland, but I could probably get a few more days off given the circumstances. Let me know if you'd like me to come down and help. I know your mum isn't back for a long time. Trust you to have him early.*

Yes, trust me.

Mum messages. She's tried another phone call and a video call without luck, but at least we can still communicate in words. She's asking if I want her to fly back. I don't have to think twice about that. No. Although I do really, of course.

It's mid-morning, I've had breakfast, staggered to the bathroom a few times, changed Matthew's nappy repeatedly, winced while I've had another go at breastfeeding – really not too sure about it. Baby is in the crib and asleep, his little lips puckered up and I'm lying back with my eyes closed. I have the curtains pulled around me for privacy and peace, although I have chatted to a couple of the other mums, they seem nice. They both had their babies yesterday and they're going home today. I hope they don't kick me out today.

I'm just dozing, residing in that blissful place between coma and consciousness when the curtains are ripped aside. It's my student midwife Anji from the labour ward again.

'I hear you had a bit of a tough time last night,' she says, standing over Matthew and gazing at him. 'Worth it though, eh?'

'Yes, he is.'

'Thought I'd come and see you. How are you? Has the doctor seen you yet?'

'Doctor? No. Been poked around by plenty of midwives though.' I have and I feel as though my body is not my own, especially my boobs and below the waist.

'I think he wants to check on your stitches. You had so many, didn't you?'

'Did I?' It might explain why I feel as though my left leg is attached to my right buttock, but I'm not saying anything in case it sounds as though I'm complaining. I'm not. Everyone has been amazing.

'He'll be round later. Congratulations. I'd better get back to my own ward.' And then she's gone, closing the curtains behind her.

I lie back and attempt to doze again but no luck. At least I'm resting, my eyes are closed and I'm comfortable, sort of.

The curtains are whipped open again. A nursing assistant this time. It's so obliging of them all to wear name and job title badges. She's come to take my temperature and blood pressure.

'I'm not ill,' I say, a bit irritated. 'Am I?'

'No. And we want to keep it that way. No infections.' She laughs a little. I don't.

I lean back on the bed after she's gone and close my eyes again.

Matthew stirs in his crib. I grab the side of it and wheel it back and forth. Please, I just want ten minutes sleep. He settles back down. Peace and quiet, apart from the general hubbub going on outside my curtains. But I can ignore that. I feel myself relaxing into sleep.

Then the curtain is ripped apart again, bright light from a window bursts onto my eyelids.

'What now?' I snap, forgetting myself.

'Doctor just needs to check your stitches.' It's the same nursing assistant from earlier.

I open my eyes and there he is. The dishy doc, isn't that what Pearl called him? He has no hat on this time but he's still wearing a mask. I take a good look at him, or at least what I can see of him above the mask. He has dark brown eyes and fair hair. That's when I realise it's the same bloody guy from the pub and the hospital corridor who chased after me when I dropped my phone.

He's definitely stalking me.

And now he's going to ferret around in my fanny. Again.

I put my hands over my face and mutter, 'Feel free.'

He steps to the side; yes, I part my fingers slightly so I can see what's going on, while the nursing assistant pulls back the covers and exposes my bits. There is no privacy and no dignity here.

Grow up, I tell myself.

I close my fingers; I don't want to see any more.

He's soon down there poking around. Please go away.

'How does it feel?' he asks.

'Like you've stitched my left leg to my right buttock.' Well, you asked.

'Really? Let's have a closer look.'

Oh God. Why didn't I just say fine?

He's down there for ages, and with a torch. A torch. If that's the correct medical term. But surely a torch is a torch.

'No, it's fine. Just a bit tender, I expect. It'll heal

well.'

'Thanks.' Now go away.

'You should stay in another night. Let it get a good start on the healing. Make sure your other half looks after you when you get home.'

'Thanks.' I'm not telling him there is no other half. I'm not telling anyone here because even though I'm shit scared of going home alone I don't want to stay here indefinitely where it seems anyone can lift the covers and ferret around in my fanny. Going home alone is the lesser of two evils.

The covers are soon pulled apart and I hear retreating footsteps. Good, they've gone. I lift my hands from my eyes, only *he* hasn't gone. He's staring down at my baby and my baby is staring straight back at him. Great, so they've woken him up too.

'Baby okay?' he asks.

'I think so.' Then I realise how very ungracious and rude I am. He's only doing his job after all. He must see a dozen frilly fannies a day. I really need to get a grip. 'Thank you for getting him out so quickly and safely.'

I think he smiles; his eyes certainly crinkle.

'Err, yes. All in a day's work.' With that he turns and leaves but he doesn't get far before the nursing assistant stops and speaks to him.

'Going anywhere nice for your two weeks off?' she asks.

'No, just doing a few jobs around the house.'

'Oh yeah, you've just moved, haven't you? Have fun. I'd rather fly off to the sun but we can't have everything we want, can we?' She laughs then bustles off.

He walks away slowly, stops, glances back at me – shamefully I'm still watching him – then finally goes. I do wish he'd closed the curtain behind him. I debate whether I can be bothered to get up and do it myself.

I don't know why he kept staring at me. Have I grown another head? Maybe I'm deformed *down there*, though Gary never said anything and he certainly would have. Maybe I'm deformed now when I wasn't before.

Matthew cries. My boobs tingle. Now it's time to have another go at this breastfeeding malarky. I'm still not too sure about it.

The morning passes in a blur of attempting to breastfeed, wincing when he latches on, wincing when I need to go to the toilet, knocking back painkillers whenever they're offered and in between that, chatting to the other mums. I watch enviously as two go home, although I'm glad it's not me yet.

I message Pearl on her work phone since that is the only number I have and wonder if she'll pick it up, what with it being a Saturday. But she does.

How are you? she asks. *And how is your lovely little baby boy?*

I'm a bit sore, I confess. *Baby is lovely. I'm definitely calling him Matthew.*

After the dishy doc, lol.

No. No.

Thought I might come up and visit this afternoon. Visiting starts at two pm. Would that be okay? Or are your family coming then?

That would be great, I message.

Then I message Kerri and Carol-Anne on our WhatsApp group, sending photos and keeping the birth story details to the bare minimum. I really don't want to frighten them.

They want to come up together this afternoon too, so I tell them four pm, which should give Pearl plenty of time to come and go.

I've had a shower. It was a frightening experience. It's the first time I've seen my post birth body in its entirety, though fortunately there are no full-length mirrors here. I knew my baby bump wouldn't disappear instantly but I still look pregnant. And my boobs look fit to explode – and my milk hasn't even come in yet. And my face looks like shit, my skin is grey and spotty. I can't wash my hair here because I don't have my hairdryer. Anyway, that would take too much time and I didn't want to be long.

I was nervous about leaving Matthew on his own, even with the curtains pulled around the bed. Someone might steal him. I looked for a nurse or midwife to look after him but they were all bustling around and busy. In the end I entrusted another mum to keep an eye on him.

I feel relieved when I get back to my bed and he is still there.

'Safe and sound,' the other mum says. 'Not a peep out of him.' She picks up her own baby then, handling her with an expertise I can't imagine ever having. 'My third,' she says, watching me watching her. 'Your first?'

'Yes. Is it that obvious?'

'No.' She smiles. But I know she's just being kind.

I want to cry. I will not cry. Instead I get my makeup bag – a reduced travel one – from my hospital bag and attempt to make myself look more like me.

By the time Pearl arrives I'm feeling slightly better. Although, after doing my makeup which definitely lifted my mood I then had to feed a hungry Matthew. I'm still not sure about breastfeeding. Would it be a crime not to do it?

Pearl arrives alone, her eyes light up when she sees Matthew in his crib. I'm sitting on the chair by my bed, a little bit of a wincing experience and I almost wished I'd stayed lying on the bed, but I'm not actually ill, am I?

'You look great,' she says, handing me a little brown paper carrier bag.

'What's this?' I peek inside.

'Fruit,' she says. 'I think you need it. I saw that white bread toast they were feeding you last night. So I thought I'd bring something better.' She's right, this is better. Peaches, grapes, apples and plums glisten from inside the bag.

'Thank you. That's so thoughtful.'

'Yes, we have a little organic shop by us.'

'Great.' Now I don't know what else to say. 'Thank you again for last night.'

'No problem. I wasn't expecting it but actually I sort of enjoyed it. Gave me and Harshad plenty to talk about.'

'Cool.' I dread to think what they talked about. 'Was he okay about you being here?'

'Of course he was. He's my boyfriend not my keeper.'

'Absolutely.' This is the most awkward conversation ever. 'Did you get parked okay today?'

'Yeah, Harshad drove.'

'Oh, is he hovering, waiting for you?'

'No. We parked. He's sitting out in the corridor; it's too cold to sit in the car without the engine running. We had a frost today, didn't we?' At least this visit is going to be short if he's waiting.

I've no idea about the weather. I haven't even looked out of the window. My bed is furthest from the window and I've had the curtains drawn around my cubicle most of the day. Even now they're not fully open.

'I'll go and find a chair unless…' she eyes the bed.

'Oh, sit on that.'

She doesn't need telling twice. Matthew wriggles around and opens his eyes. Pearl's face, though not actually inside the crib, is suddenly very close to his.

'He's got brown eyes. Wow. I thought babies all had blue eyes when they were born.'

'Apparently not.'

'You've got blue eyes. What about his dad?'

I don't answer and that provokes an awkward silence.

'Can I hold him?' Pearl asks, her face going all gooey; a look I've never seen on her before.

'Yes.' I haul myself up from the chair. That leg is

definitely lassoed to the opposite buttock and it's an effort to get up.

'You okay?' Pearl asks, seeing me wince.

'Yeah. Great.' Liar.

I place Matthew in her arms and he's soon cooing at her, the little traitor. He hasn't cooed at me, not once. When he's in my arms all he does is seek out my boobs.

'Makes me want one,' she says. I suspect she didn't mean to say that aloud. 'In due course, obviously. I'm too young at the moment. Things to do, a career to work on.' She gives me an odd sideways glance.

'Yeah. Well, don't wait too long. I'm sure it's easier when you're younger.' If I remember correctly, Pearl is about twenty-six or twenty-seven.

'Harshad's keen on a family too.' Another unguarded comment. She realises what's she's said and quickly adds, 'Though that's a long way in the future. Can I take a photo of you both before I go. Just to show everyone at work.'

'Do they know? Did you tell them?'

'Yes, emailed the sweepstake group this morning. Claimed my prize.' She laughs.

'Sweepstake?' Of course they'd be running a sweepstake. 'How close were you?'

'A week out but far closer than anyone else. Also only seven ounces off the weight. I thought he'd be bigger given your si....'

'Yeah. But he was big enough, thanks.'

'Yes, scary when they put that vacuum thing in you. Woah, never heard of that.'

'It's not uncommon.' Please don't make me think about it.

A head pops around the curtain. 'Ah, lovely,' the nursing assistant says. 'You'll probably go home tomorrow so don't forget to bring up the car seat.' She looks pointedly at Pearl. 'Would you like me to take a photo of the three of you.'

'No,' Pearl and I say together, a little too forcefully.

'Car seat,' I mutter. I hadn't even thought about how I'm going to get home. I feel my heart start to beat a bit faster. Panic.

'I could bring it up. It'll have to be tonight though because me and Harshad are off to ComicFest tomorrow early, just for the day.'

'ComicFest?'

'Yeah, you know, cosplay and all that…' She giggles nervously.

'Tonight would be great.' I give her my keys for a second time and all the details and thank her profusely before she leaves.

Just as she's pushing the curtains aside she turns. 'I don't suppose Harshad could come in and have a peak at the baby, could he? Just a minute or so?'

'Oh course. Absolutely.' Oh God.

He's in and out in no time. He looks as embarrassed as I feel, if his ears are an indicator – bright red.

Then I'm alone and Matthew is hungry again.

'It'll make the milk come in faster,' the experienced mum in the next bed tells me. 'All that feeding.'

'Yes. Good. Not sure I want to continue if I'm honest. Is that an awful thing to say?'

'No. No.' She shakes her head and I think she's about to launch into a *breast is best* tirade. 'You have to do what's best for you and your baby. I breastfed the first one, spent most of the first two months crying, me and the baby.' She gives a little laugh. 'Then my mum gave him some formula while I was asleep. Best thing ever. Never even tried with number two and not doing so with this one either. You do what's good for you.'

'But they seem so keen here.'

'Yes, well they're not the ones coping with sleepless nights, sore boobs and a hungry baby, are they?' She winks at me and I feel a lot better.

When Kerri and Carol-Anne visit I'm thrilled to see them, though not as thrilled as they are to see Matthew. They both have a hold and coo over him; at least he doesn't coo back this time.

'He's just so gorgeous. Aren't you lucky. No time to even think about it.' Kerri nuzzles Matthew again. 'I love the smell.

'Don't get too close he hasn't had a bath yet.'

'Oh yes,' Carol-Anne says. 'They advise to wait as long as possible.'

'The girl in the next bed says she'll be bathing her baby as soon as she gets him home. I might do the same.'

Carol-Anne raises her eyebrows; I'm not sure whether it's a question or a criticism.

'Look,' I say, pulling his hat off. 'He's got all this

hair and it's gunked up. Not nice.'

'I think he's blond under there,' Kerri says. 'I thought you went for a dark donor.' She has the sense to whisper the last part.

'I did. But…' I shrug.

Right then, Matthew who's been asleep the entire time they've been here opens his eyes.

'My God, they're so dark,' Kerri says, before going silent.

'He's still beautiful though.'

'He is.' Kerry nuzzles him again. 'Are you feeding him yourself?'

'For the time being,' I say, wondering when I'll be able to get some formula. Maybe I'll do an online supermarket shop when I get home and order some then. In the meantime I'll carry on with breastfeeding.

Of course they want the full horror story of the birth. I've already decided to spare them some of the gory details, especially the stitching up, but they press so hard for details that I tell them everything.

'Well Garth is not filming *that*.' Kerri sounds almost angry.

'It probably won't be like that for you. You're much younger than me.'

'Did they say that was a factor?'

'I don't know. My age was mentioned but I can't remember the context.'

Not long after they've gone Pearl arrives with the car seat, but she's not alone. Harshad is with her. He hovers in the background and smiles nervously as Pearl stows the seat and the wheels under my bed.

'We brought your car back to your place too,' she says. 'Harsh drove it. It's on your drive now.'

'Thank you, thank you so much. I'd completely forgotten it was still at work.'

'He folded all the boxes off this,' she points at the car seat which I hadn't even unpacked yet. 'And stuffed them in your garage. Hope that's okay.'

'Yes, brilliant. Thank you again. You've been great, Pearl. You both have.' I nod at Harshad who's shuffling around as though he just wants to get the hell out of here.

'What time do you get out of here tomorrow?'

'I don't know. Mid to late morning, I think. I have to wait for the doctor to give me the all clear.'

'Mmm, will it be dishy doc?' she whispers.

I hope not. 'Doubt it. There are so many.' Truth is I've only seen him.

After they've gone I start to worry about tomorrow. A part of me hopes that they won't give us the all clear to go home because another day in here feels preferable to being on my own at home. If he'd been born on time, or later, it would only have been a short while before Mum and Tim were home. But now, it's weeks. Over a month.

Mum messages me later and tells me she's going to try a video call. But it doesn't work. I message that I'll probably go home tomorrow. She asks again if I want them to fly home early? I say no, most definitely not. That cruise has cost them a fortune, all of the lump sum from Tim's pension has gone into it. It's a once in a lifetime holiday and I cannot make them abandon it for me, even if they want to. I can manage, I tell them, I've a friend helping me.

There is no friend and I don't know how I'm going to manage.

It isn't the dishy doc who says I'm good to go. I smile my gratitude but inside I'm crying.

Then there's the question of how I'm actually going to get home. I can't ask Pearl because she's away at her comic festival thing all day. I won't ask Kerri or Carol-Anne because I really don't want to admit to anyone that I have no one. They all think that someone else is helping me out.

Shit. Why am I letting pride come before a fall? I'm so stupid.

I pack everything up slowly. One of the other mums sends her husband over to help put the car seat on the wheels when she sees me struggling. Pride makes me want to bat him away – I don't need a man – but sense gets the better of me. Just lifting the car seat had me wincing in pain. How long will these stupid stitches trouble me?

I'm nearly ready when Matthew decides he wants a feed. I'm almost grateful to pull the curtains around me and sit back down with him, even if it does involve a lot more wincing. My boobs are so painful and my nipples are red raw.

Eventually there is no more putting it off. I'm ready. Baby is ready. Everything is packed. I pull my phone out and start scrolling through taxi firms. Then decide that I can't make that call here. I need to wait until I'm at least away from the ward.

I say a few goodbyes and slink out.

'On your own?' The nursing assistant from earlier frowns at me as I pass her in the corridor.

'Friend's gone on ahead to bring the car close,' I lie. 'It's so cold out there.' I have no idea how cold it really is.

She nods and smiles. 'It is, that wind is vicious. Do you need a hand now?'

'No, no. Everything under control.' If only that were true.

I get all the way to the main hospital reception before I get my phone out again and start scrolling for taxis.

The first one says it'll be a half hour wait. I decline and move onto my next choice, and my next. After that I decide to call the first one back. Their wait has now increased to forty-five minutes. I book it and slump onto a bench; grateful they have seating here. Matthew, mercifully, is sound asleep thanks to that feed he had before we left the ward.

My phone pings. It's a text from the taxi firm. The wait is now an hour. No, that's wrong, it's supposed to go the other way. This isn't going well. I feel overwrought, emotional. How the hell did I ever think I could cope on my own? I can't even get us home. This wasn't the plan; I wasn't supposed to be on my own. Mum and Tim should be here. Is it too late to call Sue and beg for help? Or Kerri and Carol-Anne?

Pull yourself together, girl. He was so worth it. I look at him, my beautiful baby; he is so worth it. I can cope.

No I can't. I can feel the tears pricking the back of my eyes. I am not going to cry in public. Not here. Not now. It's the hormones, I tell myself. No, it's not. It's the situation.

I close my eyes and rest my chin on my hand; I must look like Rodin's The Thinker – now that's a bizarre thought. I'm all over the place.

Someone plonks themselves down beside me on the bench. Go away.

'Are you okay?' The voice sends tingles down my spine.

Is he talking to me? I'll have to answer. 'Yes, fine thanks.' Now go away.

'Waiting from someone?'

I want to say mind your own business, instead I turn and look at him.

It's him. Dishy doc. I recognise the hair and the eyes. But now he has the mask off he looks quite different and yet also familiar.

'Oh my God. Matt? Cardiff Hen Do Matt?' Just my luck.

Fifteen

He opens his mouth to speak but I never hear his answer because it's drowned out by the fire alarm. The alarm is right above us and Matthew jerks awake and starts crying, not that I can hear him. I feel as though my head is going to explode.

Matt stands up. He jerks his head at me to do the same, then reaches down and picks up my bags at the same time kicking the brake off Matthew's wheels.

He urges me outside where, although the wind is biting, at least the alarm isn't so loud.

'We need to get out of here before they lock the place down. Last time I got stuck in the car park for two hours.'

'But the hospital could be on fire.' I think of all those babies newly born or not even here yet. The tears course down my cheeks. I'm crying like a baby and so is Matthew.

'They'll stop whoever's collecting you from getting in now.'

'They're not here yet. Another hour. Anyway,

what about all the patients, the babies?'

'It probably a false alarm, it was the last time. Don't worry, they have procedures for this.'

'Shouldn't you be up there helping?'

'I am helping.' He looks at me pointedly. 'Come on. Let's at least get out of this wind and sit in my car.' He yanks the hood up on Matthew's car seat and urges me to go with him.

I haven't got the energy to refuse. I also don't have a viable alternative. People are coming out of the hospital now so there's no way I can go back in and it's too cold to stand here.

We zip around a few corners and suddenly we stop by his car.

'We'll put your baby in the back,' he says, opening the door. 'Do you want to get in the back with him?'

I nod. I feel spaced out, as though I'm in some alternate reality.

'I'll put the wheels in the boot or they'll blow away or get knocked over.'

Once inside the car with all the doors closed I feel relieved, although my stitches are hurting. But at least inside the car Matthew settles down and dozes back off.

'Look, I'm keen to get out of the car park before they lock it down. Do you mind if I just drive us out of here?' He doesn't wait for an answer, but starts the engine.

I click on my seatbelt and notice that he's already belted Matthew's car seat in.

We head out of the car park, away from the hospital and then he pulls into the car park of the pub where Mum and I went after my scan visit. The pub where I thought I saw him and then dismissed it as madness. But it looks as though I was right.

We can still hear the alarm, but just as he turns the engine off it stops. He pulls out his phone and flicks through it.

'Yep. False alarm,' he says. 'Third in two months. They really need to sort that out. The one time when it is real no one will take any notice.'

'No,' I mumble.

'Are you okay?' He turns around and looks at me.

I'm dazed. I'm tired. I've just had a baby. My leg is stitched to my buttock. Of course I'm not okay. 'Yes.'

'My escape seems a bit ridiculous now,' he says. 'Do you want me to take you back? They won't be locking the place down so your lift will get able to get in okay?'

I don't answer. I really don't know what to say. He stares at me for a moment.

'Or I could just give you a lift home,' he says. 'And you could just ring your… person and let them know.'

'Yeah okay.'

He smiles. I hurriedly text the taxi company and cancel my taxi.

'Baby okay?' He glances over at Matthew.

I nod slowly. 'What happened to your hair?' Is it really Matt from Cardiff or his hairy doppelganger?

He runs his hand through his blond locks and smiles. 'It was a charity thing, for cancer. You know, get sponsors, shave your head. It grew back.'

'You never said.'

'It really didn't seem relevant. Also, I didn't like it. But you seemed to not mind.' He shrugs.

'No. I didn't mind.' I actually rather liked it. He has a nice shaped head so it looked good.

'Where to?'

'What?'

'Where am I taking you? Where's home?'

I give him the address and, although he tries to hide it, he does a double take. He drives right to my door without me having to give him directions, which is a first because usually even taxi drivers need a bit of a prompt.

My car is on the drive and he pulls up alongside it.

'You okay to get out while I get the wheels?' he asks.

'Of course.' Only it takes longer than I expected as I try to suppress the ouches and ows.

He's already put the wheels and my hospital bag by the front door by the time I've managed to get myself out of the car.

'You get the door,' he says. 'I'll get your baby.' He reaches in and undoes Matthew's car seat.

I stand there rummaging in my bag for the keys. I definitely have them, don't I? Pearl brought them back. What did I do with them? Finally I feel them at the bottom of my bag.

'Oh, lovely. Let me see.' My neighbour, who I rarely ever see, is scuttling up the drive towards us. She looks at Matthew asleep in his car seat then stares at Matt before smiling at me. 'Congratulations.

He's just like his daddy, isn't he? How lovely. Enjoy this time, it soon passes.' With that she scuttles off again.

We stand there, Matthew still asleep, Matt and I red-faced.

'Sorry about that,' I mutter, finally extricating the keys from my bag and wincing my way towards the front door.

He doesn't say a word, just follows me.

Home. I've never been so happy to be home, if a little apprehensive. I step inside and wait for Matt and Matthew. I hold out my hand to take the car seat from Matt but he shakes his head.

'Let me take him inside for you.'

I step aside and point towards the living room but he seems to know exactly where to go.

'Can I give you some money for the petrol?' I ask.

'No, no. I was coming here anyway.'

'Were you?' Even I can hear the alarm in my voice.

'I have a confession to make. I live just around the corner. I couldn't quite believe it when you said your address. My house is a bit of a dump, though same layout. I'm renovating it.'

So I wasn't mistaking the double take. I smile at him and think, off you go now. Then Matthew starts to cry. It's that horrible, urgent *feed me* cry that I've already come to recognise and by boobs start to tingle.

'Oh, someone's hungry,' Matt says.

'Yes, it must be at least two hours since I fed him. Well, barely two hours.'

‘Why don’t you go and see to the baby and I’ll make you a cup of tea.’

I want to say no thanks but I can’t. I could murder a cup of tea.

‘Okay, but make mine milky,’ I tell him. I shut the front door and go to see to Matthew while Matt locates the kitchen. I slyly watch as he shrugs off his coat, no long wearing the scrubs I’ve seen him in so much, but black jeans and bright, white t-shirt. I remember his body from Cardiff and feel myself blush. Idiot. You’ve just had a baby for pity’s sake.

I settle down on my sofa and attempt to get comfortable with Matthew. He’s stopped howling so loudly but every time I get him near me he starts that snuffling, rooting thing and I can’t get him to latch on and feed properly. I’m struggling. I’m a failure.

I look up and Matt is standing in the doorway holding two cups of tea. He sees my face. Yes, I’m crying, but silently so that I don’t alarm my baby.

Without a word he puts the cups down then grabs a couple of cushions from the other sofa and wedges them under Matthew’s head. I could die from embarrassment but I’m also grateful when by baby finally latches on and feeds.

‘Thanks,’ I mutter. ‘Good that you’re here and such an expert.’ I’m not being sarcastic yet it has that tone about it.

‘I’m no expert as I’m sure you must know but I’ve seen the midwives do that enough times. Obviously, it’s sunk in.’

He sits opposite me and drinks his tea slowly while I feed Matthew who after five minutes dozes off. I sit him up, my hand under his chin just as I've been shown in hospital and pat his back. He lets out a loud burp which wakes him up and Matt and I both laugh. I start pulling the cushions around to the other side but Matt jumps up and does it for me.

'Round two,' I say, cringing.

It doesn't take long for Matthew to have his fill and I sit him up again. I look longingly at my mug of tea.

'Shall I take him while you drink your tea?' Matt asks.

'Yes, please.' What the hell? He's a doctor, I have to trust someone.

Soon Matthew burps again and then lays in Matt's arms cooing up at him. Little traitor; he still hasn't cooed at me. I study them over the rim of my mug as I sip the sweet concoction.

'How many sugars?' I ask.

'Two. Thought you could probably do with it. It's what I do when I work long shifts.'

'Very healthy, and you a doctor,' I say, but I smile and wink.

Wink? Wink? What am I doing? Am I flirting with him?

'I know. We're the worst.' He looks down at my baby in his arms and there's no denying that he could easily be taken for his father. They look very alike. Same hair, same eyes.

That's when I get that sinking feeling. Could he possibly be? No, Roger is the birth father. Roger the sperm donor who is very fertile and has high motility, or something. Roger and Sue, my son's godparents.

But Roger has blue eyes and dark hair just like me. That's why I chose him. I didn't want a cuckoo in my nest.

I shake my head.

'You okay? Everything okay?' Matt asks. 'Do you want him back or shall I put him in his car seat?'

'No. Wait.' I zip – who am I kidding – stumble out to the hallway cupboard and find the baby nest thing that I bought months ago. Once back in the living room I start to unpack it. It's a struggle, the packaging doesn't want to comply.

'Let me help you.' Matt jumps up with my baby, hands him to me than takes the baby nest. He soon has it unpacked. He places it on my sofa and I lay Matthew down in it.

'That's better. He looks much more comfortable. Thank you.'

'No problem.' Matt picks up the packaging and folds it neatly before heading out to the utility room where I keep my recycling boxes.

I lean back and close my eyes. Then I hear him opening and closing cupboard doors in the kitchen. What's he doing? He reappears in the doorway.

'Are you hungry?' he asks. 'I could rustle you up something. You've got stuff in your fridge that's okay.'

'Err, um…'

'Sorry. I expect your friend will be round soon. They can sort that out for you. Sorry, I'm intruding.'

'No, you're really not. I'd love something to eat.' I force a smile, it's an effort because I'm so damned tired. 'And obviously make yourself something.'

Half an hour later we're sitting at the table eating cheesy pasta. It's simple, filling and tasty and I'm so grateful to him. He tucks into his too.

'That's the best meal I've had in days,' I say.

'Which says more about hospital food than my cooking.' He laughs before jumping up and starting to clear up.

I let him. I know I shouldn't but I do.

'Do you want me to take your bag upstairs before I go?'

He's going? I don't want him to go. Of course he has to go. He's been at work, he's probably exhausted. I nod about the bag and he runs up the stairs with it.

Then he's back. Grabbing his coat. He stands over a sleeping Matthew staring at him. I wonder if he's thinking what I am, wondering?

My phone is on the coffee table and he picks it up. It's locked of course so he hands it to me.

'If you unlock that I'll put my number in it. Then you can ring me anytime you need anything.'

I do as he says and watch him type his number in. He hands me back the phone.

'Ring me, anytime. I mean it.'

I nod. 'Thank you. You've been an amazing help.'

He leans over and hugs me, cheek to cheek. It feels oddly natural.

'Ring me, okay.'

Then he's gone. I check my phone and he's put himself in as Hen Do Matt. Minutes later Matthew wakes up and needs another feed.

Oh God.

When I go up to bed a while later I notice that Matt has pulled the baby crib that I had in the corner up to my bed. He's put the bedside light on and pulled back the covers. I'm both impressed and a little creeped out. But overall I'm relieved and grateful.

I do manage a few hours' sleep but it's constantly interspersed by crying baby, feeding baby, changing baby – that is pure delight in the middle of the night, I now know what poonami means – and all accompanied by me wincing.

I make it downstairs in the morning, even that seems to take forever, and after settling Matthew in his nest I venture into the kitchen for breakfast.

There's no milk. Not surprising since there wasn't much anyway and we finished it off with milky teas last night. That means no cereal for breakfast. I look in the bread bin, no bread, just a rather dried up crumpet, but at least it's not mouldy. I pop it in the toaster. Then Matthew starts to cry so I rush into the living room. He cannot possibly be hungry, can he?

But he is. I only fed him less than an hour ago. I think today is the day my proper milk is supposed to come in and I hope it's more satisfying that what he's currently getting. I settle down and feed him, yet again. I'm gagging for a drink as I've haven't even had a sip of water. Once he's sated, I have to change his nappy again. Then, finally, he's okay to go back into the nest while I see to myself. I'm not even dressed, no shower, nothing. I haven't even cleaned my teeth but sating my hunger and thirst is top of my list.

I down a glass of water then turn my attention back to the stale crumpet. The toaster has popped it up which is good, but what is not so good is that because it has sat so long it is now rock hard. I fling it in the bin and hunt through the fridge, maybe I can scramble some eggs. But there aren't any.

I was supposed to go shopping on Friday night, instead I had a baby.

Then Matthew starts to cry.

And so do I.

I cannot cope.

I rush into the living room and pick him up and as soon as I do he stops crying. I rock back and forth until he drops back off then put him in the nest. He cries again. I pick him up.

Maybe I need to tell Mum that yes I do need her to come home early. I can't do that, can I?

There's a knock on the door which I decide to ignore. I'm not dressed; I'm still in my nightclothes and dressing gown. And there's baby sick down the front of me. But the knocking persists.

I stagger to the door, baby over my shoulder, stand behind it and crack the door open a little.

'Esme, I've brought you a few supplies.' Matt is standing in front of me holding two supermarket bags. 'I noticed you'd run low on a few things.'

I fling the door open and welcome him in. As I close it behind him I catch sight of myself in the hall mirror. Who the hell is that witch? I look like shit. I feel like shit. I don't care.

'Did you get milk?' I ask as he heads for the kitchen.

'Y..e..s,' he says gingerly.

'Good, because I'm so bloody hungry, I'm desperate for some cereal.'

He grins, producing a four pint from one of his bags.

The cereal is already in the bowl from my aborted attempt at breakfast earlier. I eye it while Matt quickly puts the shopping away. How weirdly domestic this feels. He's got bread too, and more crumpets. I could hug this man. Except I have an armful of baby.

He folds up the bags, then smiles at me. 'Would you like me to hold him while you eat?'

'Yes please.'

'What's that smell?' he asks as I hand Matthew over.

I sniff my baby then shake my head.

'No, it's burning, burnt.'

'Crumpet, got side-tracked.' I nod at Matthew. 'It's in the bin now.'

'How was last night?'

I shrug. I could cry but also I'm so happy that he's here helping me, however short lived it might be. 'Exhausting,' I reply.

'I hear that, from other mothers.' He wanders off while I pour milk on my cereal; I really cannot get it into my mouth fast enough. I'm just boiling the kettle and popping bread into the toaster when he comes back.

'He's asleep in his nest thing,' he says.

'Did you want coffee or tea? And toast, would you like toast?' I feel almost hostess like.

'Yes, please, and whatever you're having.'

'I'm having coffee. I can have one, I think.'

We're soon sitting at the table eating breakfast together and it reminds me of the breakfast we didn't share in Cardiff. The proper goodbye we didn't have and his note pushed under my door with his number that I never called.

Why would I? It was a one-night stand and I never thought I'd see him again.

'I know we never exchanged much information that night,' I start, after a second slice of toast. 'But did you live in my town then?'

'Yes, but only just. I'd started my new job at the hospital and was living in rented accommodation. It was why I couldn't take any more time off, why I had to rush off that morning, I'd only been working at the hospital a week.'

I nod slowly. 'Yes, I see. But it was no strings, wasn't it?'

He looks away, then glances over at Matthew. 'Did you get my note with my phone number?'

I could lie. I easily could. 'Yes.'

'But you didn't contact me.'

'No. Why would I? We were a fling. We agreed that. Didn't we?'

'Not that I recall. Not in so many words. No.'

'But we understood it.' Shut up now. I don't want to rake over our one night of amazing sex that wasn't even the result of excessive alcohol.

He stares into my face, it's unnerving. 'Would

you like me to hang around so you can have a shower and get dressed?'

'Would you?' I ask. 'Would that be okay?' He's not going to kidnap my baby, is he? He's a doctor. I know where he works.

I run upstairs, well run is a stretch. I stagger upstairs as fast as my stitches will allow and after a hasty tidy up of the bedroom, jump in the shower. Nothing compares to the luxury of your own bathroom after a couple of nights in hospital. Nothing. I wash my hair and after a hasty go with my super hairdryer I start to feel almost normal.

I'm wearing leggings and a long sweatshirt when I go downstairs.

Matt smiles at me. Matthew is still asleep and Matt has cleared up the kitchen. I think he might have vacuumed too.

'You look better,' he says, smiling.

'I feel better. More human.' I don't like to mention the stitches again, it's too much like a criticism of his work.

'Is there anything else I can do?'

I shake my head. 'No, you've been amazing. Thank you so much. How much do I owe you for the shopping?'

He shakes his head, then changes his mind and tells me. I hunt around for my handbag, find my purse. But inevitably, I don't actually have enough cash.

'Owe me,' he says with a smile.

Then he goes. And I wish he hadn't gone but of course he has to. This has nothing to do with him.

Five minutes after he's gone he messages me. *Ring me or message me if you need anything. Anything at all. Don't hesitate.*

You have work, I message back.

I have two weeks off, renovating my house. Ha ha.

I don't want to keep you from that.

I will need breaks, believe me, I will. You'll be doing me a favour.

I send back a few smiley faces then decide I need to do some washing while Matthew is sleeping.

Later, when I'm looking through the cupboards and making a list for my online shop I find a tin of baby milk. He's bought it. He must have because I haven't. That's why he was hesitant when I asked about the milk.

I hold the tin in my hand. How do I feel? Insulted? Annoyed? No, relieved. I have a backup plan if the breastfeeding fails. Somewhere, and I'll have to hunt them out, I have bottles and a sterilizer too. I make a mental note to find them after I've done my online shop.

I cannot get a delivery date for three days. Three days because they don't have enough drivers. How absolutely, bloody ridiculous is that? But I can collect it in two hours. Can I do that? I've just fed Matthew again and this time I know my milk has come in because after he'd gorged himself he puked half of it back up again, fortunately on himself and not me. Now, even though that was three hours ago my boobs are full and tingling again. Can I nip out and pick up my shopping? I leave the online shop hanging on my tablet and pick up my phone.

He did say to ask him for help. This is help, isn't it?

He answers the phone immediately.

'Can I be super cheeky?' I ask, sounding flirtatious when that's the last thing I want to be.

'I'm sure you can.' There's a smile in his voice.

'Can you pick up my online shopping, they can't deliver for three days, the slots are all full.'

'Course I can. Text me the details.'

Five minutes later there's a knock on the door. It cannot be him, can it?

It's the midwife, checking on me and Matthew.

I think we're okay, I tell her. And I let her think that my partner is off collecting the shopping. Almost the truth. I don't want social services called because I'm on my own. Would that happen? I'm not chancing it.

Sixteen

He arrives with the shopping. He's all smiles as he brings in the bags, one after another.

'Would you like me to unpack?' he asks, seeing me holding Matthew over my shoulder. I've just fed him, yet again.

'Yes, please.'

'Hover, so you can tell me where to put stuff.'

I watch as he quickly puts everything away. He's nice. I mean, I thought that in Cardiff, but he's kind, thoughtful, helpful. I wonder if we could have been something if we'd met years ago.

'Where did you live before you came here?' I ask, which probably seems as though it's come out of nowhere to him but I'm wondering where he's been all my life. Is that corny?

'Nottingham. Then Oxford, briefly. I've moved around a lot for work. I plan to settle here though.' He gives me an arch look.

'Why's that?' I'm genuinely curious.

'Great job prospects. Housing is good and reasonably priced, especially after Oxford.' He looks at me again but this time there's nothing showing behind those eyes, he's guarded now. 'I need to remember to take my bags back with me,' he says, folding them into a collapsing pile.

'Yes, of course.'

'Would you like me to make a cup of tea?'

I nod, why not?

'How are you both?'

'Doing well, according to the midwife.'

'Ah, when was that?'

'A few hours ago. Gutsy here has already regained his birth weight, so that's good.'

'How premature was he again?'

'Four weeks or so, I think.' Now I'm the guarded one. 'I'm going to put him in his nest now. Do you want to bring the tea through. Help yourself to biscuits too.'

I'm sitting down when he comes in. In true man style he's balancing a packet of biscuits under his chin while carrying a mug in each hand. I stop myself from commenting. Gary used to do the same. It isn't quite so annoying seeing Matt do it. To be fair even Tim does it.

'Ask me then,' I say, because I know he wants to. I can feel it in his words, his looks.

'What?'

'The elephant in the room. Or, I should say, the baby.'

'Why don't you just tell me?'

So I launch into the insemination story, the whole thing including the failed IVF, the wanker on my drive and finally Roger and Sue. He sits and listens and doesn't comment until I've finished.

'So you did this the night before we met?'

'Yes. You might wonder why I then did what I did with you, I wonder it myself. I have no excuse, I wasn't drunk. It just happened. It certainly wasn't in my plan to have a one-night stand with a stranger.'

'Nor mine.' He looks at me intently.

I look away and neither of us speaks. I suppose it's a lot to take in, and in the retelling it sounds a little tawdry, desperate even.

'You wanted a baby very much.'

I nod because I'm close to tears and speaking might set me off. I need to keep calm. I need to stay rational.

He looks at me, then over at Matthew. His brow furrows.

There's a knock on the door, insistent, loud. I get up, wincing as I do so.

'Flowers from work,' I tell him when I come back holding a giant bouquet.

He leaps up and takes them from me. 'I'll put them in water for you. You sit down. You look in pain.'

'Not pain, just sore. You lassoed my leg to my arse.' I'm joking, aren't I?

'Would you like me to take a look?'

'No. No.' Definitely not, not now. 'The midwife says it's healing well despite how it feels.'

He looks at me slowly. 'Well, if, you know…'

'Thanks.'

'I should go,' he says, getting up and taking the flowers away. 'I've left the plumber working away,' he says when he comes back.

'Oh, yes, right. What's he doing?'

'Central heating. It was supposed to be done last week while I was at work but no such luck, he got delayed on another job so now I'm freezing and it's preventing me from doing other jobs.'

'You've no heating at all? But it's so cold outside. That wind.' I shudder at the thought.

'An oil-filled electric radiator, so not all bad.' He leans over and hugs me then finds his coat, pulls it on to go.

'If you can't bear it, feel free to come round here. Just message me first.'

'Okay,' he says. Then he's gone, grabbing his supermarket bags on the way.

And it's only after he's left that I realise we never got to the big question; is he Matthew's father? Maybe it's not occurred to him. I'm sure it has. It's certainly occurred to me. Especially after my neighbour said how alike they are. They are. Same colouring, same puckered, generous lips. Matthew is more like Matt that he is me. And he's absolutely nothing like Roger.

I finally get to have a video call with Mum and Tim. I'm glad it's at home because, inevitably, we're all crying, including Matthew.

'How are you managing?' Mum asks.

'Friends have been great.' Not sure Pearl is my friend as such, but she's proved to be a good and reliable colleague. She messaged me this morning asking how I was and if there was anything she could do. It will have been her who organised the work flowers. And Matt, I don't know what category to put him in. But whatever it is, he is certainly a help, one hell of a big one.

'How's feeding going? What did you decide to do?'

'Breastfeeding at the moment. Seeing how it goes. My friend bought some formula and I've fished out the bottles and steriliser. So I have a back-up plan.'

'That's good. Good to have a choice.' I already know that Mum had to breastfeed me even though she was reluctant. In hospital it was forced on her and once out, because of her circumstances and her age and my flakey father, Dad Dan, she couldn't afford to buy formula milk. She admits that long term it was probably better but there were times when she hated it and cried in pain. I know that feeling well. But I ordered some breastfeeding nipple shields and balm online and they should arrive tomorrow. I'm pinning all my hopes on them otherwise it will be formula for my little man. I'm not making my own life, and subsequently his, a misery for a principle I don't necessarily subscribe to.

After the video call and my absolute insistence that Mum and Tim must not cut their holiday short, I decide to make some food. But first I have to feed the hungry baby. I wonder if there's something wrong with him because that's all he seems to do. In one end and out the other. The midwife said this stage was normal when I asked her. Okay, so if it's normal how long does this stage last? She just smiled at me and said, who knows?

Not me obviously, and not her.

I've just put Matthew in his nest having fed, burped and changed him for what seems like the twentieth time today when my phone rings.

'Hi, Esme.'

'Hello, Matt.'

'I have a favour to ask of you.'

'Go ahead, I owe you.'

'My electricity's gone off. Something the plumber did and the electrician can't get here until tomorrow morning…'

'That sounds awful.'

'Not ideal. I wondered if I could come and cook dinner, for both of us obviously. Unless you've already eaten.'

Why not? 'Yes, absolutely. Come now.'

It takes him less than five minutes to get to me. He must live very close.

He has the supermarket bags with him again, only two this time. 'Food.' He holds one up. 'Clean clothes.' He holds the other up. 'Can I be cheeky and have a shower.'

'Of course.'

He's soon in the kitchen messing about with my oven and sorting out the meal. I leave him to it. Matthew is fussing again and struggling to settle.

'I've just put something in the oven, okay if I shower now?'

'Feel free. Help yourself to whatever you need.'

It takes him ten minutes, then he reappears smelling fresh, hair wet, and wearing a cosy tracksuit with socks and slippers. He looks as though he's ready for bed.

He serves up a meal with vegetables and a giant pork chop each. My God, I'll never eat all that.

Seeing the look on my face he says, 'Shit, you're not a vegan or something are you? I never thought to ask.'

'No. No. Just a lot of meat.'

When I say that we both laugh in a flirty way. Not my intention at all and I suspect not his.

'Yeah, they come in packs of two and they are big, but… Anyway, you should be eating plenty of protein, it'll help you heal quicker.'

I can't finish it, but what I do eat is lovely. Then he finds a tin of rice pudding, I didn't know I had, in one of my cupboards. Afterwards, I'm feeling stuffed.

'That was good but I'll have to be careful I don't fill this loose skin up with food or I'll never get back to normal.' Oops, too much information.

He looks over at me and smiles. Then he clears up, and I let him. Matthew is sound asleep now and I flick the TV on, searching through Netflix and Amazon Prime for some inspiration.

He sits on the sofa opposite me. He watches Matthew for a moment or two who, maybe sensing his gaze, wakes up and starts bawling.

'He can't be hungry again.' I sigh. 'As soon as he gets near me he smells it and there's no peace.'

'Shall I hold him?'

I nod. Why not? I love my baby but I do feel a bit like a cow. I don't think I'm the natural earth mother type.

'Thanks for getting the formula,' I say. 'I haven't used it yet but it's good to know it's there and I can. I never planned to breastfeed. I would have got some formula in readiness if I hadn't been caught off guard.'

Matt smiles and nods at me as Matthew settles in his arms and goes back off to sleep.

They're like peas in a pod. I've wiped more of the gunk off Matthew's hair and he definitely has the same fair hair as Matt. Matt lays Matthew back in the nest and I cover him with a blanket.

'So,' Matt starts, his voice a whisper. 'We started a conversation earlier but it was cut short.' He looks at me meaningfully. I know where this is going, where it has to go.

'Yes.'

'I've wondered if it's possible I could be Matthew's father.'

'Me too. He does look like you.'

'What does this Roger look like.'

This Roger.

'Dark hair, blue eyes, like me. It's part of why I picked him. So my son would look like me and not some stranger. Colouring-wise, I mean.'

'Yes. Understandable.'

We both stare at Matthew for a little too long. Longingly, maybe, on Matt's part.

'How would you feel if I was his father?'

'I don't know.' I don't add depends what you want. The whole point of me going it alone was so I could go it alone. 'How would *you* feel?'

He opens his mouth to speak then closes it again. I can see some inner turmoil going on in his head; it shows on his face. 'I don't know,' he says, eventually. 'I think we need to find out before we discuss what it means. Discussing it without knowing could lead to all sorts of trouble.'

He's right. We could make all sorts of assumptions and then be wrong. Then what?

'I'll order a paternity test,' he says. 'Do you mind if I get it sent here? I don't have a hall floor at the moment and anything that comes through my letterbox disappears into an abyss.'

'That's fine.'

'Whatever happens,' he says, glancing at me then looking away. 'I'd like to think that we'll still be friends.'

'Me too.'

'Do you want to do this soon or wait? I'm very aware that you've only just given birth and your hormones are all over the place. I'm willing to wait if you want to.'

'No, Dr Matt, let's do it now.'

He nods and pulls out his phone, it seems now is right now, immediately.

'Is it possible though? We used condoms, didn't we?'

'We did. They're not one-hundred percent infallible. I don't know. We'll only know if we do the test.'

I'm starting to think it might be better not to know, but it's too late now, he's already ordered the test. From the speed he's done it I think he's already looked this up; it certainly didn't take him long to find one online.

He's already thought about it. So have I.

'I should go,' he says, standing up.

It's only about nine-thirty but I'm tired and Matthew will wake up soon for feed number one hundred today.

He collects up his stuff, puts on his coat, while I sit and watch. 'Is there anything you need me to do before I go? Carry Matthew upstairs?'

'No, I can manage, thank you.' I jump up. As I do I feel something ping. 'Oh,' I yelp.

'Are you okay?'

I take a step, then another. It no longer feels as though my leg is attached to my buttock. 'Yes. Actually better than okay.'

'What do you mean?'

'Less sore.'

'Then why did you yell out?'

I shake my head. He may be a doctor but I don't want to have this conversation with him. But he's waiting, concern on his face, professional concern and determination. His doctor face.

'Something pinged,' I say, glibly. 'It's fine now. Feels much better.'

'I need to look,' he says.

'No.'

'Yes. You could have ripped yourself.'

'But it feels so much better. So much more comfortable.'

'I need to look.' He dumps his bags, takes off his coat. 'Please. I'm worried about you.' He has such a determined look on his face that I don't think he'll give up.

'Tomorrow,' I offer.

'No. If there's something wrong we'd have to sort it out tonight.'

I let out a little laugh. 'How. I'm not into sewing myself, do you have your emergency kit on you?'

He doesn't laugh. It seems he doesn't see the funny side. He just raises his eyebrows.

'Okay. Upstairs. And I need five minutes to…' I'm not saying clean myself up, sort myself out, I'm not.

He picks up Matt and carries him upstairs. I go to the bathroom and emerge five minutes later with a towel around my lower half.

'On the bed?' Matt asks, nipping into the bathroom after me and washing his hands. He doesn't close the door and I can hear the water running for ages. 'I used your nail brush,' he says when he comes back. 'Hope that's okay.'

Urgh, what is he planning on doing?

I lie down, put my knees up and close my eyes.

He dives in. This is excruciating. He's a doctor, he's a doctor, he's a doctor, I repeat in my head. He gets his phone out.

'You're not taking a photo.'

'No, I need some light.' He switches on the phone light and dives back in. This is the second time he's had a torch up there.

He moves my legs about. He ferrets. I close my eyes and pretend he's the midwife. He's taking ages.

'Is something wrong?' I ask, eventually.

'No.' He wraps the towel around me. Goes off to wash his hands again. 'Everything looks okay,' he says when he comes back. 'I can see a broken stitch but it doesn't seem to be problem, or a major stitch.' He frowns then.

'Major or not, it's the one that tied my leg to my arse.' I feel relieved in more ways than one. I've got my dressing gown on and I'm heading into the bathroom myself.

He's hovering on the landing waiting for me when I come out.

'I'd better go now. Do you need to lock up behind me?'

I nod and follow him down the stairs.

He pulls on his coat, picks up his bag. I open the front door.

'Oh.'

It's raining so hard it's like a power shower. It's hitting the ground straight on, straight down, which is why we haven't heard it. The wind has obviously dropped now.

'Do you have an umbrella I could borrow?'

'In my car, I think.' We both look out. 'You'd be soaked before you even got it up.'

We both stare out for a second or two, watching the rain hit the pavement. I shut the door and lock it up for the night.

'Stay the night. Spare room is all ready. Mum made it up so she could stay.'

He waits and I can see him debating the idea internally. 'Okay, thank you.'

I show him the room, the small bedroom. Tim

moved the double bed and put it up before he redecorated what was to be Matthew's bedroom. It's against the wall but fine otherwise.

'Bigger than I thought,' he says. 'But this house is the same as mine, isn't it?'

'Don't know, never seen your house.'

He turns and looks at me. Smiles. 'You must, when it's a bit civilised.'

'Look.' I yawn. 'You don't have to go to bed now, I am, but you please yourself.'

'No, I will. I have to get up early. Plumber and electrician round at seven.'

'Seven?'

'Yeah. Good of them. So I can't be late. Hopefully the rain will have stopped.'

'Didn't even know it was forecast. That said, the whole real world is passing me by at the moment.' Right then, Matthew starts crying.

'You go,' he says. 'Can I get you anything before I go to bed?'

'A glass of water would be good.'

'I'll turn all the lights off downstairs too.'

I go off to feed Matthew and settle us both for the night. Matt brings in a glass of water, stares at what potentially could be his son – I'm still not sure how I feel about that – then gives me a quick kiss on the cheek before going to his own room. Not sure how I feel about that either. Mostly good, maybe.

Inevitably I feed Matthew in the night – I can't wait for that nipple balm to come – but must still be asleep when Matt leaves because when I do get up, his bed is made and he is gone.

He sends me a text at about nine.

Hope I didn't wake you. Thanks for letting me stay, best night's sleep I've had in a while. Electricity is back on now and rumour has it there may be a functioning boiler today, though sadly not fully functioning heating. Maybe tomorrow. Let me know if you need anything.

I'm conflicted; I feel sad that he won't need to sleep here again tonight but also relieved. I can't think of anything I might need today, he picked up my shopping and that was the main thing, so I message back a quick thanks and leave it at that.

Kerry and Carol-Anne came round this afternoon. They're both on maternity leave now. The plan, that is the original plan, was that we would have lovely long lunches and enjoy our freedom while we could. They're doing that; I'm not. But I'm also not complaining.

The nipple balm and shields arrived not long before they did so I slathered the balm on liberally and it seems to have taken the sting out of feeding. I had to feed Matthew while they were visiting and it was good not to wince to the point of crying while he fed. I'll try the shields later when I'm on my own. I know Kerri, or rather Garth, is keen on breastfeeding so I wouldn't want to put her off. Carol-Anne is like me, not too sure. I'm still in that camp, although if this nipple balm continues to do the trick maybe I'll persevere. I have to admit that not getting up in the night when it's cold to come down and make a bottle is one of the obvious advantages. Not counting, of course, the obvious health benefits for Matthew.

'Have you got one of those machines yet?' Carol-Anne asks. 'You know, the milk making ones?'

'A pump,' I ask.

'No, not for you, for making the bottles. Takes a few minutes and does it at the right temperature.' She looks at me as though I'm insane and I know why. We discussed this at length not so long ago. How could I have forgotten?

'Of course. No. It was my intention to buy those sort of things now, you know, when I was taking long lunches with you two.'

I'm wondering now if I should buy a breast pump? Maybe if I pumped more he'd get more than I wouldn't need to feed him so often. I'll ask the midwife tomorrow.

'How sore are you?' Kerri asks, nodding between my legs.

'Oh, it's getting better. Hardly feel it now.' Which isn't actually true, but since yesterday's ping, it is definitely more comfortable.

'At least you didn't have a caesarean. My cousin had one and could hardly stand up for month, doubled over she was. Did you know you can't drive for about six weeks; you can't lift heavy things. I hope I don't end up having a caesar.'

'You've got Garth to run around and do heavy lifting,' Carol-Anne says. 'Poor old Esme hasn't got anyone until her mum comes back from her travels, have you?'

'I have a couple of friends helping me out.' It's

true, I do. Pearl, although her involvement has diminished, and Matt.

'Oh,' Kerri says, looking affronted. 'Aren't we your friends? We can help out, can't we, Carol-Anne?'

'Of course. But we're probably not a lot of use, are we? Look at us. A couple of little barrels. I can't go more than half an hour without going to the toilet.' She stands up. 'Talking of which I need to use yours now.'

When she comes back down, she's grinning.

'Ahh, who's the dark horse then?' She flops down on the sofa next to me.

'What do you mean?'

'Man's electric razor in the bathroom. Hope it's not Gary's.'

'Hardly. He's a married man now, expecting his own baby.'

'Oh yeah. Not that you'd want that loser, would you? So, come on. Whose is the razor?'

I'm not telling anyone about Matt so I lie. 'Gary left it behind so I use it to do my legs and bits now.'

They both laugh.

'Well, you go girl, because that's an expensive razor, I bet you get a close shave with it.' She laughs and Kerri joins in.

Closer that you think, actually.

'Fitting that you're using his expensive razor to shave your fanny,' Kerri says, giggling.

'Not at the moment.' I watch their faces as I say, 'Too sore.' Mean, but they started it.

After their visit I'm exhausted. So, once I've fed

Matthew and make myself a doorstep sandwich I go to bed. Yes, it's only seven-thirty but I have to grab my sleep whenever I can because I know I'll be up in the night. This is something I never expected would be so exhausting, I used to be able to party into the small hours with the best of them, but this is another level of exhaustion.

It'll pass, I tell myself. Because he is so worth it, my tiny little bundle, my son.

'You should think about taking a little walk,' the midwife says. 'It's quite pleasant out there today. Wrap baby up well and yourself and just take your pram around the block a few times. Do you have a nice park nearby?'

'Not too far.'

'A bit of fresh air would do wonders for you both. And you're healing very nicely.'

I've decided not to tell her about the ping, if Matt says it's okay, it's okay.

'I won't need to come again unless you really need me,' she says. 'Just ring if you do. Any other problems with feeding and the like, ring the health visitor team.' She pushes a leaflet at me.

At the front door, she turns to me again. 'Yes, you should definitely get out. Take it easy. Ten minutes will do for the first time. Bit of fresh air will help baby sleep, too.'

I nod and agree and close the door and think, no way am I doing that.

An hour later I'm going out of the door. I have the pram part on the wheels. It's a struggle to get it out through the front door and I wonder why I am doing it, having decided so staunchly that I wasn't. But Matthew wouldn't settle after his feed and maybe the motion will calm him off to sleep.

And I have a good excuse, I'm taking Matt's razor back.

Seventeen

It's weird pushing a pram. I thought it would be like a shopping trolley but it's not. I cannot just kick the wheels if it doesn't go in the right direction.

To be fair the pram steers better than a trolley but although the wheels are the exact same ones I used with the car seat it feels very different.

'Hello again.' My neighbour pops up, she has a little dog with her today and is heading back towards her own home. 'First trip out solo?' she asks.

'Yes.' I pull a little apprehensive face.

'Where's your lovely man today?' With that she peers inside the pram at a soundly sleeping Matthew. 'They sleep so well in the fresh air, don't they?'

I decide to only answer that part of her question. 'Yes.' I rock the pram back and forth.

'So where did you say your lovely man was?'

'Busy,' I say, with a smile. I don't have to tell her my business; I hardly know the woman. I think we've spoken more in the last few days than we have in the last five years.

'Better get on, Buster wants his food,' she says,

yanking the lead on Buster who looks more like a Fifi, and together they trot off.

I amble around the corner, not sure at all which house is Matt's, but it actually takes no time at all to identify it. In the corner of a smart and quiet cul-de-sac his is, I assume, the one with a skip and a plumber's van on the front drive.

He's right, his house is the same style as mine, except that his is detached where mine is semi-detached. No doubt his neighbours are glad of that, because even from here I can hear the banging and clanging going on. Several downstairs windows are open – they look new – and then someone shouts 'Fuuucckk,' really loudly. Maybe his neighbours are not so grateful. I turn and walk away; I don't think now is a good time to visit.

I wander on past and head towards the little park near us. Park is probably a grand word, it's more scrubby grass but there are a few swings and a climbing frame. I imagine Matthew playing on this in a few years. I'm able to walk a circuit around the park then I do it again for want of somewhere else to go. There's a Tesco Express another ten minute or so walk from here but I think that's a trip for another day. Anyway, after my big online shop, I don't need anything just yet. Gary always used to go there for milk or bread when we ran out, he always came back with a packet of biscuits, he also never walked but drove. I've only walked it once since I've lived here. I suspect that will change now. Pram walking has definitely settled Matthew, he's out for the count.

Is he still alive? The thought hits me in the gut and I double over before reaching in to pat his face. I hover, if he's asleep will my touch wake him? But if he's dead, then what? Right then, probably sensing my proximity he puckers his generous lips. He's fine. Panic over. I withdraw my hand and start walking again, allowing the motion to calm me down.

Spring is just attempting to creep in and there are a few daffodils bobbing in the breeze. The grass is looking less grey and more green. I hope the summer is nice; I imagine taking Matthew out into the garden every afternoon, picnics maybe. Not that he will be old enough for that.

I turn and wander back towards home. As I pass Matt's house I notice the plumber's van has gone but the windows are still open. I edge closer, wondering if now would be a good time to call. I have my excuse; I have his razor. I edge closer. I'm not committed, I can always walk on past. Easy.

I find myself on his drive. I can hear music. He's probably playing it to soothe himself after whatever went on to cause the swearing. Was it him or was it the plumber? I imagine him saying, 'Alexa, play something calming.' It's nice, whatever it is. Piano, classical. It's loud and it gets louder as I creep closer.

I knock on the door; I'm doing this. Why am I so nervous? Maybe it's not his house. Maybe 'round the corner' is the other way. But I find myself knocking anyway. The music probably drowns out my knocking. I knock again, there's no doorbell. I turn to walk away. This wasn't a good idea. I manoeuvre Matthew's pram around. The music stops but I'm already facing away.

'Hello, Esme.'

I turn back. It's him, it's Matt. He's beaming at me.

'Hi,' I say, flustered.

'Everything okay?' He glances at Matthew's pram.

'Fine, yeah, fine.'

'Your leg and your arse okay today?' he asks, deadpan.

I narrow my eyes at him but his comment makes me smile.

'You left your razor in my bathroom, I thought you might need it.' I start fumbling under the pram, produce it, then hand it to him.

'Would you like to come in?' he asks. 'I've actually got some floorboards down here now.' He points to his hallway.

I nod and he comes round and takes the pram handles. 'Let me,' he says, shunting Matthew forward, then lifting the pram over the front door step.

We shuffle down his hallway and then into his massive living-room.

'Is this the same as mine? It seems enormous.'

'I think so. Layout is definitely the same. Excuse the mess.'

'Yeah,' I say. 'That's a big piano.'

'Baby grand,' he says.

'You play?' Of course he does, who else would be playing?

'Yes.'

'Was that you playing just now? When I knocked.'

'Yes, just making sure the environment hadn't damaged her.'

'And I thought you were calming yourself down after all the swearing.' I giggle, I can't help it.

'You could hear it from your house?' He looks horrified.

'No, I walked past about half an hour ago. When I heard it I thought then was probably not the best time.'

'It wasn't me; it was the plumber. He had all the radiators full blast, hence all the open windows, we went from freezing to tropical in no time. Then one sprung a leak. So we're back to no heating now. I should shut the windows now it's cooled right off.' With that he goes around closing them.

'Show me round?' I ask, pushing Matthew's pram out of the way and putting the brake on.

The house is the same as mine, the layout exactly the same. There's not one room in the place that is anywhere near finished. He's obviously halfway through painting the largest bedroom.

'How do you live in this and go to work? I mean, do you get enough sleep?'

'Yes, bed's comfortable and I'm usually so knackered I could sleep anywhere. It's no worse than anywhere else I've lived in that respect.'

'Is this the first house you've bought?'

He nods. 'I was always moving around with work. So I always rented. I'm putting down roots here.' He gives me another one of his arch looks but I don't probe. 'Cup of tea?' he asks. 'We do have electricity now so I can boil a kettle.'

He makes me tea and we perch on a sofa covered in a dust sheet.

'Your playing was wonderful.'

'Thanks.'

'So good I thought it was Alexa or something. Have you ever played professionally?' Who am I to judge? But it was good.

'Used to play in a band at medical school, but I don't think you'd call us professional.' He smiles at the memory.

'A band?'

'Yes. A four piece. Violin, drum, piano and guitar. We did wedding gigs and things like that. Supplemented our student debts.'

'Wow. And you've kept it up. And you have your own grand piano.'

'Baby grand. A long-ago birthday present from my parents. I do love it though, playing. I might hit a few bum notes but it's very soothing. She's been in storage for years but it's good to have her back.'

'Play some more,' I urge.

'No, no.' He shakes his head, smiling.

'Go on. You know you want to.'

He shrugs, gets up, arranges himself on the piano stool and starts to play. I don't recognise it but it's very soothing, lovely. I feel myself start to well up. What's the matter with me?

He stops. 'You okay?'

'Yes, sorry, I don't know what came over me there.' I sniff, wipe my eyes with the tips of my fingers. 'What was that?'

'Just a piece I made up long ago.' He puts the

piano lid down and stands up. 'Not meant to upset people though.'

'It didn't upset me, it moved me.' Now I feel I have to defend myself. 'And don't forget I've just had a baby.'

I get up and take my mug out to the kitchen where I find only the sink unit with a kettle and microwave balanced on top of it. There's an ancient old fridge stuffed into the corner.

'Kitchen fitters start tomorrow,' he says, coming up behind me. I feel his warm breath on my neck. I like it. But we've already established that my feelings, emotions, are not to be trusted. 'I've been clearing out the old units. They're in the skip out the front.'

'Yes,' I say, closing my eyes and enjoying his proximity, probably in a way that isn't appropriate given that he's my doctor. Although he's not now, not really, because I'm no longer in hospital. Anyway, we've already been intimate, months ago, eight to be precise. 'You can't really make a meal in this mess,' I say, stepping forward and away from him. 'Come to mine. Eat with me.'

He looks cautious, guarded, then he smiles. 'Okay. But I'm cooking. You need your rest, not to be running around after me.'

'Suits me,' I say. 'I'll probably be feeding his little lordship all evening anyway.'

And so that's how it's been for the last three days. He comes every evening and eats with us; he insists on cooking and I don't argue. I square it with myself by believing that Mum would have done everything for me if she were here. I square it with myself because Matt might be Matthew's father. Is that why he's doing this? Keeping in with me, looking after me because I'm looking after his son? He's changing most of the nappies now and last night we gave Matthew his first bath together. Once washed it was obvious how very fair his hair is. Matt hasn't stayed overnight again though. As he said, he has early starts and it's not fair to wake me and Matthew. He's a nice man, a kind, considerate man. He's nothing like Gary.

I feel a connection that's not just about my baby. I hope he does too.

'It's here,' I tell him when he arrives on the evening of the fourth day. 'The paternity test. It came this morning.'

We both stare at the package I've left sitting in the middle of the dining table.

'Should we do it now?' he asks.

'Might as well.'

'Is Matthew asleep?'

'Yes, and for more than two hours.' I grin, so pleased with myself for feeding him enough that he can sleep longer. The combination of the nipple shields, balm and perseverance means I'm getting the hang of this breastfeeding lark. I might just continue.

'Now would be a good time then. Before he has a mouth full of milk and baby vomit.' He starts to unwrap the package, quickly reading the instructions. Then he washes his hands before laying everything out.

'Try not to wake him up.'

The deed is done, the tests are in the post. I had to supply my DNA too so that I can be eliminated from the result. Apparently the result can be as accurate as 99% doing it this way. Now it's just a waiting game. We haven't discussed what will happen if the test is positive, or indeed if it's not. I'm beginning to wonder if we should have just left it a little bit longer before finding out. But that's probably just me being selfish. I need his company, his help, his support. I feel comforted by the fact he's either here or he's just around the corner.

Sue and Roger are coming for a visit today. They're desperate to see Matthew in the flesh. They're excited and so thrilled I've agreed to them meeting him so soon. Apparently most of the other mums made them wait weeks or even months. I'm not making them wait just in case Matthew isn't Roger's biological child. It might be now or never. So far I haven't told them there's a possibility he might be Matt's. What's the point? He might not be.

When they arrive late morning I feel a little guilty for not offering to let them stay overnight. It's taken them two hours to get here and it'll take another two to get home. That's four hours driving in one day. But, I remind myself, some people do that every day for their daily commute to work. But if they stayed overnight I'd have to change the bed because Matt has slept in it. I'd also have to tell Matt not come round in the evening. Although it won't be long before he doesn't need to as his kitchen is coming on well, he says.

I haven't been round there again because of the dust, debris and noise but I will once it's finished. I am managing a daily walk with Matthew though and that seems to be doing us both good. It helps that it's starting to warm up a little, spring is definitely busting out all over.

They've been in the house for just five minutes and they've spent the entire time cooing over a sleeping Matthew. We've only been back from our walk about twenty minutes and I'm expecting him to sleep for another hour. I know Sue especially would like to get him out, but she hasn't asked and I haven't offered. I'm trying to get him into a routine because according to the baby books the sooner you start the better.

'Tea?' I ask. 'Or coffee?'

'Toilet,' Roger says. 'Is it upstairs?'

I point him in the right direction and slyly watch as he ambles up the stairs.

'Is Roger all right?'

'Oh, yes. Just the driving takes it out of him now. Age. That and his feet.' Sue titters and I feel guilty. 'And it was bad, we left after the rush hour but the rush hour seems to be all the time and every day.'

'I'll make tea,' I say, not wanting to get into this conversation.

When I come back into the room Roger has taken his shoes off and Sue is massaging his feet on her lap. At least he's kept his socks on.

'I hope you don't mind,' Sue says. 'Roger taking

his shoes off. His feet play him up something terrible.'

'No, that's fine.' It isn't, it really isn't. Having your wife massage your feet is something you keep for home, your own home.

Finally Sue lets go of Roger's feet and he swings them back to the floor. He's wearing grey woollen socks, old man socks. He has bunions, even through the socks they are very obvious. His other toes don't look too good either, like a bag of pickled onions bobbing about. Thank God he kept his socks on. I hope Matthew doesn't inherit those if Roger does turn out to be his biological father. I think of Matt's feet, definitely preferable.

After we've drunk tea and eaten a few biscuits I tell them that they absolutely must stay for lunch – I've made a quiche. I haven't, Matt made it. It's one of his 'dishes', baked salmon, roast beef and spag bol being the others.

'But real men don't eat quiche,' I said, quoting something I heard a long time ago and can't even remember when or where.

'That's the title of a book,' he said, 'About male stereotypes. By Bruce Feirstein, I think. 1982.'

'What? Really? That's before I was born.'

'Me too. Yep. Looked it up after hearing it said so many times. So, I'm not a real man.' He shrugged before getting back to beating his eggs and grating his cheese. I only have to warm it up today.

They both keep looking over at Matthew. I don't blame them, that's why they came. To see the fruit of Roger's loins. Although, obviously, no loins were involved, not on my part anyway. Eventually I think I must get Matthew up for them.

'Who wants him first?' I ask, looking at Sue who nods vigorously.

Roger has a kind of bemused look on his face and I wonder how interested he actually is. Not that it matters.

I lift Matthew out while he's still asleep and put him into Sue's arms. Her face lights up. Matthew, obligingly puckers his lips.

'Ahh,' she says. 'Those are some lips.' She smiles then looks at me and frowns. She doesn't say anything but it's obvious to both of us that neither Roger nor I have thick lips. Mine are thin to the point of meanness, thank God for plumping lipstick, not that I'm wearing any today.

'Isn't he cute, Roger. Look at him.'

Roger nods and agrees that yes, Matthew is cute.

'What other names are you calling him?'

'Matthew Haste,' I say before realising that she means second name, middle name. Is she hinting that she wants him to be a Roger? Are there lots of babies with Roger or Sue, if it's a girl, as a middle name. The thought bothers me. 'Other than that, not decided yet. I haven't even registered the birth.' And there is a reason for that but I cannot possibly tell Sue and Roger what it is.

Matthew starts to stir on Sue's lap and she gets excited. She touches his cheek and he immediately turns his head, rooting for milk no doubt.

'I think he's hungry,' she says, her voice singsong. 'Can I feed him?'

'Not really. Sorry. I'm breastfeeding him.'

'Wonderful, wonderful. Isn't that wonderful, Roger?'

Roger nods and agrees it is. He looks to me as though he'd rather be anywhere but here.

Matthew opens his eyes, his dark brown eyes. Sue stares at them, nudges Roger, then looks at me. Yes, I have blue eyes and Roger has the bluest eyes I've ever seen. I hadn't realised quite how blue; they're film star blue. When I met Roger and Sue on the night of the (possible) conception it was in a darkened pub and restaurant. But today, the light is good and bright in my living room and Roger's eyes shine out.

'Well, look at his eyes. Obviously brown eyes run in *your* family.'

I just smile. What can I say? No, they don't.

'And look at his hair, it's blond,' she says, stroking it. 'Does he take after your dad?'

I immediately think of Tim who is grey now and mouse before that, then correct myself and remember that Dad Dan did have fair hair the last time I saw him. So I nod and smile.

This is cringe and I feel so duplicitous, but what can I do? He might well be Roger's baby. Matthew's colouring and lips might have nothing to do with Matt.

'Do you want to hold him, Roger?' I ask, thinking it might be his one and only chance.

'Sure,' he says, not looking sure at all.

Sue hands Matthew over and arranges him in Roger's arms so that they both look comfortable and

Matthew dozes back off to sleep.

I sit back, I hadn't realised that during this I have been sitting on the edge of my seat, quite literally.

There is no resemblance at all between Roger and Matthew. Nothing. This is not at all like it is when Matthew is on Matt's lap.

'He looks comfortable. Shall I make lunch before he starts bawling for a feed?' Truth is I just want to get out of here. And let them have some time alone with Matthew, who may or may not be related to them.

Lunch is quick and easy thanks to the premade quiche and some shop bought salad, throw in some baby potatoes and crusty bread and we're good. Matthew, happily, does not wake up for feeding even after I take him from Roger's lap and put him in his nest. He even allows me to clear up and make coffee before he makes his demands known.

I feel self-conscious when I feed him so sit in the swivel chair – ironically this was bought at Gary's insistence, but since I paid for it, I kept it – and turn away from them. Fortunately I'm getting so good at this and so is Matthew that it doesn't take long to sate him.

'Did you want to do a nappy change?' I ask Sue, who jumps at the chance. Roger shakes his head just as quickly.

'He's a beautiful big boy, aren't you?' she says to Matthew who coos back at her. 'Was he definitely premature?'

'Oh yes. Four weeks.' I don't want to say any more because if I'm too insistent that he was conceived that night we met and it turns out that Roger isn't the father, we're all going to be embarrassed and I will look like a right liar.

I'm not a liar. Just confused.

I've gone over and over than night when Matt and I met. We had sex, there's no denying that, and twice because we used both of the 'stag party' condoms, but did we do it again without one? Was one leaky? Is that the right word? Will I be pleased if Matt is the father? I think I might be, except that it will confer rights on him that he wants. Not something I originally planned. Will I be disappointed if Matt is not Matthew's father? I think I might be. What will happen with me and Matt? Is there a me and Matt? Despite our night together we've done nothing since – how could we? I've just had a baby. But there's not even been a kiss. Matt has hugged me in the same way he might hug his mum or a female friend, he's kissed me on the cheek too, ditto the mum and friend thing, but that's it. He hasn't initiated anything more intimate. Neither have I.

Sue has another long cuddle with Matthew who falls asleep in her arms. Roger doesn't seem especially interested, checking his phone more than once while Sue puts her finger in Matthew's little hand and he clenches it. I like that too, it's so cute.

'We ought to get going,' he says. 'Beat the traffic. Roads look fairly clear at the moment.' So that's what he was checking on his phone.

'Of course.' Sue gets up and puts Matthew back in his nest. 'Just use your loo,' she says, heading upstairs.

When she comes back Roger goes up again.

I've just fetched their jackets for them, and Sue is hovering over Matthew saying a final farewell when the front door bursts open and Matt calls out.

'Finished early so I thought I'd come and keep you company.'

Sue and Roger both jerk their heads in his direction as he comes through the living room door.

Sue does a double-take, her eyes flicking between Matthew and Matt. Yep, there's no mistaking the similarity, though it could still be entirely coincidental.

'Matt,' I say, smiling. 'These are my friends Sue and Roger. Matt is a doctor at our local hospital, he actually delivered Matthew.'

Matt, probably not registering who Roger is, steps forward and shakes hands with them, smiling and charming. I hadn't told him they were coming; I don't know why.

'Well, it's been lovely,' Sue says, regaining any composure she might have lost when she saw Matt. 'Nice to meet you, Matt.' She glances at Matthew again. 'Have you known each other long?' It's such a loaded question.

'No,' we both say, perhaps a bit too quickly.

'Better get going,' Roger says. 'Traffic and stuff.'

I follow them outside and after hugging them goodbye before they get into their car, I wave them off. I feel a bit shitty about everything. But what can I do? Or say?

'I've just realised who that was,' Matt says, when I go back inside.

'Roger.'

'*The* Roger.'

'Oh shit. Hope I didn't make it awkward for you. They didn't leave because I arrived, did they?'

'No, they were just going anyway.'

'What did you tell them?'

'Nothing. There's nothing to tell yet, is there? We don't know, do we?'

'But Roger isn't going to have any part in Matthew's life, is he? I mean, that was your arrangement, wasn't it?'

'Yes. Yes. Absolutely. But, I don't know, Sue questioned if Matthew was actually premature. I assured her he was. I don't want them thinking I was messing them about.'

'In what way?'

'I don't know.' I give a little shudder. 'It was all a bit cringe to be honest. Sue commented on Matthew's colouring, not like me or Roger. I felt really duplicitous.' I feel tearful now. I don't really know why. I stop speaking and press my lips together to stop any silly crying from getting out.

Matt steps forward and hugs me. Really tight. It's nice. I find myself wrapping my arms around him in response. We stand like that for a long time, just hugging in my living room. It feels normal, comforting. Then I pull back. I glance up at Matt and he looks down on me and smiles slightly. Then it happens.

We kiss. Properly. World stopping, room spinning, all the clichés.

After the kiss of the decade, no century, I have to

go to the loo. The lid is up and so is the seat and there are sprinkles everywhere. Yellow ones. Roger. His aim evidently not very good. He was last in here, after Sue because I'm sure she would have cleared it up if she'd seen it. I'm liking Roger less and less.

Eighteen

Matt stayed the night, all night. He slept in my bed.

We kissed, we cuddled, we snuggled. We didn't do anything else, obviously. How could we? I've just had a baby. He did get up and change Matthew's nappy after I'd fed him. Both times.

I loved it. We felt like a proper little family.

We haven't had an in-depth conversation about the future because we're both on edge about the paternity test results. I so want it to be Matt. Not sprinkle-willy-pickled-bunion-toes-Roger. How horrible am I? But Matt did say before that he hoped we'd be friends, no matter what the outcome. I'm hoping for more than that. I *think* he is.

'How long do you think it'll be before we get the results?' I ask him over breakfast. He doesn't have to leave early today because he's working on his own, painting and decorating. The plumber and the carpenter have finally gone and left him with working heating and a decent kitchen. Now everything needs painting. And he's only got three days before he goes back to work.

'I don't know. It said one to two weeks.' He takes a big bite out of a piece of buttered toast. The butter runs down his chin and I have to resist the urge to get up and lick it. How mad.

'It's already a week.'

'Nearly. Anyway, there's nothing we can do about it. We'll just have to wait. I'll have to go soon, all that painting. I'd much rather stay here, but…'

'I know.'

'Shall I come round this evening?'

'Of course.' Why is he even asking?

He gets up, washes his hand and face at the sink then comes and gives me the biggest hug possible. Then strokes Matthew's face, not that Matthew is aware of it because he's sound asleep.

'I'll see you later,' he says, kissing me briefly on the lips.

I stand at the door and watch him walk away. I feel like a teenager in love. Not a forty-year-old knackered new mum.

It's after two pm when I notice the post on the hall mat. Honestly it's taken me all this time just to get showered, dressed, do a load of washing and tidy up. I used to be able to do all these things before going to work at eight am. Oh, and I had to change Matthew's entire outfit twice after a double poonami disaster. But I'm presentable now and so is he, so that's a bonus.

I'm getting us ready to go out for a walk when I find the post. It's a letter addressed to Matt but I know what it is because of the return address is on the back. Our paternity test results. I want to open it. I'm fighting with myself not to just rip it open and find out, but that wouldn't be fair. We should to this together. Anyway, it's not addressed to me.

I manoeuvre the pram into position to go through the door and pull on a lightweight jacket. It actually looks nice outside today and according to the weather app on my phone the temperature is a balmy eighteen degrees, which is positively scorchy after our cold winter. I'm wearing non-maternity leggings and a loose-fitting, long t-shirt and they don't look too bad. But I'm so looking forward to getting into my pre-baby clothes. It'll probably take months but I'm determined to not get downhearted.

I don't even need to do my jacket up because the sun is so warm. I stuff the letter into one pocket, my house key in the other and set off round to Matt's. As well as the excitement of the letter I'm looking forward to seeing his new kitchen.

It takes minutes to arrive at Matt's. The front door is propped open and music is leaking out onto the street. I think he's playing the piano again, although it sounds different to the last time. Sort of plonky and jaunty; maybe that's *Alexa* playing this time.

As I approach the door I see why it's propped open. A piece of paper is taped to the step saying: WET PAINT. He's made a nice job of the door, it's navy blue and very shiny. The music continues and since there's no knocker to knock, I position Matthew's pram in front of the step and put the brake on. Although I will be able to squeeze through without touching the door there's certainly not enough room to get the pram through.

'Matt,' I call out, not wanting to shock him if he's up a ladder painting, but my voice is drowned out by the music.

I slither inside, very aware that the navy-blue paint will ruin my pale jacket. I breathe a sigh of relief, turn and check on Matthew, who's sound asleep, and then continue on into the living room.

Matt is playing the piano. I stand there and do not speak because he's not alone. Sitting next to him, very close and cuddled up to him, and playing the piano too, is a woman with long, blonde hair. I step back slowly so that I'm back in the hallway, but I can still see them through the gap between the door and the frame. I glance back at Matthew; he's fine.

They've stopped playing and they both laugh. I'm watching them and they don't know I'm here.

'So thrilled you're here,' Matt says, wrapping his arms around the woman and kissing her forehead before giving her a big squeeze which makes her squeal with delight.

She wraps her arms around him too and they giggle together, heads together.

'Another?' she asks. 'One hand. Yes.'

They giggle again and then start to play the piano one hand each, while keeping the other hand firmly around each other's waists.

I slink back out of the house. Kick the brake off Matthew's pram and skitter down the drive as fast as I can.

He's a lying bastard. He's as bad as Gary. This is the hairdryer scenario all over again. Well, maybe not exactly the same, but the deceit and treachery are.

I'm run-walking back home now as fast as I can without tripping over or tipping the pram over. Why oh why did I ever think that there could be a future for me and Matt? I'm just an idiot. A stupid, hormonal, post-birth-giving fool. He was only being nice to me so that he could find out if he was Matthew's father. Then he'd make demands and want to be involved, who knows, he might even try to go for custody. I'd have to share my baby with him. And her. She's probably barren and that's why he was so keen.

I'm scurrying along so quickly that I don't see my neighbour in front of me.

'Whoa,' she calls, as though I'm a bloody horse.

'Sorry. Sorry,' I whimper – so I am a horse. 'In a hurry.'

But she doesn't move out of the way, she just skirts around the pram and stares inside. 'Isn't he a beauty. Just like his daddy.'

She has no idea what a double hit that is. Or maybe she does. For a start off Matt may not be his daddy, in fact he is definitely NOT going to be his daddy and secondly, is she implying that Matt is beautiful and I'm not? Cheeky bitch.

I move to get past her and the movement, or maybe it was the previous lack of movement wakes Matthew up. He starts to cry, it's his urgent, haven't been fed for days cry, even though it's just over two hours. My boobs tingle, I feel the throb. I need to get home.

'Oh dear,' my neighbour says. 'I think you're leaking.'

I look down. She's right; milk is oozing out from both my breasts, spreading across my t-shirt. I start to scuttle away but she has to have the last word.

'You need breast pads, dear. Industrial strength.'

I cannot answer her because I don't want to scream 'fuck off,' in the middle of the street.

By the time I get home Matthew has nodded off again. I get the pram inside and expect him to wake and start crying, but he doesn't. Even peering right inside and up close at him doesn't disturb him. So I deadlock the front door behind us, put the chain on, rip my jacket off and scuttle upstairs to change my clothes.

I remove the breast pads which didn't do much of a job. I wonder if there is such a thing as industrial strength?

Once back downstairs, I yank the paternity letter from my jacket pocket. That's when I notice the little streak of navy-blue paint on the sleeve. It's ruined; that's his bloody fault too. Bastard.

Should I open the paternity letter? I stand there waving it across my face trying to calm down while I debate this with myself.

No.

I remove the rarely-lit giant candle from the zinc bucket on the hearth and throw the letter into it. I hunt around for my candle lighter, it takes me a full five minutes to locate it. Then I set fire to that fucking letter and stand back to watch the flames lick up the sides of the bucket, blackening the inside and making the room smell of burning dust.

There. Done. Now we'll never know.

To hell with you Dr Matt and your blonde floozy. You can go the same way as Gary the cheat. Off. Out of my life.

I do not need a man.

No man is required in my life.

Other than Tim who never lets me down. But let's face it he's the exception that proves the rule, isn't he? Just look at Dad Dan. Another useless arsehole.

Matthew carries on sleeping so I take the opportunity to ring the registry office and make an appointment to register his birth. There will be only one parent name on that birth certificate and it will be mine.

'Two weeks?' I hear how screechy my tone is. 'Haven't you got anything sooner?'

'No, sorry.' The voice on the other end sounds bored. No doubt he has this conversation frequently.

'Okay.' And we agree a date which I will be keeping firmly to myself.

Afterwards I feed Matthew and prop him up in his bouncy cradle which I've wedged onto the kitchen worktop so I can make myself beans on toast. I'm not in the least bit hungry but I am fully aware that I have to eat to make sufficient milk for my baby. And since I've come this far, I'm going to carry on. I was going to make something nicer for Matt and me but what's the point now? It'll just be cooking for one from now on and for the foreseeable future, until Matthew starts to eat real food.

I've dozed off with Matthew in my arms. He's had a huge feed and is sound asleep too. We were warm and comfortable and cosy and now I'm shaken awake by a knocking on the door. I take my time placing my baby in his nest then go to answer the door which I crack open just a little, leaving the chain on.

'Hey, did you get my message? Sorry I'm late. My key wouldn't turn.' Matt stands there smiling at me.

'I don't care how late you are. I never want to see you again. Do you understand. Never. Never ever knock on my door again. Or attempt to contact me again. I'll consider it harassment and will report you to the police. Do I make myself clear?' I feel pleased with my little speech; I've had plenty of time to practise it in my head.

He stands there blinking and speechless. He doesn't even attempt a defence because there is none. Even though he doesn't know that I saw him and his girlfriend, he does know what he's been up to today and that's probably enough to make him feel guilty.

Finally he rallies himself, shaking his head in puzzlement. 'What's happened? Are you all right?'

'I'm fine. Do not contact me again. Ever.' With that I shut the door then dash into the living room so I can see what he does. He just stands there, then after a while he wanders away.

Don't pretend you don't know what you've done,

because you absolutely do, I think, just as he glances back. Don't think you've fooled me. I will not be subject to any man's will or con-artistry. Is that even a word?

I wish Mum was here.

In the kitchen I check my calendar; eighteen more days until she comes home. Eighteen more days and counting.

This is the second day I've had a headache. After I'd checked via Google I found I could take paracetamol while breastfeeding and that's what I've been doing and while they work initially, the headache just keeps coming back. And today I don't feel very well, sort of fluey. Typical. I've got no one to help me and I feel shit.

On the plus side even if Matt was still in my life he wouldn't be available because he's gone back to work today. Good. I have to admit, though only to myself, that I'm missing him. And not just because I don't feel well. I feel so conflicted. How can I miss a lying cheat? I'm missing Matt more than I missed Gary and he lived in my house and we were engaged for a year. It makes no sense. And it's not as if I don't know what Matt did. I caught him red-handed; I never actually caught Gary in the act, the evidence against him was circumstantial.

I think the headache is stress. What else could it be? Unless it's a brain tumour. Don't go there, I tell myself. I'm being a bloody drama queen now. Drama llama, Gary's words. I wonder if his child bride has given birth yet? No, she's got months to go, hasn't she? I don't really know; she might have had a baby before me… What?

Matthew starts to cry; my boobs start to throb and I realise I've been rambling on inside my own head.

I'm wincing as I feed him, especially on the left side. I must be getting immune to that nipple cream which I thought was so good and I can't find the shields. I'll have to amend my review of the balm now. That's why they kept urging me to review it; an email almost daily until I did. It's because it stops working after a while.

I'm rambling again.

At least Matthew is settling into a pattern. Good boy. He sleeps a lot now. Though it might be all the paracetamols. I haven't exceeded the dose, have I? Because he'll be getting some of it. No, he's fine. Bright-eyed and finally cooing at *me*. It's good, he's good.

I'm still rambling.

And my headache isn't going away today.

I take him upstairs, put him in his crib and watch him doze off. This is our routine and now I'm jumping into the shower.

My left boob is red. All down the side. What the hell is that? It feels like a sting. How can I have been stung? I saw it in the shower and in the mirror it looks even worse. Once I'm dried and dressed I'll be ringing my GP surgery.

'There are no appointments left today,' the receptionist sounds so bored. 'Ring tomorrow at eight.'

'I don't think I can wait until then.' I've already had to explain to this non-medical person what my symptoms are – so she can allot the right doctor to me – now she says no appointments. She could have just said that to start with.

'As per our terms and conditions which I think you heard when you rang…' she's referring to the four-minute monologue I had to hear before I could get in the queue to speak to her. '…if your symptoms are urgent you should go to Urgent Care.'

'But I've just had a baby.'

'Try the midwife then.' And then she puts the phone down. Hilarious. In their monologue they say they won't tolerate rudeness to their staff, doesn't appear to work both ways.

I wish I could ask Matt.

No, you don't, he's nothing but a lying, cheating, dog. What? What am I thinking?

I ring the midwife but her phone goes to answerphone. I start to leave a rambling message then lose the will to live and give up. Then I ring 111 only to listen to another long, rambling message – they ramble on worse than I do at the moment – which says ring 999 if it's urgent. I don't think it's that urgent.

Is it?

As the day goes on I don't feel any better. I consult Dr Google. It appears I might have mastitis. I thought only cows had that. My boob is throbbing and so is my head. I've got the shivers now too. I can't mess around any longer. I try the midwife again, another answerphone message. I can't chance going overnight, can I? What if something awful happens to me? What if I faint with Matthew in my arms? I'm catastrophising of course, but…

I can't trust myself to drive. I haven't driven since I had Matthew but only because I haven't needed to. And now I can't. I call a taxi. That's the safest way.

It's heaving at the hospital urgent care centre. Why did I expect anything else? I join the queue at the reception desk.

'Is it for the baby?' she asks, glancing at Matthew who, fortunately, is asleep in his car seat. 'Only we have a separate area for children and it'll be much quicker.'

'No, no, it's for me.'

'What's the problem?'

So I tell her in full hearing of the rest of the queue behind me and probably the whole waiting room too.

'Take a seat. You'll be called. We're very busy.'

I sit down on the end of a row and park Matthew next to me, that way I'll able to wheel him back and forth and hopefully keep him asleep.

I glance around the room, careful not to stare at anyone, just as I don't want anyone staring at me. Most of the injuries are exactly that, injuries, with blood and ice packs. The man next to me has a towel wrapped around his hand; it's soaked in blood. I'm not blood phobic but the thought of what's beneath that towel makes me feel nauseous. And I think I can smell it. Blood. I turn away and gulp air but it's hot in here. I look towards the door. It's cooler outside and I could just stand there for a while.

I get up, wheel Matthew towards the door. Miraculously there's no longer a queue at Reception and the receptionist spots me.

'Are you leaving?' she yells.

'No. No. I just need some air.'

She nods. Then points to a sign. 'No smoking on hospital grounds,' she yells loud enough that several heads turn.

It's cooler outside for which I'm grateful. But I so want to sit down and there are no seats out here. Also, despite her shouting about the smoking and the numerous no smoking signs, people are out here smoking, then stubbing their butts out on the ground. I used to smoke, like most kids I tried it, but I gave up twenty years ago. I don't mind the smell of fresh smoke but the stench of stale smoke on people who smoke is truly horrible.

I turn Matthew away from the smokers, pulling his hood up. But we're downwind of them and there's no escaping it. Where is that receptionist when I need her. She should be out here shouting at them instead of me, a non-smoker.

The smoke is making me feel light-headed. I need to sit down. It's cool out here, I know it is, but there's sweat around my hairline. Cold sweat.

And now I'm seeing stars.

Nineteen

The lights are so damn bright when I open my eyes.

'Ah, how are you doing?' The nurse, or doctor – they all wear scrubs – smiles at me. She's wearing a name badge but it's out of focus. 'You were very lucky. An off-duty member of staff saw you and rescued you when you collapsed. We're sorting you out now.'

I don't know where I am, then I remember.

'My baby.' I sit up suddenly, feel woozy and flop back down. 'Where's my baby?'

'He's fine. A member of staff is wheeling him around to keep him asleep.

'Can she bring him back here now please.' I don't want to sound panicked but I am.

'He's fine. I'll find him in a minute. You need to rest now and let the antibiotics do their job.'

That's when I notice I'm hooked up to a drip.

'What have I got?'

'Mastitis. And it's got quite a hold. Still, this will sort you out.'

'I thought only cows got that. I've seen it on

Countryfile.'

'Now you know better.' There's a little laugh in her voice. 'I'll see where your baby is.' She disappears, pulling the curtain closed behind her.

The drip is dripping slowly into me but it's not working fast enough; I still have a headache. When the hell will that go? But I don't feel sick any longer, probably because I'm away from the smokers.

The curtain bulges and Matthew's car seat and wheels appear.

'Thank God,' I say. 'Thank you.' I don't even look at the member of staff.

'You're welcome,' Matt's soft voice says.

'You. It had to be you. Are you still trying to steal my baby?'

'What? I've never tried to steal your baby.' He's not wearing scrubs, he's in normal clothes. He looks sad, his face looks hollow, his eyes sunken; maybe he's just worked a long shift.

'You don't need to hang around, I'm fine now.'

He raises his eyebrows and makes a 'doctor face,' you know the one, like he knows much better, which I admit, he might. 'You're not fine.'

'Ah, there you are.' The original nurse/doctor comes back in. 'Did you know our man saved your life.'

'Exaggerating, Angie,' Matt says, smiling at her.

'Well, he caught you as you fell. Stopped your head from hitting the concrete. Could have been nasty. Anyway, how we doing with this drip?' She fiddles with the tube in my arm. 'Okay, you can go home as soon as this is through. We've got more antibiotics for you to take with you.'

'Thank you. Thank you so much. What about feeding my baby? Can I still do that?'

'Yes. In fact if you can bear it, that's probably the best thing to do. Or pump that side if you prefer. See how you go.'

'Where's my handbag?' I say, not really asking anyone in particular.

Matt retrieves it from underneath Matthew's car seat and hands it to me. I fish around for my phone but I fumble about with it, struggling to concentrate.

'Can I help?' the Angie asks.

'No. It's fine. I just want to ring a taxi to get home. I didn't drive myself up here so don't have my car.'

She glances at Matt then at me.

'Just as well, I wouldn't recommend driving until you're feeling one-hundred-percent. And a taxi isn't necessary, is it Matt?'

'No. I'll take you home.'

'No thank you.'

Angie looks between the two of us, watching for a reaction from either but neither of us speaks.

'Okay,' she says. 'Do you have anyone else at home to look after you?'

'No, she doesn't,' Matt answers for me.

'Right. Don't know what's going on here with you two, but if there's no one at home then you'll have to stay, at least overnight. As usual we're pushed for beds so it's unlikely we'll find you a bed, so you'll probably spend the night on a trolley in the corridor because we'll need this cubicle soon. Is there anyone who can take the baby for you? Not ideal for him to spend the night in a corridor.' Is she in cahoots with Matt?

'I'll ring someone else,' I say, fumbling with my phone again.

'I can look after you,' Matt says. 'Wouldn't you rather be safe and comfortable at home?'

I don't answer him. Then Matthew starts to cry. My boobs tingle, well the left one starts to throb more, and Matt obligingly lifts my baby out of his car seat and hands him to me.

So now I'm breastfeeding my baby with an audience, but I don't care any longer. Matt hovers by the side of the bed his hands out as though he's going to catch a rugby ball.

'I won't drop him,' I snap.

'Better safe than sorry,' Angie says, shaking her head before leaving us alone.

After I've fed him I feel even more exhausted than before and I still have my headache.

'He needs changing,' I say, leaning back and closing my eyes momentarily.

'I'll do it,' Matt says, lifting Matthew from me. I keep my eyes closed and let him get on with it, pulling the changing bag from beneath the car seat. I'm just so tired.

'Here you go, drink this.'

'What? What?'

'You were asleep. I let you sleep. You're dehydrated so drink this.'

'What is it?'

'Water.'

'Where's Matthew?' I panic after taking a few gulps.

'He's asleep. Sound asleep.' He nods to the corner of the cubicle where Matthew is indeed sleeping in his car seat.

'Right,' Matt starts. 'Now is not the time or place to discuss what the hell is going on but I do think you need to go home, get some proper rest and let me look after you. Do you really want to spend the night on a trolley? And what about Matthew? Much as I'd love to I can't stay up here all night looking out for him and you.' He looks annoyed, really annoyed, but he's keeping his voice calm.

I just shake my head in response.

'I think your high temperature has made you confused, delirious maybe.'

'I'm not delirious, I know what I saw.'

'What?'

'I know what I saw.'

Ignoring me he just continues, 'So what do you say? Shall I take you home now?' He waits while I think about it, although to be fair I'm not really thinking about it. The lure of my own bed is far too appealing. 'Let me look after you both in the comfort of your own home,' his says, his voice soft, quiet.

'Okay. But don't think it changes anything.'

I'm on the sofa, propped up by cushions and snuggled under a fleecy throw. I have to admit this is so much better than the threatened hospital trolley. Matthew is in his nest beside me.

'Drink that,' Matt says, putting a cup of milky tea down in front of me. 'We need to get your fluids up. How's the headache?'

'Improving.' And it actually is. Maybe they gave me painkillers in hospital, I really don't know.

'Okay, I'm going to cook us something to eat. You need to eat a proper meal so you can take more antibiotics and I'm bloody starving after my shift. Have you actually eaten anything today?'

'Can't remember.' I don't think I have. 'You don't have to do any of that. You can go home now.'

'Stop it,' he says, though kindly. 'I'm staying until I'm satisfied you're okay. Why didn't you call me?'

I shrug. I can't just unsee what I saw and I can't stand liars and cheats. I won't be taken for a fool.

He shrugs then too. He looks even more tired than I feel. Then he goes out to the kitchen and I pick up the remote and flick the TV on.

'Food's ready,' he says, shaking me. I must have fallen asleep. 'It's on the table. And you haven't drunk your tea.' He shakes his head.

I feel shaky as I totter to the table but I bat away his hand as he attempts to help me. I'm ungrateful I know, but I won't be fooled by another cheat.

He's made spaghetti Bolognese; he did say it was one of his dishes. I can't help but smile when I see it. There's a big glass of water too, and a packet of pills.

'When do I take these?'

'Eat that first. I'll tell you when. They're there as a reminder.'

We eat in silence and I admit I really enjoy it. I'm

starving, not that I really realised. After the meal he escorts me back to the sofa, bringing the water and tablets too.

'Drink the water please,' he says. Then he goes off and clears up. I let him. He owes me.

After I've fed Matthew again I let Matt get him ready for bed. I know I'm taking advantage of him and I still don't trust his motives. Unfortunately I'm just too tired to dismiss his help.

'Come on,' he says. 'Let's get you both to bed.' He helps me upstairs, carrying Matthew for me.

When I finally get into my own bed the sense of relief is unbelievable. Matt puts Matthew in his crib.

'I'm sleeping in the spare room.' He waits for me to argue but I just don't have the energy. 'If that's okay with you. Shout if you need anything. Don't be too proud to call out.'

I nod. It's easier than arguing and then he can just go.

'I'm leaving your door open so I can hear if you need me.'

'Whatever,' I mutter, sounding like a teenager.

'Hey, Esme. Do you want to feed Matthew or do you want me to make him a bottle?'

'What?'

'He's crying, he's hungry.' He's also being soothed in Matt's arms, but nothing compares to his mummy's arms, or her milk.

I can't believe I haven't woken; I never sleep through his hungry cry at night. 'I'll feed him.'

Matt arranges Matthew in my arms, then flops down on the bed beside me. He's careful to keep his distance. He has the bedside lamp on on his side and as I study him, his eyes closing before he jerks himself awake, I notice he's wearing only a thin t-shirt and boxer shorts. He looks drained.

'How long was your shift?'

'Huh? Twelve hours which ended up as fourteen. Lucky I was so late, or I wouldn't have been passing when you fell.'

I don't answer, instead turning my attention to Matthew.

Matt changes him and puts him back in his crib while I make my way to the bathroom. Matt's standing, waiting, when I come back. He hovers while I climb back in.

'How are you feeling?'

'A bit better. Headache's finally gone.'

'That's good. I'll be back with your antibiotics. Left them downstairs, should have brought them up.'

When he comes back he stands over me as I swallow the tablet and drink the water. Satisfied he wanders round to the other side of the bed to switch the lamp off. I snuggle down before it's even off. I'm still so tired.

It's early morning. Matthew is stirring but not crying yet. I wriggle around and sit up. Matt is asleep on the bed beside me. How long has he been there? He's not under the duvet, which is bunched around me just how I like it, and he must be cold. He looks cold. I reach over and touch his bare arm; he's cold. I hope he hasn't died in my bed. Don't be stupid. I unravel the duvet and lay it over him. He wriggles his shoulders and lets out a little sigh. I should tell him to get out, go to the spare room, or better still, go home.

I wish I'd never seen him with his lover. Because that would make it all right? Not.

I feel a lot better this morning. After a quick bathroom visit I lift Matthew out of his crib, climb back into bed and feed him. He gurgles contentedly in my arms afterwards.

And Matt sleeps on. He looks peaceful, comfortable. To think not so long ago we did this and we felt like a little family. I feel so saddened by that thought.

I get out of bed, change Matthew then get back in because it's early and the heating hasn't come on yet so it's cold outside the bed. Anyway, why should I have to get up just because *he's* here.

After a while Matthew falls asleep in my arms and I put him back in his crib. Matt sleeps on. I snuggle down. I must doze off because when I open my eyes again Matt has gone.

I take advantage of Matthew still being asleep and grab a quick shower.

Downstairs the curtains are already open when I carry my baby through to the kitchen.

'Oh,' I squeak when I see Matt just switching the kettle on. He's wearing different clothes and his hair is wet. 'You're still here.'

'Yes. You were sound asleep and so was Matthew,

so I ran home, showered and changed. I'm back to see how you are.'

'Much better. Thanks.' Now push off. I need to get my key back off him.

'Why don't you sit down; I'll make us breakfast.'

'You don't need to hang around, I'm fine.' I wedge Matthew into his bouncy cradle on the worktop. He's awake now, but not screaming for a feed.'

Matt pulls out the cereal he knows I like, a bowl and the milk from the fridge. I sit down at the table.

'You gave me quite a fright,' he says. 'When you fell, when I saw how ill you were. Why didn't you call me?'

'Why would I?'

'Because, because I thought we were…' he hesitates, hunting for the right word. 'Friends.'

'Yeah, I thought that too. Seems we were both wrong.'

Right then Matthew decides he's hungry. I haven't even got the first spoonful in my mouth and he's already yelling.

'You eat that, you need to eat. And take a tablet.' He plonks the packet down next to me. 'I'll walk him around and distract him until you're ready.'

I let him. It's easier than arguing. And I am hungry.

Ten minutes later I'm on the sofa feeding Matthew while Matt sits on the opposite sofa watching me. I don't care. There's nothing on my body, or indeed up inside it, that he hasn't seen. He's a doctor. It's not personal.

Finally Matthew is sated and Matt jumps up to take him, sitting with my baby on his lap, patting his back until he burps. I hope he vomits all over Matt's clean clothes. It would serve him right.

'Do you want to talk about it?'

'What?' I snap.

'Whatever's gone on between us to cause this. Whatever I'm supposed to have done that I'm totally unaware of.'

Okay. Okay. 'I saw you.'

Matt waits for me to say more, I drag out the silence.

'Playing piano with your girlfriend.'

Take that, Dr Matt.

Twenty

He doesn't deny it, just looks at me. Stares even. Burps Matthew then puts him in his nest.

'When?' he finally asks.

'When? When? Does it matter when?'

'Just curious.' He shrugs then, which really annoys me so I twist the knife.

'When I came round with the letter, the paternity letter.' I allow a smile to creep onto my lips.

'What did it say? Where's the letter now?'

I can't stop myself from glancing over at the bucket, the ashes still inside, the candle still on the hearth where I plonked it.

'You didn't?' he says, jumping up, peering inside the zinc bucket, then at me. 'What did it say?'

'Don't know. Never opened it. Now we'll never know.'

He rolls his eyes.

'Don't do that at me,' I snap again. 'And why didn't you tell me you had a girlfriend. You're as bad as Gary, he was a liar and…' I'm about to add cheat when I realise that Matt hasn't been cheating on me, on us, because there has never really been an us. He's been cheating on her *with* me. We were a one-night stand and then friends of convenience, especially for me if I'm honest.

'I've obviously not made myself or my intentions very clear,' he starts before I cut in.

'Oh, your intentions are crystal clear, especially in hindsight. You thought you'd see if you were Matthew's father then the next thing I'd know you'd be wanting him for you and your barren girlfriend.' There, it's said. Take that, Dr Matt.

But he doesn't answer. He gets up instead and puts his hand on my forehead, then he grabs my wrist and takes my pulse. And I let him before coming to my senses.

'Get off. What are you doing that for?'

'I'm concerned about you, but you don't seem to be running a temperature.'

'Fuck off,' I mutter, hoping that my baby won't hear it and grow up thinking his mother is foul mouthed.

Matt flops back on *his* sofa. 'I'm going to give you the benefit of the doubt because you have been ill, more ill than you realise and you've had a raging temperature that has probably affected your thinking.'

'Don't patronise me. And don't try to pass this off as me hallucinating because that's what you're trying to do, isn't it, you gaslighter?'

I see a smirk on his face appear before he quickly looks serious.

'No. No, not at all. But your actions are starting

to make sense now. The person, woman,' he corrects himself. 'You saw me cuddling was my sister.'

'Oh right, like that's plausible.'

'She turned up announced for a few hours the other day. I haven't seen her since before I moved here. She lives in France with her family, that's her husband and three children. She was suddenly over here on business, a last-minute attendance at a conference in London, and she had a spare day, well half a day really, took the train down and turned up at my house to surprise me.'

'What if you hadn't been there?' Because he could have been at work, that was more likely, wasn't it?

'She checked what I was up to the day before when we spoke on the phone. I thought she was ringing from France, not London.'

I believe him. He looks so earnest, so honest. No wonder he thinks I'm batshit crazy, not that he's said that.

'And,' he continues. 'I can assure you that the prospect of looking after another baby is the farthest thing from her mind. Her youngest has just turned eleven and Martha, that's my sister's name, is just starting to get her career back on track.' He follows this with the smallest of hopeful smiles.

'You were very cuddly,' I mutter, defensively.

'It's almost a year since I last saw her. We talk a lot on the phone, but… We've always been close but since our parents died…'

'Sorry,' I say, feeling like a lunatic now. I cannot bring myself to admit it to him just yet but I can see that I completely overreacted. I had no idea his parents were dead or even that he had a sister. Now I feel really bad.

'So you came round and saw us but didn't tell us you were there?'

'No, and I got your stupid front door paint on my jacket.'

Now he looks confused. 'I'd love for you and Martha to have met. She had to get back to London for an evening conference dinner otherwise...' He shrugs and sighs. 'And I didn't bring her round to see you in the afternoon because, selfishly, I wanted her all to myself. Why didn't you let me know you were there?'

'I called out but you were playing the piano together, then giggling and cuddling and I thought… Well, you know what I thought.'

'Oh God,' he says, sighing again. 'Cards on the table, I adore you. Liked you the instant we met that night in Cardiff, certainly very attracted to you which I think was obvious. Left you my number when I had to run off. Hoped you'd call and kicked myself for not having the nous to get yours first. But you never called so I thought you weren't interested. Then when I bumped into you again… What can I say? Even if I did have my head up your…' He makes a face that I think is covering a snigger.

Now it's my turn to shrug.

'How do you feel about me?' he asks.

'Quite like you,' I mumble, looking at my hands.

'Don't give anything away, Esme. And, just for the record I did say that no matter who Matthew's father is, I wanted to be around. I meant you. And him.'

'Did you say that?'

'Yes.'

'I probably thought you meant as friends.'

'If that's what *you* want. I'd like more. But I'd settle for friends.'

So now I've friend-zoned him without even trying.

'I don't know.' Or at least I don't think I do. I'm so bloody confused.

'Of course you don't know. You've just had a baby, your hormones are everywhere, everything is new and the last thing I wanted to do was pressure you into committing to a new relationship. I'm waiting for you to…' He looks around the room for inspiration, his eyes falling on the ashes in the zinc bucket again. Then he frowns. 'Recover,' he says.

'Recover,' I echo.

'Yes. Not the best choice of word but the best I can come up with at the moment. Sorry. I'm still tired from work.'

'Don't you have work today too?'

'No, I have a few days off before my next run of shifts. That's how it works.'

'I expect you want to get on with your painting and stuff.'

'Not urgently. I'd rather spend the time with you. I don't want to leave you just yet, you've been ill, although you do seem to be recovering well. But even so…'

'Do you plan to stay here?'

'I'd like to. Is that possible?'

I hesitate.

'And not because I don't have heating, or a kitchen, or electricity, I have all those things now.'

'You didn't try very hard,' I say.

'What?'

'When you came round and I told you to go. You just went.'

'I didn't. I came back the next day, I knocked and knocked and your nosy neighbour came over and told me to stop making such a noise and that if you didn't want to see me I just had to accept it, baby or not.'

'Oh no. Sorry. Maybe I was in the shower.'

'And I messaged you repeatedly but you never replied. And don't forget you threatened me with the police.'

'I blocked your number.'

'I suspected that.'

'I'm sorry about the paternity thing. We could do another one.'

He shakes his head.

'You don't care? You don't want to know?'

'Of course I do. We can just request a duplicate letter. I'll email them in a minute. If that's what you want?' He looks at me, he looks tired and worn down. I'm making him feel like that.

'Okay. What if you're not his father?'

'Changes nothing. Conversely, if he is mine that's a bonus.'

'Email them then. Do it now. I'm so sorry I've been such a cow.'

'You haven't. It's a tricky time. I understand.' I actually think he does too.

Matt stayed last night, in my bed. We snuggled up like a proper family and it was just like it was on that one night before I got mastitis, before I mistook his sister for his lover. But without the kiss. We've agreed to take it slowly. We've talked and talked. Trivia mostly, but I now feel I know all about his family and his parents and their deaths. I even managed to have a shower while Matthew was awake because Matt looked after him. I know I can't get too used to that because he'll be back at work in a few days but I've enjoyed it today. I even blow-dried my hair again.

'You look so much better today,' Matt says, when I venture downstairs nearly an hour later.

'Hair,' I say, pointing at it.

'It is.'

'No, I've washed it, made it nice.' I don't want to talk about drying my hair with Matt.

'You look great, hair looks great, always does.'

I roll my eyes at him.

'Hey, if I'm not allowed to do that then neither are you.'

'What?'

'Eye rolling.'

I roll my eyes again and we both laugh.

'By the way,' he says. 'I've cleaned the paint off your jacket.'

'Oh, thanks.'

'After breakfast, do you want to come round and

see my place now? You haven't seen the kitchen, have you?'

'Yes and no.'

We wander round but it's more than an hour later because I have to feed Matthew and Matt has to change him. He's good at it. As we leave my house Matt turns to me.

'We have to be back by two-thirty at the latest.'

'Do we, why?'

'Because the paternity test result is being couriered here today.'

'How did you do that? You only emailed them last night.'

'And I spoke to them this morning. I might have let them believe that we never received the original.'

'That's bad.' But I giggle anyway.

'Yes, well I didn't want to tell them that my crazy girlfriend burnt it without opening it.'

'Is that what I am?'

'Crazy?' he says, his eyes twinkling.

'Your girlfriend?'

'I'd like that.'

'Oh.'

'What do you think?'

'Girlfriend seems such a pejorative term for a forty-year-old.'

'Woman friend then?'

'Nah, stick with girlfriend, boyfriend.'

He hugs me right there on my doorstep just as my nosey neighbour opposite steps out of her front door.

'I bet she's been waiting all morning to do that,'

Matt says, kissing me again.

'I'm sure she has. Let her live vicariously through us.'

'Oh, listen to you and your big words.'

His kitchen is lovely, of course it is. His whole house, although not quite finished, is like something from a show home. It helps there is little furniture and no junk lying around too.

We're back at my house now, waiting anxiously for the courier. Two-thirty comes and goes.

'Courier's late.'

'Five minutes,' he says, glancing at his watch, the Tag Heuer.

A knock on the door makes us both jump.

Matt goes because it's addressed to him and he has to sign for it. He brings it back into the living room. Sits down next to me.

'Ready?'

I nod.

He rips the envelope open then pulls out the letter, smooths it open on his lap face down, then spreads it over both our laps, face up. We read together.

Matt falls back against the sofa, silent. I reread the letter. I steal a glance at Matt. He's silent and crying.

'Well I'm thrilled,' I say which sounds so trite.

'Me too.'

Twenty-one

Months later

Matthew is six months old today. And he looks even more like his daddy than ever. Although, I'm happy to report, while his eyes are dark brown like Matt's, they're shaped just like mine.

Mum and Tim are constantly popping over, taking Matthew out for walks, showing him off to their friends. They're such proud grandparents and Mum finally admitted that she never thought it would happen to them; they'd always thought I was a career girl.

They adore Matt, and he adores them.

We're still marvelling at Matt being Matthew's daddy. How the hell did that happen? Neither of us can recall any mishaps with the condom or indeed not using one. I put it down to fate, Matt puts it down to manufacturing. Whichever of the two it is doesn't matter because we have Matthew now and nothing could be better.

Matt offered to help me tell Sue and Roger that

Roger wasn't Matthew's daddy. I did consider it but decided it would be rubbing salt in the wound. Doing it over a video call was bad enough without Matt being there.

Roger was quite sanguine about it but Sue was so disappointed, but at the same time delighted that I'd found a suitable man. That's what she'd called Matt, a suitable man. She said she guessed the minute Matt turned up because the resemblance was so obvious.

'This has been the loveliest day,' Sue says, giving me a hug before she and Roger leave.

'I'm so glad you could come. I know it's a long way for a day.'

'Oh, we've booked a hotel twenty miles further on. Roger has a duty to perform tonight.' She winks at me. It seems his lack of success with me hasn't put them off. 'Last one,' Sue says, sighing. 'Because if this one is successful, he's fulfilled his quota.'

I think Sue's more bothered by this than Roger.

'Lovely wedding,' Roger says, kissing me on the cheek. 'Lovely man too, well done there.'

'I hope you said similar to my husband,' I joke.

'Of course.' He winks at me.

'They seem like a nice couple,' Mum says as she joins me on the drive to wave them off.

'Where's Grandad,' I ask. Referring to Tim as Grandad is the easiest thing in the world.

'Collecting everything up with Matt. They're going to load the car in a minute so we'd better get indoors and out of the way or they'll have us helping.'

We trot inside and hide out in the kitchen with Matthew while Matt and Tim do the loading. Eventually it's time to kiss our son and his grandparents goodbye. I cannot even bring myself to wave them off in the car. Mum and Tim have babysat plenty of times here, and taken Matthew out for the afternoon, but this is different.

It's the first time he's been away from me overnight and I know I'm going to be more bothered about it than he is. But it's our wedding night, the start of our two-day honeymoon. We're not going far, just around the corner to Matt's house. Just for the change of scenery, just for the novelty. Matt hasn't slept there in months and he's having it valued soon with a view to selling it.

'They've gone,' Matt says, coming back indoors. 'Don't get upset.' He hugs me. I know I'm being silly, but there you go. 'Come on, let's get round to our honeymoon house. We've got some work to do.'

I roll my eyes, then he rolls his. Then we pull on our coats and trot off.

It's been a weird time since Matthew was born, apart from having a baby which is the most life changing experience in the world, I met the love of my life. Although, obviously, I'd already met him. I can't believe how I feel about Matt, nor he about me. We're like two sides of the same coin. Not that we agree on everything, far from it. We bicker. We argue. We make up. But we have each other's backs. We love each other through the good and the bad.

That's why I did what I did; I asked him to marry me. And he said yes. It was only two months ago.

Our wedding was tiny, and on a Thursday. When I was with Gary I'd imagined a full-on church and reception affair, but with Matt none of that mattered. I realised that it wasn't the getting married that was important, it was the being married. Pearl asked me why, in this day and age, we were bothering. Couldn't we just live together like normal people? It was a good point and I couldn't explain the why very well. We just wanted to be tied tight, legally, permanently. A quick, but nonetheless lovely, Registry Office wedding and a wedding breakfast curtesy of *M&S* buffet platters back here. It was the easiest option because then Matthew's naps wouldn't be interrupted.

Because it was a Thursday, Pearl (and Harshad) couldn't come. She was attending her first board meeting as HR Director. Yes, Pearl is the new HR Director. David has gone, he retired – some say he was encouraged to retire and it was long overdue. I find it almost impossible to reconcile the mouse that sat in the corner of the office crunching data and updating the company intranet to the dynamic woman Pearl has become. She'll be my boss when I go back to work, a better one that David, I suspect.

Kerri and Carol-Anne came, they brought their husbands and their babies along too. It was nice to see them all. Matt gets on really well with Ollie and Garth. Garth even made a little video of our ceremony, which was nice of him. He does like his videos although he never did video Kerri giving birth because his phone went missing for two days. Funny that. Martha, Matt's sister, couldn't make it over, but we're going over to France for a two week stay next month.

'Wow.' I laugh as Matt lifts me up and dumps me inside his house.

'Over the threshold,' he says, panting.

'I'm not that heavy.' I play slap his arm.

'You're not heavy at all.' He wipes his brow of imaginary sweat.

'House looks amazing,' I tell him. He's kept me away for the last week, wanting to surprise me for tonight. There's champagne on ice in the fridge, canapés, chocolates and balloons.

We take the champagne upstairs with us.

'Candles,' I exclaim as he goes around the room lighting them. 'And rose petals on the bed. My new husband is so romantic.'

He grabs me and kisses me, swirling me around as we fall laughing on top of the rose petals.

'Nothing is too much trouble for my new wife.' There's a twinkle in his eyes.

'Good. Well, we'd better get down to work then.' Now there's a twinkle in my eye. 'Because for this next one I would like a girl.'

CJ MORROW
Sooo
Not
Looking
For a
Man
And with an attitude like that,
never likely to find one!

CJ MORROW

Blame it on the Onesie

The hot guy upstairs thinks she's a weirdo in a frog suit

Printed in Dunstable, United Kingdom

79235296R00173